The

Wife

ALSO BY ANNA MANSELL

How to Mend a Broken Heart

The Lost Wife

anna mansell

bookouture

Published by Bookouture
An imprint of StoryFire Ltd.
23 Sussex Road, Ickenham, UB10 8PN
United Kingdom
www.bookouture.com

ISBN: 978-1-78681-234-6
eBook ISBN: 978-1-78681-233-9

For Mel G, because I love that you loved it

PART ONE
JANUARY 2012

Chapter One

Ed

My wife gave me strict instructions in the event of her untimely death: no crying, no drinking, no sympathy sex with an ex. Her final crushed-velvet curtain should fall before a congregation wearing *'Glitter-red shoes and sky-blue gingham, make that bit obvious on the invites, Ed.'* We didn't establish the protocol regarding funeral invites as such, because, you know, why would we?

A big fan of *The Wizard of Oz*, she also wanted the original version of 'Ding-Dong! The Witch is Dead' played for a cast of perma-tanned small people to dance down a specially installed yellow-bricked aisle. I didn't consider the logistics, or how impossible promises would be, because she wasn't going to die. And now my head pounds, disbelieving tears replaced with dry, gut-wrenching sobs of pain and reality, which means I've broken promise one: no crying.

Despite crisp winter air stealing my breath, I can still detect the stench of whisky and wine and anything else I've found around our house, searching for something to dull the pain. Except no amount of alcohol works, it just makes me feel guilty that I'm drunk in charge of a baby. Promise two: no drinking… broken.

Maybe I should be grateful that I've no energy, will or inclination to break promise three. Ex or otherwise.

Four pitch-black-suited men lower her walnut casket six foot under-ground, and I resist sinking to my knees. I want to go down with her. I want to hide six foot under. I want this all to be over. I want the pale and solemn faces that surround me to leave. They're another reminder that I did not do what she wanted: no gingham, no red shoes. I feel the punch in my heart again; on each and every level, I've got this wrong.

I've blocked out the vicar's words, until now: 'Let us commend Ellie Moran to the mercy of God…' It's too much.

My head feels a safer place. Sifting through memories that keep her alive, if only for a few more moments. Ignoring the questions I have about how we came to be here. Today is not the day.

The night she tabled her dark-humoured request was our house-warming, not more than nine months ago, a night of love and laughter and friends. After years of graft, we'd finally finished our forever home. We were on our third bottle of Chianti – drink shared among the group – and conversation flowed as easily as the wine. Ellie's laughter infected us all to the point we could barely string a sentence together as we threw equally dark suggestions into the mix: a wake on a ranch-style farm; wind machines; a crafted prairie-house coffin; and my personal favourite – ashes scattered by Glinda the Good Witch. It's easy to be flippant when you're invincible.

'We now commit her body to the ground…'

Happy memories flood and splinter the ache in my chest, sending it shooting through my body. We were going to die when we were old, we'd always said so. We'd agreed.

'Earth to earth…'

We'd share a life together, raise a family. We'd enjoy a lengthy retirement ticking items off a bucket list, once-in-a-lifetime trips had she not done them already… patience was never her strong point.

'Ashes to ashes…'

Maybe *that's* why she was in my brother's car? Because she couldn't wait until I got there.

'Dust to dust…'

If I hadn't been stealing an hour's sleep, despite her being the one up all night with Oli, she'd have asked me to take her out. We'd be together. She'd be alive. I wouldn't be left with little else than a note on the kitchen table: *Gone for fresh air, won't be long. X*

'In the sure and certain hope of the resurrection to eternal life.'

We'd waved off our party guests, finally alone in our newly renovated forever home. Ellie had pendulum-waved an empty bottle in my direction. '*Open another,*' she'd said, with a wink meant just for me.

'*Perhaps I should dress as the Tin Man,*' I'd joked, popping the cork from another red.

She'd flirted with the idea. We'd laughed. Later that night, we'd conceived Oli.

'Amen.'

Mourners gather round. Faces I know, a few that I don't. Simon, my brother, stands with Mum and Dad on either side. His eyes focused on the middle distance, he's here but he's not present. Lisa, his wife, stands behind them. Does *she* wonder why they were together that day? Has he explained? To her? To anyone? He hasn't to me, he hasn't even tried.

I rest my lips upon the softness of Oli's newborn skull. When he arrived, less than two weeks ago, he and Ellie shared the same smell. If I take a breath, it's almost like she's still here. Beside me. Holding my hand as we say goodbye. So, I don't take that breath. I can't.

Why did I strap him to my chest when I can barely breathe as it is? All 8lb 6oz of perfection, snuffling like a truffle pig in his sling. Perhaps I shouldn't use him as a tiny human shield.

I said I didn't blame Simon. That's what I told Mum and Dad. I said I knew it was an accident, that the investigation will prove that.

But even accidents can be avoided. Can't they?

The vicar nods at me. With Bible in one hand, he offers his other out, palm up, inviting me forward. One step is enough to bring her resting place into view. I drop two crimson roses, their velvet petals deep and plush, down on to the brass plate with her name. One from me and one from our boy. My breath catches and my eyes sting. A stifled cry behind me makes me pause, and another moment of clarity presents: muddy wet layers of newly dug soil surround her, a smell we once loved. Gritty. Earthy. Evocative. On rain-soaked mornings we'd step outside and take a deep breath, our senses full. Because then the smell signalled life, new beginnings, the future. Now? It's dirt and damp. It smells of the end. The End. A smell that will forever remind me that Ellie hated burials. Yet here I am, in the grounds of a church in Nottingham, laying my wife to rest. If anything happens to her Versace dress she'll be furious. It's her favourite. *Was* her favourite.

ELEANOR JANE MORAN-FITZGERALD (ELLIE)
16TH DECEMBER 1976 – 14TH JANUARY 2012
WIFE. MOTHER. DAUGHTER. FRIEND.
R.I.P

Chapter Two

Rachel

Making the walk from hangover to the local shop is hellish. Mo can't structure a sentence, the smell of stale ale repeats with my every breath, and it's freezing out here. Like properly, properly, freezing.

We can't do this any more. We're too old for it. We should probably have stayed at home… last night, if not this morning. I reckon I could've cobbled a breakfast together from whatever we have in the cupboards, then I wouldn't have to be dressed, in the cold light of day, smelling faintly of lady sweat as a result of overenthusiastic vogueing down our local nightclub. I swallow back a burp and Mo shoots me a disgusted look.

Icy fog hangs over the church steeple. Car after car weaves the tree-lined road with blatant disregard for double yellows. There's a hearse parked at the front of the queue, right outside the church gates. 'Lots of people,' I say, nodding at the giant congregation huddled by an open grave. 'Is that a good sign or not?'

'What?' Mo grunts. 'Are they mourning the loss, or dancing on your grave, d'you mean?'

'She speaks,' I announce, sarcastically. 'And no, Mo, that's not what I meant.' I push my hair away from my face before ruffling it back to cover up cold ears again. We walk on in almost silence, except for Mo loudly sucking bubble gum into her mouth to distract me from the memories the odd passing funeral can invite. I look down to the flagstone pavement; it'll be sixteen years, later this year. Sixteen quick-long years since I buried Mum. I was twelve. No age is good, but twelve is really shit. You've generally got enough on with the gangly legs and emerging hormone-fuelled attitude. Losing a parent and then years of bundled angst are not a magic combination. Nor are the years of anger I felt towards an illness that, at the time, swallowed our lives just as much as it did hers.

'Do you know, I never knew that my dead granddad had a twin brother until Mum's funeral.'

'What?' Mo spins around. 'I did not know this!'

'Yeah. Sat down on the pew, Mum's coffin before us all, and this bloke who – as far as I was concerned at the time – was the grandfather we'd buried two years before, sat beside me to pay his respects. Mum's entire service was overshadowed by me wondering if anyone else could see this ghost of a man beside me.' Mo fails to stifle a giggle. 'It's alright, you're allowed to laugh. To be fair, it was probably the distraction I needed at the time. Funerals can be grim.'

'Grim. Sure. That's the word for it. You know, your family are the gift that keep on giving!'

'Hmm...' I say, pointedly, because I think she's maybe forgotten that currently, if my family were a gift, they'd be the equivalent of a £5 book token that my eleven-year-old self wants to swap for a shopping spree in Topshop.

Mo pushes open the door to our local Tesco Express. 'Mission hangover cure begins!' she declares. 'Bread, hot dogs, ketchup, crisps, chocolate, full fat Coke by the litre! What do we need?'

'A time machine back to the hour before that final bottle of Prosecco in the club?'

'Prosecco? It was a freebie from the DJ! I dread to think of its actual origins, because it definitely wasn't made from Italian grapes.' She swallows with a grimace. 'Eurgh, drinking that was a bad move.'

'You're probably right. Okay, we need all of the beige carbs in our basket,' I say, but Mo's not behind me. I retrace my steps to find her staring out of the window, face awash with vacant expression.

'What?' I ask, catching sight of my reflection in all of its morning-after-the-night-before glory.

Her eyes scan up and down the road, beyond a passing tram. 'I was just wondering if I could stomach sushi, then thought I saw someone I knew. Black-suited and booted, like they were on their way to that funeral.' She strains to see past the promotional posters in the window.

'*Can* you do sushi?' I ask, suspiciously. *I mean, who does raw fish on an empty stomach?*

'Nah, don't think so. I'd do pretty much anything for a finger buffet though.' She winks, last night's mascara clumping her lashes together.

'So, what? You're trying to get an invite to a wake now? Classy.'

'You know me, Rach! I love a cheesy pineapple hedgehog.'

'I'm more of an open cob kind of girl myself. But not at a stranger's funeral, so come on, let's get what we need and split.' Mo nods her head in agreement, sauntering off to pick up things off the shelves, dropping them into the basket: Alka-Seltzer, Coco Pops, two bags of Doritos, followed by a third because it's 'buy two, get one free' and Mo can't resist a bargain. 'You pay, I'll meet you over at The Pitcher for hair of the dog.'

'Nope. Can't,' I answer, taking my card out and swallowing another disgusting burp.

'Okay, DVD then. Shotgun *Pretty Woman*.'

'Hey! My birthday, my choice!' I protest.

'You know full well that shotgun trumps birthdays. You snooze, you lose,' shouts Mo, picking up the pace and leaving me behind as she stomps down the back streets to our city-centre flat. I look back over to the church, send my love to Mum up in the sky, and skip on to catch Mo up. *Pretty Woman* it is. But I'm totally following it up with *A Chorus Line*. That'll teach her…

Chapter Three

Ed

Mum's polished black court shoes click around the kitchen. She's not a natural homemaker, never has been, so she keeps picking things up and looking at them before putting them back down, or moving them somewhere else with the statement, 'I don't know where they belong.' As if cupboards couldn't be opened.

She goes to reach for the steriliser then stops. Then sighs. I can't hear her sigh again. I don't want it. I want her to leave so I can go up to our room. Wrap myself in our cream cotton sheets; sheets left unchanged because Ellie slept in them. I want the fading smell of her perfume to wash over me as I sink into our bed. I won't sleep. I haven't since Simon called, not properly. Distress, fear and hurt poured down the phone line as he told me what had happened, the horror yanking me from gritty-eyed, new-parent slumber. Since then, I've laid in bed, my mind wandering away from reality. It's not sleep so much as wakeful dreaming about our life together, until a noise plucks me back and the pain hits me all over again.

'Keep the cat away from Oli,' Mum says eventually, as Floyd twists through her legs, reaching his tail high for her attention. 'Cats can smother a newborn.' She looks down on him, accusingly, not a fan of public displays of affection from people, never mind things with four legs. Floyd chases after her as she clicks away, before rubbing his head on her shin, then darting out of the cat flap.

Oli suckles the last of a clumsily prepared bottle, my hands tired, shaking. I shift to rest him on my shoulder, muscles aching as I rub his back the way Ellie would each time she fed him. She'd celebrate his burps as if we'd bred a genius.

Mum reaches across the table for a muslin cloth to tuck under his chin. 'Put this here,' she instructs and it irritates me that I forgot. Mum sighs again, looking around. Her hands rest on the counter top. 'Can I at least tidy a little before I go, Edward?'

She wants to for her sake, not mine. She wants to occupy herself before she finally takes her leave. She could just go.

'I could just clear this side, maybe wipe it down for you?' Her hands reach out to a pile of Ellie's post.

'Leave it,' I hiss, making Oli jump on my shoulder. Her hand retracts as if her fingers burn. 'Sorry. But, don't touch it, please,' I say. Mum goes towards a candy-striped box, one of Ellie's famed memory boxes, left out on the side. 'Don't touch anything.'

Redundant, she stands in the middle of the room, uncomfortable, uncertain.

Just leave, I want to say.

'I appreciate your help with all of this, and the funeral…' The words stick in my throat and I turn my back, hiding my face as I lie Oli down to sleep in the Moses basket we excitedly chose the night she finished work for her maternity leave. 'I just need to be on my own.'

'Your family are here to help, Edward,' she says, quietly. Her voice has the clip of elocution that makes everything sound harder than perhaps she intends.

'I know.' I don't turn to face her.

'And your brother,' she adds. I give a shallow nod this time. 'He is devastated, Edward. I really think you two should talk.'

'We will,' I say, mainly to appease her, but she prickles at my response, no doubt picking up on the fact that I'm not committing to when.

'I know he is not always easy to talk to at the moment, Edward. I know you've tried… before… But, this is different now. You're brothers. You need each other. You must work through this.' She pauses, giving me time to agree with her. To put a timescale on when I'll make contact with him. 'Edward?'

I'm not sure what she wants me to say. I've already told her I can't yet. I've explained that I need time. I've asked her to try to understand, however difficult that may be.

Oli lets out a murmur and I pick him back up again. 'Sometimes you need to let them cry,' she advises.

'Sometimes you need to listen to your children,' I answer.

She pauses for a moment, then, taking my point, reaches for her coat and bag with a formal nod. 'You don't have to do this alone,' she says, hooking her belongings into the crook of her arm. 'There are ways to get through this.'

Words, I'm certain, that could only ever come from a person who hasn't dealt with grief on this scale, ever in her life. It's not her fault, I realise that, but neither is any of this mine. Simon, on the other hand…

Chapter Four

Rachel

Since dramatically falling into our feather-filled sofa – an old house-warming gift from Mo's mum and dad – I basically haven't moved. We've done *Pretty Woman*, *A Chorus Line* and argued over *Bridesmaids* vs *Dirty Dancing*. As if that's even a competition! (*Dirty Dancing* EVERY time!) The cliché of single girls and chick flicks makes me itch a bit, but what else are hangovers good for?

Mo has crawled off the sofa in search of her onesie, leaving me to glance around the blank canvas that is our flat. Surrounded by empty crisp bags and chocolate wrappers, it's clear that we live like students… minus the shared-house grime and road cones. Okay, it's possible I'm sweepingly generalising about student accommodation, but certainly our place looks like that freshers' flat I ended up in after a particularly misjudged night out. Turns out the fresher in question wasn't as 'talented' in the bedroom department as his friends had suggested, or maybe I just fell asleep because I was really, really tired.

I shudder at that particular morning-after memory, picking up the birthday card that arrived from Dad in the post this morning instead.

Dad. I haven't spoken to him all day, which is unheard of. I've been a bit distant for a few days, in fact, which is out of character since we lost Mum. It's just that... well, I don't really know where to begin. I don't know how to tell him what I'm feeling, partly because I don't know exactly what I'm feeling. Or why. Except that it started when he told me he was putting our family home on the market, which – and I accept this is somewhat dramatic – made me feel as though I'd have no home to go to if he did. I moved out years ago; it shouldn't matter. And yet, somehow, it does matter. Which makes me feel confused and guilty in equal measure.

'We should get fairy lights,' I shout to Mo, like that's all that's required to sort the flat (and my mood) out. She's reverted to grunting and I can hear her doing so as she wades her way through a pile of clothes that will definitely be on her bedroom floor... one clean pile, one dirty... and a very fine line between the two. Apparently she knows which is which, but for someone so organised and professional at work, her level of scruff-dom never ceases to amaze me. I persevere. 'You know I love a fairy light, Mo! And they'd totally brighten up this room.' Ideas start to flow as I imagine draping lights and throws around the place, focusing on making a (not so) new home here, given that the other one is on its way out. 'In fact, why stop at lights?' I clap, excitedly. 'We should decorate!'

Mo is still huffing and puffing in her room. It's unclear if that's because of my ideas or the state of her floordrobe. I pick through Mum's old magazines on the wonky coffee table, ones that Dad gives me from her obsessive collection every now and then. From the first ever *Elle* magazine from 1985 to some random collectors' ones about Egypt, she had thousands. There's an old 1970s interiors one somewhere in this pile. 'How long have we lived here? Eight years? Maybe it's time we put our mark on it?' I say, lowering my voice from a shout as Mo walks back into the room. She's unsteadily vertical, nursing a Doritos baby in her belly.

'I blame you, Rach. I told you that third bag was a bad idea, I've no self-control,' she groans.

'Did you?' I ask, eyebrows raised, because what she actually said as she threw them in my direction was: 'Fuck it, open that last bag, would you?' Mainly because we were watching *Dirty Dancing* and she knew I was about to cry at Patrick Swayze singing 'She's Like the Wind.' That song gets me every time.

I flick through the magazine. 'What's that new craze everyone's on about? Hygge? How do you pronounce it? Hig? Hug?'

'Hue-guh.'

'That's the cat! Maybe we should decorate like that. Like the Danes?'

'Rachel,' she groans – at her discomfort I think, rather than me, 'hygge is a lifestyle, not a colour swatch for your wall.' She's always been smarter than me with this stuff. 'It's about embracing peace and tranquillity. Nature. Good food. Good friends. We're there already, aren't we?' She kicks one of the empty crisp packets out of view with a look that suggests she's blaming it for the aforementioned discomfort… as opposed to herself for single-handedly eating the contents, which, frankly, I admire. 'I think that's what your dad wants you know, Rach. Peace and tranquillity. That's why he wants to move to one of those wooden lodge type places.'

'Have you seen it, Mo? He showed me a picture. It's not a lodge, it's a bloody caravan!'

'Caravan. Lodge. Whatever. If he's happy, does it matter?'

I know she's right, I really do, but I can't help my first response. Maybe I need to work on how long I let my inner child stamp her feet for.

'Of course' – she sidles into the sofa beside me – 'you'd know how important it all was if you spoke to him about it.'

'Who says I haven't spoken to him?' I say, mock aghast.

'Rach, if you're not talking to me, you're usually on the phone to him, or exchanging text messages. Since he told you about the house you've all but cut off ties.'

'It's only been a few days!' I mumble.

'Yeah? And how many times have you gone that long without talking before?'

I put down the magazine in exchange for the local paper which somehow offers more distraction from her line of questioning. 'I still think we should decorate,' I mutter into its pages.

Mo takes a tea light out of our stash in the coffee-table drawer and lights it. 'There, hygge. Nailed it. So, I'll ask you again, have you spoken to your dad?'

'Local black spot takes new mother's life,' I say, reading out the headline. Mo fixes me with a stare, so I scowl in her direction, flicking the pages with pantomime force until I find the full story a few pages in. 'Paramedics got the baby and driver out, but they couldn't save the mother.' I carry on reading as Mo folds her arms. She's probably giving me one of the stares she has when she disapproves of my behaviour. I pity her future children. 'The driver was the woman's brother-in-law.'

'Nice try, Rach. Yes, that story is awful but, more to the point, when did you talk to your dad now Richard's not there?' Mo gives my brother his Sunday name, ignoring the pained look on my face. 'Your dad's on his own for the first time since...'

'Jean next door is about,' I say, not wanting to think about the last time he was on his own.

'Sure, because that's the same as one or both of your children.'

'Jean's lovely!' I say.

Mo goes into the kitchen and starts banging cupboard doors, probably in search of something to drink. 'God, I bet Rich's having the best time,' she says. I shrug as she comes back through with a pint of water. 'I've always wanted to travel,' she announces. I look up sharply, because not only is she on stony ground with this subject matter, but she is categorically NOT a backpack traveller.

'Since when? As if I can see you trekking the Annapurnas!' My voice is loaded with the sarcasm of someone who knows that Mo is, at best, a three-star-hotel kind of girl, ideally four or five.

'Ha! Got your attention, though,' she says, smugly.

'Look, how many times do I have to tell you? I don't begrudge Rich leaving Dad on his own.' Well… I might begrudge it a little bit. 'It's just that' – I growl into a cushion that rests on my knee – 'I don't know why Dad suddenly wants to move on. I don't think I want to help him pack up the house. I don't know why he can't just stay there forever.'

'On his own? In a five-bed semi?'

'Rich will be back before he knows it.'

'Rich is away for a year, Rachel. At least.'

'But Mum's still there with him!' I say. Mo drops back onto the sofa beside me again and I swear I detect a look of gratification that she has made me say what's bothering me out loud. 'If Dad moves out, what happens to Mum's memory? To our memories of her there, in the family home? With us all, together?'

'Your memories don't go because you leave the house. Christ, Rach, you haven't lived there for years. Moving out wasn't exactly hard for you, was it?'

'Dad told me I had to. He said I had to build a life of my own. And I could hardly let you rattle around this old place on your own.'

'It's a two-bed apartment, Rach. I'd hardly be rattling.'

Irritated that she won't let me get away with momentarily behaving like a child, I turn back to the newspaper. 'Campaigners are calling for new safety measures on that part of the road. It's the fifth fatality in three years.'

'Okay, okay, sorry. I know it hurts. But maybe that's why you need to talk to him.'

'Talk to who?' I ask, my inner child being a dick again.

'Father Christmas,' she sighs, taking the paper from my hands and throwing it onto the coffee table as she stands. The rush of air blows out the tea light, then wafts an empty chocolate wrapper onto the floor. I wonder how many days it'll stay there for.

'It's your birthday, Rach. You need to talk to him today. Or, better still, go to see him.'

'I guess.'

Mo pretends to tidy things up a bit, but I sense it's a ruse to pick at this conversation. 'Your brother said there'd already been a viewing on the house, you know.'

'When did you speak to him?'

'We Facebooked. He didn't get a response from you yesterday and he knew you'd been upset about the house stuff so he was checking you were okay.'

'I'm great.'

Mo flops back down onto the sofa beside me, ramming a finger into my side at the exact spot that always makes me laugh. 'Get off, you know I hate that!' I giggle.

'At least you've got a smile on your face, you miserable bugger! Come on, let's get in the car and go to see your dad.'

'I'm probably still pissed.'

'Okay, one night this week maybe?'

'No,' I say, petulantly. 'Besides, it's my birthday, shouldn't Dad come see me?'

'Wow, I think it's your maturity that I admire the most.'

We fall silent, before I groan at being a dick and shuffle to get comfy again. 'I told him I was out all day,' I admit. 'I sent him a text to say thanks for the card.'

'Rach!'

'I know, I know. I just… I don't know what to say to him. I can't explain it.'

'You're allowed to tell him how you feel,' she says, which invites sledge-hammering guilt into my consciousness. 'You just can't expect him to live his life by your requirements.'

Once again, Mo's ability to be the grown-up shames me into submission. I flick the TV channels, searching for something else to focus on. *Coronation Street. Location.* Age-old repeats of *Friends*. 'I think we're getting too old for this hangover lark,' Mo eventually, delicately, says. 'You clearly can't handle them. Maybe all future birthday celebrations should be restricted to mineral water and salad.'

'I hate salad.'

'Okay, frikadeller?'

'Frika what?'

'Deller. Meatballs. Hygge?'

I groan. 'Only if it's the ones from Ikea. With chips.'

'Now there's an idea…' She wiggles her eyebrows. 'What time does it shut?'

Chapter Five

Ed

The door clicks shut as Mum finally leaves, the house falls quiet. Ellie should now be slipping her arms around me, draping one arm over my shoulder, the other reaching beneath to clasp her hands across my chest. She should be nuzzling into my back, dropping a butterfly kiss on my neck. I should turn and hold her in my arms, like I always would, relieved to be on our own again.

How long will I still be able to imagine her like this? Almost feel her? This morning, I lost the sound of her voice for a moment and it was like losing *her* all over again. I wish she'd recorded an answerphone message, or that we'd had our wedding filmed. I wish… I wish.

I try to find the strength to move, lead-weight legs making everything twice as hard. The pile of Ellie's letters sits on the side. I reach out, hovering my hand above it at first, before letting my fingers graze, then rest on top. She was the last person to touch the letters, organising them until her return. Each envelope has her name; the top one is a small white parcel, a gift from a friend maybe?

I turn the package over, shake then gently squeeze the padding to feel the contents. If I close my eyes I can hear her: '*Ooh, a present.*' That she hadn't opened it was unusual. She'd always laboured the present-opening process, shaking, sniffing and squeezing gifts until her curiosity got the better of her and she'd tear the packets open, contents falling into her lap. That this one remains unopened shows how life had instantly changed when Oli arrived.

Should I open it?

The palms of my hands itch with the truth that she'll never see it, a reality that once again knocks air from my lungs. I gently place the package and letters into the box on the side. One of many boxes she would collect precious memories in, storing them away in her wardrobe along with diaries and boxes upon boxes of shoes. I replace the lid, pick the box and Oli's Moses basket up, before finding the strength to climb the stairs, breathless.

I place Oli's basket down on the stand by Ellie's side of the bed. I undress and get into bed, then pick up her phone, placing headphones into my ears like each night since the first that I was here alone, total silence too much to bear. Flicking through the music lets songs nudge at memories: Madeleine Peyroux whilst we ate and talked in the early days. Guns N' Roses, played loud to clean up after *that* house-warming. She played air guitar with the vacuum, I joined in on air-drums at the breakdown.

Oli's fidgeting limbs stop as he drifts off and I realise I'm hungry for the memories, ravenous, playing a few bars of a new song then moving on to the next. There's comfort in the pick and prod of raw, open wounds exposed by each song. Sarah Vaughan, 'Come Rain or Come Shine', Ellie's favourite song. The lyrics, Vaughan's striking, smoky voice, peel away layers of memories and, again, I can feel Ellie's embrace. I can feel her snuggled up beside me. Thick-socked feet holding my own together. Her fingers tracing a heart on my shoulder. Like always.

And with the chorus comes the physical, all-consuming, sick-making pain.

It's heart-punching, gut-wrenching; it's debilitating.

I put the phone down on the duvet and press the heels of my hands into my eyes, but rushing stars don't change my view. I can't escape. I can't move. I can't breathe. I can't see, hear or feel. I pick up the phone again and throw it into the box with everything else, the music still playing but muffled beneath the stash of memories. With new energy, I rip the duvet from me, leap out of bed and push the box to the very back of her wardrobe. As I let the door swing shut, Ellie's smell suffocates the sound of her music and the last of my strength. I fall to the floor, crushed. Sobbing dry tears again.

This wasn't in the plan. How will I ever live again? Why did she go out? Why wasn't I there? What could Simon have done differently to change things? Why was Ellie even in his car in the first place? And that question, above all, rings around my mind. So much so that I reach out for the landline, on her side of the bedside table. Last touched to answer Simon's call. I dial his number. I have to talk to him. Mum was right. I have questions. I need answers.

'Hello?'

It's Lisa.

'Hello? Who's this?' she asks.

'Lisa, it's Ed.'

'Oh.'

'I need to talk to Simon.'

She laughs. 'Sure, you, me, the police.'

'What do you mean?'

'I mean, there's a queue of us, Ed. But he's currently paralytic on the sofa downstairs and I don't suppose he's got a lot to say for himself.'

'He's drinking?' I ask, because we stopped Simon drinking years ago. 'Since when?' I ask, wondering how she let this happen. Lisa pauses. The phone line crackles. 'Since when?' I repeat.

'Your guess is as good as mine,' she sneers.

The phone line goes dead.

'Lisa? LISA!'

But she's gone. And I'm left with another unanswered question.

Chapter Six

Rachel

We wandered the aisles of Ikea. We ate our body weight in meatballs, despite still nursing crisp-induced indigestion. We bought two packs of tea lights and some fairy lights in the shape of stars, which we agreed we'd drape along the fireplace. I tried to persuade Mo we didn't also need a giant pack of Daim bars, which made us laugh out loud because we both knew I was lying.

By the time we got home, it was pitch-black, cold, and I was very much over my birthday. Mostly because I'd spent all day ignoring the feeling I get every year when I compare my life to Mum's at the same age. She'd stopped watching trashy films on her birthday long before that. She'd achieved stuff by now. Kids. A husband. A proper job for a grown-up. I can't for the life of me think what I've achieved. A top score on Angry Birds, and brief notoriety on Twitter when one of the girls from Little Mix (I forget which one) retweeted one of my tweets. Even the subsequent spike in followers has since fallen back down to eighty-five.

What else? I flunked my archaeology degree when I realised I didn't actually want to spend my life dusting rocks in a remote desert somewhere north of nowhere. And I know I shouldn't compare us, but Mo did media at uni, a subject we all know is an excuse to go out on the lash for three years, and now she's a £400-a-day marketing consultant working up and down the country. Where can eight months' study of Anglo-Saxon burial grounds take me? Or even seven years working as a nursery nurse?

And if either can take me anywhere, is it somewhere I'd like to be? And would it pay enough to get rid of the subsequent student debt for a degree I never finished?

I stare out of my bedroom window at the red-brick walls of buildings that surround us. A street light gives off an orangey glow, and I can't work out if our flat, nestled among office blocks, student accommodation and private flats, is somewhere magical, where anything can happen, or somewhere claustrophobic that I'll never escape from. I'm twenty-seven. Lying in a bed I haven't bothered to make today. What do I really want out of life? What do I need to do? What is the thing that will take me from plodding daily to achieving success? What does success even look like? I glance down at my panda onesie, catch sight (again) of my (still) unwashed hair, and run my tongue across fur-lined teeth. Success probably doesn't look exactly like this.

I reach for my phone, bring up Dad's number and call.

'Rachel, darling! Hello, happy birthday! I thought you were going to be back late?'

I shift guiltily on my bed, wishing I hadn't texted him to say I couldn't talk today. 'Oh, we'd had enough… came back early… getting too old for birthdays now,' I explain lamely.

'Nonsense. Though I seem to remember it was around your age when your mother decided she should stop partying.'

'Did she?' I ask, surprised at the description of a mother I don't recognise. I'd never seen her as a party animal.

'Yes! You were seven, maybe eight. You came bounding in, then jumped up and down on our bed one morning after she'd been out with friends. Told us you needed to go to Sherwood Forest to do some early research for a project at school, then looked at her, green-gilled and hungover as she was, and asked if she'd been out drinking… again!'

'Did I?'

'She was mortified. Barely drank after that.'

'I don't remember that at all. I thought she just didn't like alcohol.'

'Ha ha ha, nope! She'd probably say it didn't like her.'

'I get that,' I say, realising the drink chat was bringing back my own alcohol-infused nausea. When did I get to an age when hangovers lasted a full day and night?

'I've got your present here, love, if you want to come by and get it when you're free? And some more of your mum's old magazines. I found a load of history ones I thought you might like.'

'History?' I'm not sure why she had them, or why Dad thinks I'd like them.

'Yep. She was beginning to flirt with the idea of going to college to train as a secondary-school teacher… or whatever you'd call that now.'

'Dad, are you intentionally giving me brand-new information about Mum today, or is this stuff I've always known and forgotten about?'

'You knew your mother as your mum, I knew her as my wife. Same person, different sides. There will always be things I can tell you about her, things you never knew. It's one of the joys we still have left.'

'But she worked at that engineering firm on the edge of town. In accounts, wasn't it?'

'Yep. But only really because we didn't have the money to support her if she retrained. Biggest regret of my life, that. If there's one thing you must never do, it's to not chase after your dreams. Even if they cost money, there'll be a way.'

'Oh, Dad!' I lean back in my bed. Soft pillows swallow my body as I pull the duvet up under my chin and shift the hot-water bottle I've been cradling for comfort. 'Chasing them would be far easier if I knew what they were.'

'Come on, you must have something?'

'I don't know.' My mind goes blank.

'What would you do if time, money, access and opportunity were no object?'

'Marry Tom Hardy.'

'Rachel!'

'Okay, okay. I know, he's got a girlfriend. I don't know… what sort of a question is that?'

'It's one you should be able to answer.'

I sink further down into the bed. 'I'm probably too old for change.'

'Nonsense. Gosh, if your mother could hear you. Right, here's a task. A birthday task. Get a piece of paper, get a pen, write a list of all the jobs you could do. I bet you that, within a few days, the perfect one comes to mind. Then we just work out how to get you there. Okay?'

'Okay…'

'Great. Now, the new people in Betty and Doug's old place came round earlier. Their little girl's been baking brownies for charity. I'll save you one if you come over tomorrow for your present.'

'You didn't have to buy me anything, Dad.'

'I didn't.'

'Oh.'

'It's something I found of your mother's that I thought you might like. Might come in handy now…'

'Ooh, the suspense. I'll see you tomorrow, then, Dad.'

'Look forward to it. Happy birthday, Rachel. I love you.'

PART TWO
MARCH 2012

Chapter Seven

Rachel

It's been six weeks since my birthday, which is apparently long enough for Dad to accept an offer on the house and tell me that he would like to pay for me to go back to university. No student debt, no excuse. He called me last night to tell me the 'good' news.

The list he told me to write didn't really help, and now the offer of money has lit the blue touchpaper on a sudden rush of anxiety about the rest of my life, which, it would appear, is sending my mind completely blank.

Dad's present to me was an old briefcase of Mum's. It was a gift from her (mysteriously appearing) uncle at her dad's funeral. Complicated, but stick with me. Apparently it had been a gift from Grandpa on Great-Uncle Cyril's graduation and he wanted Mum to have it. Which was sweet of him then, and sweet of Dad now, but it was taunting me so much when I looked at it that after a few days I had to hide it in my wardrobe.

So, I'm no clearer on a job, which – as I stand here, cuticles deep in baby poo – makes me feel like an abject failure.

A text comes through on my phone and I check over my shoulder to make sure Vicky – our boss – isn't in sight. Reading it, I roll my eyes, shoving my phone back in my pocket. It's no longer just Dad. Now Mo is on one with career suggestions, the latest being sports therapist, no doubt inspired by Olympic fever (and, I imagine, the opportunity to hang around me while I treat men with thighs like Jonny Wilkinson… maybe she's onto something!). It's more appropriate than her previous suggestions, which include international civil rights lawyer (because, sure, I'm *that* smart), aeronautical engineer (so 'we can be among the first when making a new life on a new planet'), and my personal favourite: roller-coaster tester. Apparently it's a real job, but I'm not convinced you need a degree for it, just a strong stomach and excellent pelvic floor.

I pull my phone back out, tapping a response: *I was thinking lion tamer.*

To which Mo responds almost instantly with: *Is this a euphemism?*

I'm unclear what kind of euphemism she's insinuating, which – if nothing else – gives me somewhere to drift off to as I pick out the baby poo from my nails with a wet wipe.

I snort, remembering the look on our teacher's face when Mo said she was going to marry Ryan Giggs and therefore didn't need to work. For someone as smart and independent as she is now, her brief hormone flirtation with being a WAG still makes me chuckle. I guess on some level I can see the appeal… the lifestyle, the cars the… Actually, no, scratch that. I can't. I can't see the appeal at all. Total dependence on one man's career aside, I don't like champagne or football, and I flatly refuse to go bare down there… not that waxing your nether regions to within an inch of their life is necessarily a prerequisite to being married to a footballer, Premier League or otherwise… but the whole self-grooming thing is generally something I do out of necessity, not as a career.

A quiet tap on the glass alerts me to Vicky, peering through the observation window. My mind was hurtling towards the memory of an ill-gotten vajazzle and an industrial tub of Sudocrem, so her interruption is well timed. She stage whispers through a crack in the door, keen not to wake the sleeping babies. 'Can you show a new parent around this afternoon? Mr Moran. Due in at three.'

'Of course, no problem. How old's baby?'

Vicky adopts an artificially informed tone... artificial because I know she plays Sudoku on her laptop when hidden away in her mezzanine office and is usually thus distracted. 'Just him aaaand...' Note check, note check. 'Yes, and the baby' – she turns the notes upside down – 'eight-week-old, Oli.'

'Ahhh, a little one, lovely,' I say.

Phoebe, the new girl on a four-week trial, slopes back in from her lunch break. She smiles as she bites her nails and chews the reward, waiting for me to delegate a job. Another reason for my considering a move: I'm not cut out for managing people. It's not her fault, I just feel bad giving people orders. I end up doing things myself, because I'd hate it if she thought I was being overly bossy.

A word that, each time I think it, I can hear Mo shout, 'Nobody calls a man bossy!'

I cough, then try my hardest. 'Phoebe, can you finish sorting the nappy area, please? Give it a good wipe down and general tidy up. If that's okay. Thank you. Please.'

'Sure,' she drawls, not moving.

'We've a visitor due in at three. Potential new parent. Between now and then we need to be on top of the room, keep it shipshape.'

Shipshape? This is what I mean. I never use words like that in real life! There is something about managing staff that has driven me to introduce aged phrases to my vocabulary. I make a mental note to stop it. Then a mental note to stop making mental notes. I move, but Phoebe stays looking at me.

'Then if you could start with Thomas and move along that back wall, we need to change them all,' I add, slightly flustered, but then, realising that this means I won't have to change another nappy for a good few hours, I begin to see a glimmer of the appeal of management. 'There's more Milton over there,' I say with an emerging air of authority.

The passing of time is punctuated by disinfectant spraying, the room being gradually tidied, and babies waking then wailing to be fed, changed and entertained.

Soon enough, Vicky's dulcet tones echo down the corridor, past all the pre-schoolers' paintings and the rarely looked-at parents' noticeboard. I pick up Maisie – a cute and relatively chilled-out eight-month-old – taking her over to the sensory area. It always helps if the new parents see us being proactive and engaging with the babies. 'Come on, Mais, let's have a look at some bubbles.'

The door opens slowly. 'Rachel, Mr Moran's here.'

Chapter Eight

Ed

The nursery manager ushers me in. 'Mr Moran, this is Rachel. She's in charge of the baby room.'

'Ah, hello, Mr Moran.' A young woman in nursery uniform of jeans and a branded hoody flicks on some lights and bubbles for a young baby to play with. 'Welcome.' She shakes my hand firmly, and I retract it pretty quickly. 'Thanks for coming in to see us.'

I nod, looking around the room, uncertain what questions I'm supposed to ask. Would Ellie have known?

As if picking up on my lack of questions, the nursery nurse continues. 'This is where the babies stay until they're about one, Mr Moran. Then they tend to move into the next room, where their requirements for play can be better catered for. We can feed them their own food, or you can pay slightly more for our kitchen to make them food. They tend to have the same as the older children, just blended according to age. Okay?'

I nod again, scanning the room. It's immaculate, apart from a cobweb that spans from ceiling fan to window frame of the old school building. There's a row of cots; an area where presumably they change the babies; a tidy book corner with cushions all plumped... They take pride in the space, that's clear.

'We've only a few of our babies in today, hence it being just myself and Phoebe here,' she explains. 'We have another two girls who join us on the busier days. We always try to have a 1:3 ratio in this room.'

I wonder if she notices my eyes glaze over at facts I don't really understand or care about. I wouldn't even be here if I didn't have to be. If I didn't need the money.

'Wednesday does tend to be our quietest day, and Monday is the busiest,' she says.

Having reeled off her well-practised patter, both women, whose names I've totally forgotten, stand beside me in an awkward silence that is eventually broken by a kid in the corner, farting. Ellie would have howled, but my sense of humour remains absent.

'If it's okay with you, Mr Moran' – the woman who introduced me to the room touches my arm, making me flinch; do they notice? – 'I'll leave you in Rachel's capable hands for a while.'

Rachel. Remember… Rachel.

'You can spend time in the room, ask her any questions you may have. See how baby likes it, okay?' She doesn't wait for my answer and we are united by her turning her back on us and exiting the room.

'So, am I right in thinking that Oli is six weeks old, Mr Moran?'

'Ed,' I say.

'Oh God. Sorry!' She colours. 'I thought Vicky said…' She waves a hand, passing the blame on to her colleague. 'Of course. I meant Ed.' She smiles, looking at Oli. 'Am I right in thinking Ed is six weeks old now, Mr Moran?'

'He is Oli,' I say, hand on Oli's chest. 'I am Ed.' Her colour deepens. 'I was just saying you could call me Ed, not Mr Moran.'

She laughs, like a train, then stops abruptly. The fact she is so human is somewhat helpful, given that I've no idea what I'm doing. I don't feel so out of my depth. 'Sorry – God, Ed. Hello. Hi. I'm Rachel. Rubbish at being a professional and, on occasion, a grown-up!'

'Right.' Ellie always thought being a grown-up was overrated anyway. She'd have liked this girl… Rachel.

'I'm rarely rubbish at childcare though,' she adds, with a slight grin.

'Oli is eight weeks old,' I say, realising that if she's going to look after him, I need to see if they could develop a bond. Oli cries when I'm not holding him; how will she do here? I kiss the top of his head, take a deep breath, then hand him over.

'Hello, little one,' she says. 'You are a handsome boy.'

'He takes after his mother,' I say.

'Ah, very good answer, Daddy.' She coos in Oli's direction. 'So, Mummy and Daddy are going back to work and they need someone to look after you, then, is that it?'

'Well, it's not quite…' I take another deep breath, feeling the backs of my eyes sting. 'My wife' – I cough the words free – 'she passed away.' *God, it hurts, every time I say it.*

'Oh, no!' Her hand flies to her mouth, then she pulls Oli in closer to her. He doesn't mutter or mumble, but seems to almost snuggle into her. 'Ed, I'm so sorry! I can't even begin to imagine how that must be for you.' She looks down at Oli. 'And he's so… God, you must be devastated.'

That's one word, I think.

'God, that's a stupid thing to say. Of course you're devastated. Sorry!'

'It's okay.'

'I remember when my mum died, people would say things like, "She's in a better place," or, "It will get easier with time," and I remember wondering how they could be so stupid. Sorry, I should have known better.'

She offers Oli back to me, as if instinctively she sees I need him. I hold him in tight, as if my life depends on him… which it probably does. Does she see that? Given that she understands grief.

'Are you seeing any other nurseries?' she asks.

'I don't think that will be necessary,' I say. Certain about the first thing since Ellie died. 'Here is perfect, thank you.'

'We'd love to have Oli. *I'd* love to have him. And we can go at your pace, there's no rush to leave him. However long it takes to establish the new routine for you is fine.'

'I have to get back to work, I'm paid on bonuses. I can't really afford not to.'

'Ah, I see. Okay, well, we would normally do two sessions to ease him in, make sure he settles okay. If you'd rather we do more, that's fine. When you're ready, we'd encourage you to leave him so that you can both see how you do without each other.'

My heart thumps.

'It's okay,' she says, as if she feels it. 'You can grab a coffee and sit in the office with Vicky, if that's easier. It's just so that we can all see how easily Oli will settle.'

I nod, uncertain.

'Honestly? At this age, much to most parents' dismay, the babies usually don't even notice you're missing.'

'Okay.' I should probably be relieved, but wonder if that's the same for Ellie. Did he notice she had gone? Does he now?

'Let me know when it suits to have the first session.'

'Um, Friday?'

'Perfect.'

She reaches for the door, giving me my getaway. Which is good, because this is the longest I've held it together in public and I don't know how much more strength I have in me.

'Thanks for your time,' I croak, glad she turns away as I leave and the floodgates of pain reopen. *Six weeks since Ellie died. Oli is eight weeks old. Is he too young for nursery? Is it too soon for me?* I strap him into the car seat. 'Sorry, little man. But we have no choice. Let's hope your mummy would forgive me.'

Chapter Nine

Rachel

'Come on in, let me take your bag. I've made up a peg for Oli so we'll hang his things on there. Are there nappies in there?'

'Erm, yes.' He hovers by the door before handing me the bag, perhaps deciding he's not going to run away.

'We tend to put nappies into named trays too, so we only ever use the ones you bring in for him.' I stack the new pack of Huggies into Oli's tray. 'We provide wipes, though, unless you need a particular kind used for him?'

'Oh, no, I don't think so.'

'That's fine, some people just prefer an eco-version, or sensitive ones, that's all.'

Ed looks around, somehow uneasy in our surroundings. Has he changed his mind since choosing us so quickly, so certainly? Is he having second thoughts about it all? I can't imagine how he's feeling. He looks giant-like in a room full of tiny people. He moves clumsily out of the way as a pair of ten-month-old boys crawl off to make their mischief. 'They're a pair…' I nod. 'If I ever lose sight of them, you can be sure they're emptying nappies and wipes from the low-level trays round here,' I say. 'So young, yet so cheeky!'

Phoebe crawls after the boys, talking to them as she tries to scoop them both up and occupy them with some shape sorters.

'Do you want to sit down?' I signal for Ed to head over to the sensory area, usually a good place to do the first introduction session. 'Pop Oli down and see how he gets on.'

Ed does as suggested, cross-legged before Oli. I leave them both for a moment, sorting a few jobs while watching him. He is wholly focused on Oli, his hand resting on his son's tiny chest as he rocks him gently side to side, talking to him. Sometimes he breaks into a smile, just a gentle one, inspired by something about his boy. Sometimes he sighs, a heavy sigh from the depths of his boots, but quietly... perhaps so I don't hear it. Sometimes he seems to drift off, gazing at nothing, zoned out. After a while, I head back and sit down beside them, propping myself up against the wall. I pull Maisie onto my lap so that I can use her to avoid eye contact, for Ed's sake more than my own.

'How do you feel about going back to work?'

He sighs one of those heavy sighs again. 'Oh, I can't wait. I've really missed being in an office where taking the piss out of each other is a prerequisite. I think this emotional precipice upon which I teeter is the perfect place to handle jokes, usually at other peoples' wives' expense.'

'Eurgh, sounds...'

'Like a school playground full of testosterone-fuelled idiot boys?' He raises his eyebrows in question. 'Yeah, that's pretty much it,' he says, flatly.

'Jeez, what do you do?'

'I'm in recruitment. IT specialists. A job that's perfect if you like drinking, money and banter. A job that is not so suited to a man mourning his wife, I fear.'

'No.'

He rubs at his face, leaning back against the wall. 'In truth, I'd rather not go back at all, but I need the money. And Ellie…' His confidence falters. 'My wife… well, she'd be bloody furious if she thought I was lounging around feeling sorry for myself.' His smile is sad, resolute almost. 'And I need to pay for my increased wine intake somehow.' I look up at him. 'That last bit was a joke,' he adds. 'I quickly realised that drinking was not good when you had to get up with the baby.'

'Inconvenient,' I joke, which, pleasingly, makes him laugh a little. 'Well, I reckon Oli will be just fine, looking at him now.' Oli is flat out, legs bent like a frog and arms above his head in total submission. 'Is he always this chilled out?'

Ed nods. 'Pretty much. He would cry a lot, after the accident, but I don't know if that was anything to do with his mum not being there, or just the fact that I was crap at recognising the sign for hungry, nappy change or comfort.'

'Ah, yes, apparently some of them have a different cry for each thing they need. I'm not convinced, though. It's always been a process of elimination for me. Maybe mothers can tell the difference, but I certainly can't!'

Ed stares down at Oli.

'Sorry, that was… insensitive.'

'Don't worry. I'd rather someone said the occasional thoughtless thing than didn't talk to me at all. You lose a wife, you lose normal conversation. Everyone wants to know how you are, how you're feeling… if they talk to you at all. The ones who turn away are probably the worst. You know they're doing it because they've got nothing to say. That's going to be the hardest thing about going back to work. The pitying looks and the phone calls to people who probably think I've just been on an elongated paternity leave."

'How very self-indulgent of you!'

'Got to get your holidays in where you can, eh? How else can I keep on top of my box sets?'

He smiles briefly and, for a moment, I can see what he might have looked like before all this happened. Handsome. Strong. Confident, not arrogant, I think. He has the kind of hands you'd want to be held by. Arms that could wrap you up and make life okay. I realise he's staring at me and that I should probably stop analysing him. Though not before wondering if this tragedy has aged him; if the crease marks around his eyes were there before; if laughter was the cause, or if those, and the darkness beneath his eyes, are all new.

'How old were you, when your mum...' he asks suddenly.

'Twelve.' I reach behind me for some tissue to wipe Maisie's nose, stuffing it in my pocket when I'm done.

'What's it like?' he asks, looking down at Oli.

I think for a moment. 'As awful as what you're going through, but for different reasons I guess. What can I say?'

'I wonder how Oli will cope.'

I sigh. 'Well, for the most part, I imagine, he'll cope fine. Because, sadly, or maybe in some respects fortuitously – I don't know – he won't know any different. And that's awful, isn't it, but he will grow up understanding this as his normal.' Ed drops his head and I realise I've got a short space of time before this conversation unravels him. 'There'll be other stuff he'll find hard, I imagine. When kids have their mums on hand and he doesn't, but you'll work through it. Together. Look' – I put my hand on his, then wish I hadn't been quite so forward and pretend that I've got an itch to get my stupid wandering hand back – 'Oli will be okay, ultimately. As will you, eventually. Because survival kicks in. I'm not saying you'll get over it. I'd never suggest that. Just that you'll find a way to get up every day. You'll do what you need to do to live.' I stagger up, shifting Maisie onto my hip. 'Right, I'm going to leave you to it. Wake Oli, if you want to; show him a few other bits in the room, if you like. I'll check the diary to work out when you can come in to drop him off. And I promise,' I say to his startled look, 'he'll be okay!'

Ed nods, gets up and takes Oli over to the book corner. I get a text from Mo with another job suggestion, but shove it into my pocket this time. After this two-minute chat I realise I'm needed here, just for a while. Maybe this situation will help me, too. And you know, childcare's not all bad... not really.

Chapter Ten

Ed

Rachel was right about the trial session being more for me than for Oli. After my first session, staying with him, seeing her move around the room and tend to the children, I thought I was okay with dropping him off and sitting outside. But I was useless, my foot tapping on the floor of their office mezzanine like I'd had too much coffee, or speed, or perhaps both. She'd popped out of the room to assure me he was fine and, in truth, when I went back in after time was thankfully up, he seemed it. I picked him up, I tickled the spot on his shoulders that always gets a smile, and he wriggled like I knew he would, then let out a giggle. For the first time in his short life, he actually laughed. My nerves and fear and tension disintegrated as I heard what memory says was a belly laugh, but probably wasn't really. Belly or no, it made me laugh too! It made me realise that I'd not laughed in weeks, and so alien yet delicious was the moment that I tickled him again, until both he and I were laughing together... and it was the best, the brightest moment I'd had in ages. And then Rachel joined in with the laughter and the best moment, in that very second, soared up there to become one of the worst. I was sharing it with someone who wasn't Ellie. That very fact packed a punch that pushed me silent.

Rachel said she understood. She said that my tears were understand-able, that it was okay to cry, as she passed me a tissue then left me to collect my thoughts. But I felt an idiot. Not because men shouldn't cry, nothing stupid like that… it was just that the weight of my grief caught me by surprise. I wasn't prepared. I wasn't at home, on my own, where I could embrace the pain more completely. It was in such contrast to the love I was feeling for Oli, and it suffocated the feeling of being happy.

But it was the proof I needed that Oli was going to be okay. And that is why I went back this morning, to drop him off before my first official day at work. Rachel and I stood nervously opposite each other for a second, before she took control and lifted him from my arms, unhooking his bag from my shoulder. 'Go on,' she instructed, 'he'll be fine.' And I wanted to ask her if I would be too.

But how could she know, how could anyone? And even if she had answered, it wouldn't have changed the fact that after a total of ten weeks off work – two for Oli, followed by the eight I've taken to try to find some sense in this new life – I am now sat here at my desk, just wondering how soon I can leave to pick Oli up and then retreat to the safety of our home.

'How're you doing, mate?' Colleague and friend, Greg, shifts my in-tray to create space for him to perch on my desk, a steaming mug of tea in his hand. I stare at my screen, numb. 'You getting on okay?'

'If staring into oblivion, clock-watching till home time is okay, then, yes, sure, I'm good. Great. Never fucking better.'

'Stupid question then?' he asks, knowing full well the answer. 'Look, the first day back was never going to be good.' He puts his hand on my shoulder, giving it a squeeze of support. 'But it's almost over and tomorrow's another day, and then Wednesday. You'll get there, just—'

'Take my time. Be kind to myself. Go gently at first.'

'Well, that sounds a bit more new-age-hippy than I was thinking, but essentially, yes, I guess so!' I give him a look that suggests I've heard it all before. 'Alright, fair enough. Supportive friend probably isn't the most natural position for me, but I'm trying my best.' He grins at me, kindly, and I'm grateful he's big enough to ignore my mood. 'You didn't have to come back yet, you know.'

'It was this or mother-and-baby groups. I don't know the words to nursery rhymes, never mind the actions.'

'There are actions to nursery rhymes?'

'So Ellie said.' It's the first time I've mentioned her name in the office and there's a brief lull in the usual hum of work noise around our open-plan space. Or maybe I just imagine it. 'Besides, I've got contractors leaving right, left and centre. Clients who want them replacing without realising that process takes time, even if I didn't hate the idea of picking the phone up and talking to people about possible jobs. Honestly? I don't think I have the energy or interest to build it back up from scratch, but I need the money.'

Greg nods.

'Basically' – I lower my voice, tired of it all – 'I don't care. I hate this place, I hate this job, and I hate my life.' Greg stares at me until I relent. 'Maybe I did come back too soon.'

'We all thought you'd take longer.'

'We all did, did we? Good to know. Did *we* have any suggestions on how long? Does the grief recovery period change depending on who it is and under what circumstances?'

Greg shifts awkwardly. 'Sorry, mate. I'm making a hash of this, aren't I?'

I groan. Because as much as I can't cope with this job, I'm fast realising I also can't cope with people understanding my mood swings… forgiving them. Sympathy breeds the need to run away.

Greg catches sight of the framed photo on my desk. An hour-old Oli with his mum. It was the first thing I did when I got in this morning: I put this photo in place of the one of Ellie and me on our wedding day, which I couldn't look at, so placed in the drawer beside me. He lifts it up to take a closer look as he sips at his drink and I know that steam from his mug is teasing the polished silver frame. I stop myself taking it from him.

We fall silent. My leg twitches beneath the desk so I reach down to try and hold it firm, turning my attention back to my desk to perform an end-of-news-bulletin paper shuffle. Maybe now he'll leave me be.

'And, erm… how's your brother?'

I flip around to look at Greg. I can just about cope with Ellie's name being mentioned, but I've put thoughts of Simon to the back of my mind for weeks now. I can't face thinking about him; I can't explore my feelings about him. Mum has kept trying, in phone calls and visits. Telling me he's devastated. That he's not coping. I asked if that meant he was drinking and she fumbled her answer, which was all I needed to know. Her response, plus Lisa's accusation: it all means that talking to him is currently a no go.

'Ed?' Greg tries to catch my eye.

If Simon had been drinking when he drove Ellie home… That's all I keep thinking.

'Ed?'

'I don't know. I don't know how he is. We haven't really spoken. Look, Greg, thanks for the chat, but I'm busy, I need to… to do a few things before I head off to collect Oli.' I turn my back and pick up the phone as if about to make a call, though I've no idea who to.

Greg slides off the edge of my desk. 'Sorry if I got this wrong, mate. I'm crap in a crisis, but if you can put up with me saying stupid shit, I'm here if you need anything. Anything at all.'

'Cheers, I appreciate it.' I nod, picking through paperwork for an imaginary number. Greg walks away and I put the phone back in the holder as a text message comes through to my phone. I open it without looking at the sender.

Ed, I'm sorry. For everything. I never meant this to happen. I wish it had been me.

My brain fogs with the words, with confusion. A message I'm unprepared for. A method of reaching out that I can't quite believe. I read it again. And again. Is this it? Out of the blue? Weeks of no contact? Weeks of Mum telling me we need to talk and all I get is a text? My wife dies in his car and *this* is the best my brother can do? So he can put a pint glass to his lips and obliterate the memories, but he can't find the strength to do anything other than text message an apology?

I pick my office phone up again, furiously punching Simon's mobile number into it, waiting for it to connect. I tap my desk, I shift in my seat. My heart is racing. I'm angry. I'm full of rage. I'm incan-fucking-descent.

The phone connects, rings three times, then goes dead.

I dial again, pulling myself up tight to my desk in an effort to keep me still, to contain myself. The line is quiet as it tries to connect until, eventually, a generic voice invites me to leave a message after the tone. I slam the phone down. Simon might think there are words to placate this situation, but I fucking don't.

Chapter Eleven

Ed

From the office, propelled by the anger, hurt and confusion that permeate every bone in my body, I got here in no time. I launched myself out of the car and up the path to the house, knocking furiously for someone to come to the door. I knocked so hard that my knuckles still hurt some twenty minutes later. I wasn't sure what I was going to say or do when he opened the door. Part of me could feel my fingers fizz with the desire to hit, to cause him pain, but clearly no one is at home.

I return to the car to wait. While I was driving here, part of my heart had begun to feel different. Thoughts of us as kids together had flashed into my mind: the mud pies we'd make, then paste up an old metal washing line; squishing tiny red spiders on the stone wall outside our house; the grazed knees when we were learning to ride our bikes. He was my childhood partner in crime, the one who always got me into trouble, but who I always forgave, because that was my job as Simon's big brother. *Take the flack then rise above it, pinch him when no one is looking, then play on.*

With these memories came a brief softness in my heart, but ultimately the desires of my fist took over the second I saw their front door. How broken must he be to think he can avoid me for so long, avoid this conversation, then simply text an apology? That's not the Simon I grew up with. He might have got me into trouble in the past, but it was mischief not naughtiness. He was kind, really. He was thoughtful. He was the sort of person who'd tell you he was proud if you did something good, who'd volunteer to help out with jobs around the house. Sometimes I'd tease him for it, call him a square, or a suck up. But, actually, I admired him. He'd see things that needed doing before anyone else noticed.

So, I'm angry; fuck, am I angry. But I'm hurting, too. And confused. And maybe... maybe I'm even a bit worried about him. We've been gradually losing touch as the years have gone by. He's slowly built a wall around himself. He's detached – maybe from when he met Lisa – to the point now where we barely see him. We barely know him. He rebuilt his life after taking a few wrong turns. After losing confidence, turning to drink. He saw it was killing him and he fixed it. At that point, I thought we'd rebuild our relationship too, but Lisa... she seemed to want him all to herself. And so, it never happened. I lost him. I didn't know him any more. And, clearly, I still don't. I mean, what kind of person sends a text message of 'sorry', when that person killed your wife?

He *killed* my wife.

Which is why I sit here, waiting for someone to return, my itchy fingers drumming on the steering wheel. My heart is racing, my mind is fogged in disbelief.

A tap on the window makes me jump. Steamed up, I open the door to find Lisa standing on the pavement, her coat pulled around her in the cold air. The light is going, I haven't noticed that near dusk has swallowed the street, the houses. 'Ed?' she says, her eyes narrowed. Is she suspicious of *me*? What the hell for?

'Where's Simon?'

Lisa laughs, nastily, then turns on her heel and walks up to the house. I get out of the car and notice, for the first time, that their curtains are drawn and there's a recycling box of empty bottles and cans on the doorstep. 'Well,' she says, pointing to the box. 'It looks like he's drunk everything in the house now, so if recent behaviour's anything to go by, he's out to find more. Again. Like he always does.'

'Where? Where does he go?' I chase after her, knocked back slightly as she throws her handbag back on her shoulder after extracting the house keys.

'He goes anywhere, Ed. Everywhere, if you will. He goes down the Arboretum, by the tram stop up at the goose fair site. I found him in a pub down Hockley the other day, a tip off from a neighbour. Apparently he's been found curled up on the steps of the town hall before now too. You name the location, he's probably drinking, drunk or passed out there.'

She reels the facts off as if it's totally normal behaviour. As if she's numb to it because he's been doing it for so long, but to my mind, he's been sober for years. At least, that was always the message from Mum.

'Since when?' I spit. 'When did he start drinking again?'

'Your guess is as good as mine.'

'Since the accident?'

She unlocks the door, stepping inside, pausing as if she's trying to remember that far back.

It was eight weeks! I want to shout. *Eight weeks!*

'God knows, Ed. If you find out, perhaps you could let me know. I haven't been able to track him down for months. He'd disappear without a trace then turn up out of the blue. He'd ignore my calls. He'd come home, late, without a reason for where he'd been. Without routine, or purpose. He'd drink his way through God knows what.' She points down to the recycling. Apparently as evidence. 'Jesus, it wouldn't surprise me if he was having an affair, he was so secretive about everything. Good luck finding him. And if you do, good luck getting any sense out of him. I'm done, washing my hands. Our marriage is over.'

'An affair?' I say. Lisa turns to face me, staring, her face frozen in the moment. 'Who with?'

'Who with?' she repeats. She looks up and down the street, then right back at me. 'Who knows. Maybe Ellie could have answered that question, were she still here.'

Lisa slams the door shut and I start knocking again. My knuckles still sore, red raw now from knocking harder. 'Lisa! Lisa! Open the door! What do you mean Ellie could have answered? What are you talking about? LISA!'

I bang my fist on the door in frustration as a bloke passes the end of the path. 'Everything alright, mate?' he asks, blocking my way from leaving. He folds his arms and fixes me with a glare that adds fuel to my anger.

'Not really. Mate!' I labour the point.

'Well, maybe Lisa' – he nods towards the house, and I'm not sure if he knows her or is jumping to conclusions, based on hearing me shout – 'doesn't wanna talk to you.' He steps back, inviting me to leave. I glance back at the house, then at my car, eyeballing the bloke.

My watch beeps six o'clock and I realise I should be at the nursery to pick up Oli. 'Fuck!' I growl, climbing into my car. As I start the engine, the bloke perches on the wall as if to check I'm really leaving.

How dare she? How fucking dare she! That was my wife, MY wife. Why would she have the answers? Does Lisa mean Ellie and Simon were...? Ellie wouldn't have done something like that, I know she wouldn't.

Except the sound of Simon's voice when he called after the accident comes flooding back, louder than it ever was before. *Ellie was with me, Ed. Ellie was with me… she's… she's…'*

He never finished the sentence; a paramedic took over telling me where to meet them. A & E at Queens. Ellie was dead on arrival and, from the look in his eye, so was Simon. I'd asked him what they were doing… she'd left a note saying she was going for fresh air. She'd said nothing about Simon. I'd asked how they'd met up and now I realise he'd never answered. Mum had ushered me away. Was she protecting me or him? They wouldn't… would they?

No! No!

I start the car up, pulling off with a tyre spin as I head back to the city centre. If the bloke outside their house watches me leave, I don't notice. I'm dialling Simon's number, one last time. But it doesn't ring. There's no voicemail this time either. Just a dead line, number not recognised.

Pulling into the nursery car park, I shake my head, trying to rid myself of the crumbs of doubt that are collecting in the back of my mind. I rub my face, my hair, I knock sense into my skull with the heel of my hand. How could Simon let things get so bad with Lisa that she would say something like this, now, to me? How could either of them do that?

I swallow back the salty sting of tears, anger still spitting in my chest. It's nearly half past six. First day back after ten weeks off and I've achieved nothing at work. First day leaving Oli at nursery and I'm late to pick him up.

I can't do this. I need her, I need Ellie!

Chapter Twelve

Rachel

It's past six thirty when Ed finally bursts in. 'Sorry, I'm so sorry!' he says, flustered and distracted as he bends down to pick Oli up. 'I didn't realise what time it was, I…' He pulls Oli into him, holding him tight, eyes closed. He lets out a deep breath as if he's held it since dropping Oli off at eight thirty this morning. He fumbles him to his left- then right-hand side, before trying to turn him round in his arms, almost dropping him in the process. 'Shit,' he says, as I leap towards them both, pushing Oli safely back into his arms.

'Is everything okay?' I ask, taking his arm to try to steady him.

'No, it isn't. Not really. Far from it, but there we go, that's just…' He looks around for Oli's stuff. 'Look, sorry I'm so late. Let me get out of your way, I'm sure you wanna go home.' He jogs over to the peg with Oli's things on, pulling at the bag, which won't come away from its hook. 'Fuck!' he says, when he eventually liberates it only for the contents to spill and clatter onto the floor. 'I can't do this!' He stops, thumb and forefinger from his free hand pulling his eyes closed, dropping against the wall as if out of energy, sliding down it, Oli still in his arms.

I pause a second, not sure what to do. Ed swallows, wiping his eyes, kissing Oli on the head. 'Here, let me,' I say gently, bending down to pick up the dummies, bottles, nappies and spare change of clothes that lie scattered around his feet. Bag open, I rest back on my heels, folding and placing things neatly inside. The sound of my packing Oli's bag is amplified somehow. The energy in the room is thick. I glance up at Ed, who's staring at me.

'I can't do this,' he says again, quietly.

I lean forwards. 'You can,' I say gently.

'How?'

'I don't know, giving yourself time, maybe. Being patient with yourself and others. Asking for help.'

He lets out a hiccup, as if I've just suggested the most ridiculous thing in the world to him. 'Who do you think I have?' he asks.

'Okay, so I can't answer that. We barely know each other.' I laugh awkwardly. 'But, look, *I'm* here to help, with Oli at least. He's been brilliant today, so calm. You must be doing a great job, for him to settle so quickly.' His eyes fill again and I feel compelled to place my hand on his knee. 'It's going to take time.' He looks up. 'And all those other clichés, I know.' He smiles sadly. 'But let's agree at the very least, that this bit, the Oli at nursery bit, let's agree that we can do this together. I was going to leave, as it goes. Retrain. No idea what as, just something with career prospects. I'm hurtling toward thirty at an alarming rate and I'm not sure I like it.'

'Your thirties are nothing.'

'No, probably not. But it feels like something, and it feels like I want to achieve something. Let's make it this – working together to help you to get into a new routine, where arriving late to pick Oli up doesn't tip you over the edge!'

'I'm a potential achievement, am I?' Ed moves Oli to his knees. 'Hear that little man?'

'Well… for want of a better word, I'm going to say yes. You are. Let me help you find a new routine. Besides, you'll be an excuse that buys me time. My best friend and my dad are desperate to pack me off to university and I've no idea what to do there. This is as good an excuse as any for me to postpone a life decision I feel unprepared for.' He gives a shallow nod. 'Look.' I reach out to his arm, but he pulls it back and I can feel the moment moving on; he's building his barrier back up.

I get up and move away to pack up the last of the room. 'Take as long as you want,' I say over my shoulder, giving him the space I can see that he needs. 'I've got a few jobs here, some packing away. Bet you that you're ready to go before I am.' And I set about making jobs up to occupy my time for as long as it takes.

'You okay?' I ask, when Ed eventually stands up to leave.

He shrugs.

'See you tomorrow?'

'See you tomorrow.' He nods, pausing at the door before heading out of it.

I stare out of the window a moment, wondering if there is anything I could have said or done differently just now; something that could help him process whatever is going on in his mind. Then I remember how impossible it is for anyone to understand what you go through when you lose a loved one. Every experience is unique. I guess the only thing he needs, or the only thing I can give him, perhaps, is patience.

By the time I get home, I find Mo unscrewing a bottle of Pinot, then pouring a generous glass, which she promptly knocks back before breathlessly telling me she's had 'a shit of a day'. I reach for an empty glass, clinking hers so she'll pour. 'You too?' she asks. 'Good job I bought two bottles then. Get the pizza menu, meet me in the lounge in five. You can offload first, then it's my turn and, prepare yourself, I have ALL of the swears for today. Literally ALL of them.'

That's when I'm reminded how reassuring it is when someone has your back, and how good it feels to have theirs in return... especially when they need it most. And I can't help feeling as though Ed doesn't have that person.

Chapter Thirteen

Ed

Embarrassment and discomfort creep across my chest each time I think about last night, picking Oli up, and then again this morning, dropping him off, pretending my 'breakdown' – for want of a better word – hadn't happened. I avoided Rachel's eyes. I aimed for an air of efficient and grown-up, desperate to prove to her that I am not completely falling to pieces. I don't know why it matters to show that to Rachel, or to anyone, but it does. It just does.

Perhaps it's part of the mask I need to wear for work. The suit of 'in control' that proves I am ready to come back. That now is the time to find a new normal among the devastation. That I have the strength to do it.

The sweaty palms, nervous voice and sleep deprivation suggest entirely the opposite.

'Hi, this is Ed from IT. You… I just wondered if…'

People hanging up on me each time I try to make a call and offer them a job isn't helping. Three more contractors left this morning. If I dip any lower my company car is at risk. Not to mention my bonus.

'Hi, it's Ed. How are you? Long time no… oh, are you? Permanent now? Okay, thanks anyway. If you know— Hello? Hello?'

I slam the phone down, leaning back in my chair with a groan, then a yawn. I was up all night, analysing the last few months of Ellie's life. Looking for clues that prove Lisa wrong… there are plenty. The only clue to suggest she wasn't wrong is the most obvious – Ellie being in Simon's car. But that doesn't prove anything, I know it doesn't. And yet, she's not here to ask and that very fact means I keep turning it over in my mind. Trying to get rid of it, burying my head in pillows to suffocate the sound of a voice in my head saying, *But how do you know?*

I called Mum, asked her if she'd heard from Simon. Nothing, he's avoiding her now too. She said she was getting worried, thought she might have to try to track him down and talk to him. Get him to listen to her, maybe even get him help. I asked her if she knew he was drinking, and she stuttered and faltered over her answer. Yes… no… she didn't know.

The uncertainty of everything is eating away at me.

I dial another number. 'Hi, it's Ed from…' There's a torrent of abuse down the line. 'No? Right. Okay.' I hold the phone out, away from my ear, the energy to hang up now depleted.

Greg, appearing like a perfectly timed apparition, takes the phone from my hand and places it in the cradle. 'Come on, Langtry's are serving,' he says, rolling my chair away from my desk by way of invitation. 'If you get up and come with me now, I'll pay.'

I groan, but push myself out of the chair. 'There's motivation,' I grunt, grabbing my jacket. We travel silently down in the lift. I reach into my pocket to pull out my phone, just in case I've missed a call from Simon. Or a message. I tap one out to the number he called me from: *We need to talk.* But it doesn't send.

On the ground floor, through the revolving doors, the bright spring sunshine hurts my eyes. The air has that gentle warmth that comes in spring.

'Nice,' says Greg, turning his face to the sun.

Ellie loved this time of year.

Breathe.

We jog across the road, dodging a tram on its way to Old Market Square. The clock rings out on the Council House, a girl pushes past us, running up to meet a guy at the Left Lion. He picks her up in his arms and swings her round before smothering her in kisses that she passionately returns. I look down at the ground.

'Steak and ale?' asks Greg, reaching for the pub door.

'Yeah, cheers.'

I find a table, stuffing my jacket on the windowsill behind me.

'How're you doing, mate?' asks Greg, sitting down opposite me, sipping froth from his pint glass as he passes me mine.

'Well, you've saved me from another lunch of cup-a-soup and disillusion so I guess I should be fine,' I mumble.

'Oli alright?'

The mention of his name brings a rare warmth to my heart. 'He's…' But I can't quite find the words to explain exactly what he is to me right now. 'The only reason to get up in the morning' seems heavier than a lunchtime pie and pint warrants. 'He's good, cheers.'

Greg peels at a beer mat, ripping the advert clean off and folding it into a square that he fiddles and twists. 'Are you coping?'

'Ha!' I remember last night's meltdown again. And this morning, my hands shaking as I handed Oli over and Rachel tried to search out eye contact so she could tell me to have a good day. 'I'm as okay as I guess I can be. I mean, what else can I do?' I say, hoping that this makes me sound stronger than I really feel.

Greg nods, and drinks more of his beer. I wonder if he's looking for something else to say, but it's a relief that he doesn't try to fill the void in conversation with well-meant advice; a pie and a pint is exactly what I need, and nothing else.

Lunch arrives and I stare down at the plate of classic pub grub, which is also the most food I've seen on one plate in months. I pick at the pastry and mash, overwhelmed. Greg chats about his single life, the football, our boss, his plans for a new car. I let it all wash over me, instead staying focused on finishing lunch, then actually going back to work, rather than the more appealing option of sitting here and getting slowly, but spectacularly, drunk.

The break in my day proved to be exactly what was required. As five o'clock arrives, I've set up a few candidates for interviews and organised a meeting with a new client. Maybe I *can* do this after all. If I can get back into the swing of things; if I do what Rachel said, and take my time; if I'm patient. What felt like a mountainous challenge last night still seems mountainous, but perhaps I can find a way to scale it regardless. I pile files and papers in some semblance of order, preparing for tomorrow, before picking up my keys, wallet and phone and heading out of the door. I won't be late for Oli today.

The sound of my shoes echoes through the stairwell as I jog down the stairs and then across the newly polished marble floor. Pushing through the revolving doors, I check the sky for the weather.

And that's when I see him.

Simon.

Standing across the road. Staring.

My feet root, my body turns ice cold and he looks at me. *Does he know what Lisa said? Did she tell him I wanted to see him?*

'Shit, is that Simon?' Greg comes through the doors behind me, but before he can finish the sentence, a run of three buses, then a tram, passes between us and the other side of the road. I strain to try and keep sight of Simon through the rush-hour footfall that busies along the pavement, but as the end of the tram passes, he's gone.

'Was it him?' asks Greg.

'I…' But now I doubt it myself. I scan the street up and down. I check this side in case he made it across and is coming towards me. But I can't see him anywhere. Was he there or was it just someone that looked like him? 'I don't know…' I relent eventually.

Greg squints as if to get a better look for himself. 'God, how weird. If it was, he doesn't look good. In fact, I'd go as far as to say he looks worse now than he did at the…' Greg's sentence trails off as he realises he's about to talk about the funeral. We don't talk about the funeral.

'I've got to fetch Oli,' I say, making my excuse to leave. As I head up the street to the car park, I keep looking around me, just in case. If it *was* Simon, he's nowhere to be seen now. If it *was* Simon, what was he doing there, just standing, watching? Did he mean to visit, or was he passing from one pub to the next, as Lisa had suggested?

Throughout the journey across town to pick up Oli, I wrap myself up in 'what ifs', so that by the time I approach the nursery, I've lost track of focus. I'm zipping through traffic, catching sight of myself in the rear-view mirror. Eyes I don't recognise stare back: wild, tired, manic; eyes that don't belong to me any more. Or not to the man I was. The face too, older, paler, more angry. Grief and hurt are etched across my brow, my cheeks, my mouth turns down.

I lurch into the car park for the nursery, dazed. I park up and climb out. I have no memory of the journey here. Was it Simon? Surely he'd have come over if it was? I reach the heavy front door and bang on it for someone to let me in. I fly into the baby room, marginally relieved to see that I'm not the last one to be picking up. 'I made it!' I say, pulling Oli's bag from the peg.

Perhaps my face gives away my mood.

'Ed, are you okay?' asks Rachel, concern etched over her face.

'Yes, just… wanted to make sure I wasn't late.'

'You're not!' she says, peering at me. 'Are you sure you're okay?'

'I'm fine,' I lie, rubbing at the back of my neck. 'Long day. Busy job.'

'Oh, um, okay.' She takes a step towards me, seeking out eye contact that I avoid. 'Oli's had another good day, he loves the book corner, and we did some painting today, too. Well, I painted his hands, placed them on the paper and rubbed them about a bit… look.' She points over to a wall of finger-painted sugar paper, each one a mix of colours which ultimately looks a sort of streaky, greeny-brown. 'It's a tractor,' she says, but I think she might be joking.

'Great, that's…' I can feel myself going again, but I won't. Not two nights in a row.

Rachel steps towards me, reaching out as if she wants to guide me to a seat, but I need to leave. The room is closing in; this conversation is too.

'If he's ready, I'd like to get straight off. Lots to do, you know?' It's like I'm outside myself looking in, not hearing my voice in my own head. Everything's louder and quieter in equal measure. Everything's fogged.

'Oh, of course. Here… His bag's packed, his diary's in there too. We could do with some more nappies tomorrow, if possible.' She's moving around the room as I edge closer to the door.

'More nappies. Sure.'

'Here,' she says, pointing to Oli, reminding me that he's not in my arms. She picks him up from a playmat where he's gazing at an arch of dangling zoo animals. I reach to take him from her, putting him between us, protecting me, that tiny human shield again.

Silence envelops us. I need to leave, I want to run, I need to thank her for her help, her kindness, but I also want to hide.

'This is hard, right?' I eventually say, facing the door. Through the glass, I see her face reflected. A look of sympathy, of pity, it almost breaks me. 'Please, don't!' I pull open the door. 'I am barely holding it together as it is. Your understanding, your kindness, it makes things worse somehow.'

'Sorry, Ed. I guess I'm not sure I know what else to do. I get it, you know? It's as though everyone looks at you with pity in their eyes.'

'They do.'

'They care.' She comes beside me, taking the door to hold it open. 'You could talk to someone, get some counselling maybe. Take walks, read,' she says.

'I can't concentrate on anything.'

'You will. In time. And the talking might help.'

Oli gives her a gummy grin as she strokes his face, and I'm overwhelmed with gratefulness that, if nothing else, he has her in his life.

'Thank you,' I say. 'I didn't mean to offload. Again.'

'It's fine. I'd say that's what I'm here for, but it probably sounds weird.'

'A little,' I try and joke.

'If I can do anything, though.' She fixes me with a serious look. 'Anything at all.'

'Work out where my brother is?' I say, flippantly. 'Or why my sister-in-law wants to poison the memory of my wife?' Rachel's eyes widen and I wish I could take it back. 'Ignore me. I'll see you tomorrow.'

'Okay, and hey, try talking to her.'

'My sister-in-law?'

'Your wife,' she answers simply. 'I've always found it helps with Mum. When I'm stuck. I mean, I know it's not the same...'

'It's not,' I clip, then wish it hadn't come out quite so sharply. 'Look, sorry, maybe you're right. And I appreciate it. I appreciate you. It's nice having someone who understands.'

Rachel colours slightly. 'Go home,' she says, gently. 'Try to sleep. Tomorrow is a new day.'

I nod. 'Thanks, Rachel. I'll see you tomorrow.'

Strapping Oli into his seat in the back of the car, I get a tingling across the back of my neck. A sense that I'm not alone. 'Why were you in his car, Ellie?' I ask into the evening sky. 'And why would Lisa suggest there was a reason I should know about? And why won't Simon face up to what he has done and talk to me? What's going on?'

But the sky doesn't answer; it offers no defence. And, harder than that, I realise, is that my heart doesn't either. For the first time since the accident, I question more than just why was Ellie in Simon's car. Now I'm questioning her, too. And she's not even here to answer.

Chapter Fourteen

Rachel

'Rachel, I've just realised the perfect career for you. I don't know why it took us so long to work it out. Meet me at Annie's, I'm going to surprise you with the news over a burger and a strawberry milkshake.'

'I'd rather have a beer.'

'Ungrateful!'

'Okay, okay. Strawberry milkshake it is. If I agree with you, we can always progress to a beer!'

'Beer? I'm watching my waistline!'

'At Annie's Burger Shack?' I ask, incredulous.

'Shush! What you having?'

'Thin Lizzy with curly fries.'

'Cool, see you in twenty?'

'Twenty.'

I hear her pick up her bag and keys as she hangs up and can picture her slinging boots and a coat on as she heads out of the door and through the Lace Market. My mouth waters at the prospect of burger, but my heart flutters at the prospect of Mo coming up with the perfect career move at exactly the point I don't want to move. More than anything, because she will insist on knowing why I've gone cold on the idea of leaving work. Something I'm not sure I've entirely processed myself. It's just a feeling.

'Science Teacher!' Mo declares, when we meet up, placing her hands palm down on the table, fait accompli. 'It's so obvious now, I can't believe we've been faffing for these last few weeks. You like all that geeky science shit. You did a bit of archaeology—'

'Which is nothing like science…'

'Minor detail. My point is, you can do clever stuff. And science means you can teach kids how to make potions.'

'Are you mistaking science teaching with Hogwarts?'

'They're not recruiting,' she smart alecs back.

I roll my eyes just as our order is placed down before us. It makes us pause our conversation to admire the beauty that is a burger, with actual gravy, in a bun. 'Sweet Jesus, I love Annie's Burger Shack. Frankly, you could tell me any job in the world while I'm eating this; I literally would not care.'

'I know, right,' mutters Mo through burger, chips and milkshake. 'Okay.' She swallows. 'So, science teacher. I've looked it up, you can do several things. Here are your choices. Science at uni level – bit grown up – I'd avoid. Science at senior level – exams, hormones – avoid. Science at junior school, however, v. v. cool.'

'I don't know if I want to stay working with children, Mo.'

'Science, though, that's cool, isn't it?'

I take a bite of burger, gravy, mushroom, onion and beef coming together in some kind of northern symphony in my mouth. 'Mmm, I'm definitely trying the one with Yorkshire pudding next time.'

'Filth!' Mo looks disgusted.

'Filth? This from the woman with pineapple on her burger!' Mo flips me the bird. 'Anyway, is it though, really?'

'What?'

'Science. Is it really cool?' I ask. 'Surely it's the total opposite? Don't you remember that science teacher we had at school? In her lab coat and glasses?'

'The one we made cry that time?'

'Oh God, don't remind me. Worst day of my actual life.' I shudder. 'Shit, that could be me! I could be the nervous teacher being bullied by over-opinionated schoolgirls with no idea of what they're on about!'

'Hence why you'd stick to primary. They're still quite nice at that age. And you love kids, you know you do. You must, to have stayed at the nursery for as long as you have.'

'Hang on, have you been talking with Dad?' I ask, beginning to wonder if this is in fact a pincer approach. He plants the seed, Mo propagates.

'No. I haven't seen him for ages. Why do you ask? Ahhh… your dad. Hey, we should invite him round.'

I narrow my eyes, not entirely convinced. 'We probably should. And, no reason,' I say, still suspicious. I lick juice from the side of my hand before it drips low enough to reach my work uniform. 'Last time I went round, he mentioned something about teaching. It was months ago, around my birthday, in fact. I was bemoaning my lack of future compared with where Mum was at a similar point in her life. According to Dad, she always wanted to teach.'

'No way! Did she? Well, then! Even more reason to! Oh my God, this is serendipity in the making.'

'I'm not here to live her life for her, Mo.'

'I know, but how amazing would it be to achieve something like this, in her memory?'

'I don't know. I'm not sure. I don't think I could do it, you know, and besides…' I trail off, well aware that if I now tell her I'm staying put, she's going to start the inquisition. 'I feel I need to stick around for a while, at work.'

'Whatever for?'

If I tell her, she's going to get all protective of me. Try to talk me out of it so I don't relive my own grief. If I don't tell her, she's going to keep on at me… and on. Mo with a bone is not fun Mo. But she's also impossible to lie to. 'Okay, so look, here's the thing. One of the dads from work—'

'OH MY GOD YOU'RE HAVING AN AFFAIR!'

'What? No! Sssshhhh!' I look around at the wide eyes now staring in our direction. If I were them, I'd totally be listening in to the rest of the conversation, so I try shaking my head, mouthing I'm not, to clear the matter up. Not, I suspect, that it does. Because who would openly admit that to a restaurant of total strangers? I cross my heart for extra reassurance, then turn back to glare at Mo. 'Don't be ridiculous, hear me out,' I hiss.

'Okay.' She shoves a chip in her mouth, eyes wide, expectant. Ketchup skims her top lip.

'Sauce.' I point and she licks it clean with a wink. 'So, one of the dads from work is having a bad time.'

'Your problem, how?'

'Stop it. Just listen. He lost his wife, a few months ago, and he's trying to get back to work. They had a son just before she died. He was like days old, or something.' Mo cocks her head in sympathy, so I hurry the last bit up while she's on his side. 'I am helping him because I understand. And that's why I can't leave.' *The End. Move on.*

'Rachel.'

Shit. She hasn't taken the hint. 'Okay, yet. I can't leave, yet.'

'This is a bad idea.'

'No, it's not. It's a good thing. I'm doing a good thing. Something I know Mum would be proud of.'

'That's a spectacularly manipulative thing to say in order to try to get me off your back, but I'm afraid I've known you too long. It's lovely that you want to help, I think you're amazing, but this has hashtag trigger warning all over it,' says Mo, pushing the last of her food to one side so she can reach for my hand.

'How?'

'Ooh, let me count the ways!'

'Knock it off, Shakespeare.' I pull my hand back.

'Rach, look. You may be a good person to empathise with him, but that doesn't mean you are the right person to take on his grief.'

'I'm not taking it on!' I complain. 'I just think that he doesn't have many people in his life who are supporting him. And based on the last few conversations we've had, he really could do with someone who gets it.'

'What conversations?' Mo wipes her mouth and hands with a serviette, dropping it onto her now empty plate.

'At work, when he's arrived to pick his son up, or drop him off. He's been distressed, a couple of times, in fact. We've talked.' Mo raises her eyebrows. 'Like I would with all my parents, Mo. You're looking after their most precious thing. You don't just bond with the kids, you know, you have a relationship with the parents too. So we talk. And he's asked questions. I thought it would help that he knew I understood. I told him how losing Mum felt for me.' Mo sits back in her chair, straw placed in the corner of her mouth. 'I don't know what I want to do with my life, Mo. God, I wish I could be more like you with career and future planning, I do. But I'm not. Never have been. I don't want to stay at the nursery forever, that much I do know, but while I have no burning desire to follow a specific career path, and this dad needs a bit of extra support, what harm can it do?'

'But teaching, Rach. You could be totally brilliant at that. I'm telling you now, you'd be that one teacher we all remember. The one that stays with us our whole lives, like Mr Schaller for me, I just know it. You'd be amazing.'

'I don't know about that.'

'I do.'

I smile at my best mate; her belief in me has always been total and complete. When I thought I was going to fail my GCSEs, she told me she knew I could do it and helped me revise. I passed. When I thought I'd fail my driving test, because I was too nervous behind the wheel, she gave me all these tips on how to calm down, how to be positive, how to focus on the road ahead… quite literally. And I passed. And now, here, with this. She believes in me in a way I'm not sure I ever could and I don't think I'd have survived without her. In the words of Bette Midler, she's quite literally the wind beneath my [bingo] wings.

But this time? I just don't know.

Chapter Fifteen

Rachel

I gaze at reflections of blue skies and fluffy clouds caught in the Sky Mirror outside the Nottingham Playhouse. The vacant look I suspect I possess is partly because it's nice to feel the gentle heat from the sun, the kind of spring sunshine that feels much warmer than it really is because you've not had enough to get complacent, but partly... if not probably... because I'm on my third coffee of the morning. If I wasn't gazing vacantly, I'd be bending the unfortunate ear of the stranger at the table beside me. I don't mean his ear is unfortunate – they're quite nice ears, as far as ears go – I just mean unfortunate because I'd be rambling on about everything and nothing. He has a laptop and is typing furiously, I don't think banal chat is on his to do list. And I'm almost certain he doesn't care about my future career, if there is one, whatever it may be.

Oh, to teach or not to teach. That is the— 'Ed?'

Ed stops abruptly by my table. 'Rachel!'

'Hi!'

The look on his face suggests I should have let him walk on, unnoticed. That I should have kept on staring vacantly at the Sky Mirror, rather than gazing around in the hope of catching somebody's eye.

'Um, isn't this weather beautiful?' I smile, wishing my heart wasn't racing from all that caffeine.

'It's lovely.' He looks around, probably in search of an escape route.

'If you leg it across Wellington Circus, we can pretend this never happened.'

'Pardon?'

'Sorry. Nothing. You looked like… never mind. I've had two cups of coffee too many and that tends to bring me out either in hives, or drivel.' I look down at my chest. 'Today it seems it's both!'

He nods as if he understands, though I think that's unlikely.

'I'm avoiding my flatmate so can't go home yet,' I say, tapping my watch. 'But it's Saturday so no work, that's always a bonus. Just thought I'd sit and watch the world go by.' He stares, wide-eyed. My confidence seeps. 'And look, here it is, going by.'

'Right.'

'Well, anyway. Ignore me. Sorry, you've probably got somewhere to be. Don't mind me.' I pick up the menu, glancing down it for inspiration. 'I might have another coffee… or a fruit juice. More coffee could be a bad idea and I can't stomach peppermint tea, can you?'

'Not really.'

'No, horrible stuff.'

'I'm…' He signals in the direction of town. 'I've been…' This time, signalling behind him.

Oli starts to grumble in his pram and Ed looks at his watch, pushing the pram back and forth. 'He's hungry,' he says, looking up and down the street.

'They could probably warm his milk up here,' I say, relieved to have something I can talk about with confidence. 'I mean, you don't have to sit with me, it's fine.' Ed looks as though he's weighing up the pros and cons as Oli's cries get louder. He strains to see inside the café, then back down to Oli and in his bag, searching. 'Shall I ask them?'

'No, no. It's fine, I'll…' Oli starts screaming as if his throat has been cut. The pitch puts Ed further on edge and makes the man with the normal ears tut and shift the angle of his laptop, as if that will lessen the volume. Ed pushes the buggy back and forth faster.

'Go on, you go and sort his bottle out. I'll sort Oli,' I say, taking the bag off the back of the buggy and passing it to Ed.

'It's your day off,' he says, taking the bag.

'Day off, schmay off. Go on!'

I lift Oli out, distracting him with his favourite game of crazy horses. I clip-clop him gently on my knee before jigging him about quickly, singing 'Crazy Horses'. He howls with laughter. Ear guy moves.

By the time Ed gets back, Oli has all but ramped up to screaming again, no longer impressed with my distractions. I reach for the bottle and plug the gap, silence falling around us. 'There, that's better, isn't it?'

'If only it was that easy all of the time.'

'I envy babies for this. If I cried like I'd like to when I'm hungry, Mo would slap me round the face, not plug me with a burger. I hate getting hungry, makes me properly grumpy.' My belly rumbles. 'In fact, I may have to get something to eat now.'

'Here, let me, seeing as you're feeding him.' Ed gets the menu, putting it in front of me.

'Are you okay, Ed? I mean, that's probably a stupid question, given… everything, but, you seem…' I realise I'm not sure I want to end this sentence. You seem 'sad' is a little trite under the circumstances. 'Down' is no better. 'Like you've given up', possibly too close to the truth, if his slump in the chair is anything to go by.

'I'm not great, no. But what can we do? I just have to get on with it.'

'Of course, I mean, I guess so. But… well, you don't have to do all this on your own.'

'Mum said the same thing.' He laughs humourlessly. 'Did I miss a memo about available hands to help out in times of crisis?'

'Well, I mean, I'd always be happy to help, but haven't you got family, or friends who can help?'

'Sure… I mean… I had friends, but they were…' He swallows, pinching the bridge of his nose. 'They were "our" friends. And, it's too hard… now, you know?'

I nod my head, though I don't really know. But maybe that's because I had Mo, who pretty much managed all of my first few years after Mum died.

'I'm not really from a very "hands on" kind of family. We're a bit… stiff upper lip for that.'

'Something like this, though, it can change things, teach people new ways, give them perspective.'

'I admire your optimism, but it's not as simple as that.'

Oli drains the bottle in record time and I shift him onto my shoulder for winding. Ed passes me a muslin and a pregnant woman walks past, hand in hand with her… boyfriend? Husband? Who knows, but they both look at Ed and me as if they're weeks off being in the same boat as us, and I want to shout and explain: *It's not my child. Ed has a wife. I'm just helping.* Except he doesn't have a wife any more. And the explanation gets more complicated. The potential for errors in assumptions increase. I remember this happening to me, with a friend's mum. The assumption she was my mother, too, somehow instantly deleting people from history, it hurt. Ed watches them walk away, and I just know it's hurting him now, too.

'I need to go,' he says, reaching for Oli as the baby lets out three soft but purposeful burps.

'Of course.'

'Thanks for your help, I appreciate it.' He reaches into his wallet and drops a tenner on the table. 'Please, let me shout you coffee. It's the least I can do.' He moves off before I can give it back.

'Ed!' I call after him. 'Asking for help is important!' I say. He pauses, drops his head to the ground with a nod and walks away.

Chapter Sixteen

Ed

I wasn't sure what to say when Mum picked up. I'd never really called to ask for her help, because I learnt as a kid that she wasn't the kind of mum to step in during a crisis. Where some mothers would wrap their children up in aprons and love, she'd pat us on the hand as if that were sufficient affection to see us through. She'd offer us a cheek to kiss, rarely embracing us. That was just the way she'd been brought up herself.

And yet, Rachel's words kept repeating the whole time I walked from pub to park bench in town, searching for Simon. *Just in case. I can't do this alone. I don't have to.*

So, I did call Mum. Desperate, hopeful, needing someone to talk to about Simon; someone who understood, understands, what this is all about. Someone who knows him, who can give me some of that other thing Rachel mentioned: perspective.

And here Mum is, on my doorstep, responding to that call I made over an hour ago, when I didn't know what else to do... A call I now regret.

'Mum, hi.'

'I'm sorry it took me so long; the gardener was due and I had to make sure he knew what was required of him.' She walks ahead of me down the hallway, her back straight and formal; like a stranger, uncomfortable in my home. 'How's Oli?' she asks, looking around, hands clasped tightly at her waist.

'He's fine, asleep upstairs. Nursery is tiring him out.'

'That's good. He's settled in okay, then?'

'Well, it's only been a couple of weeks, but yes, he seems to be, so far. And Rachel, the girl who looks after him, she seems great with him.' The memory of crumbling before Rachel's eyes returns and my stomach twists. I cough my throat clear. 'Coffee?'

'No, thank you. I'm fine.'

'Right.'

She sits at the dining table, fiddling with something in her handbag, putting it on the chair beside her. Moving it to the floor. Picking it up out of Floyd's way as he purrs into it, then bounces up onto her lap.

'Get down,' I say, lifting him from her, but not before he's dug his claws into her cashmere scarf. 'Shit, sorry, I...' I try to smooth the snagged strands down, but she pulls the scarf back from my hands.

'It's fine, it's just a scarf,' she says, and I think she really wants to believe that it *is* fine, and it *is* just a scarf. It's not really her fault that she can't.

I throw Floyd in the direction of the cat flap and thankfully he takes the hint. Not sure what to say, I clatter domestically around the kitchen instead: flicking the kettle on, unloading the dishwasher, setting the steriliser.

This is ridiculous. She's my mother. She's Simon's mother. She might not be able to help how she deals with life, but this time I need her to step up.

'I saw Simon.'

'Did you?'

Does she seem surprised? 'I came out of work and he was across the street.'

'What did he say?'

'Nothing, before I could reach him he disappeared. The road was busy, I couldn't cross. He was there one minute and gone the next. He looked a mess.'

'I see.' She thins her lips.

'Have you seen him?'

She shakes her head.

'Or spoken to him at all?'

'Not properly, not for a few weeks, maybe longer. He seems to have...' She looks down at her perfectly manicured hands. 'He seems to be struggling to communicate.'

I resist suggesting that it's a family trait.

'He hasn't been good since... the accident,' she says, eyes still down. 'I think his old problem may have resurfaced.' Mum never had worked out how to say that he had a drink problem out loud. Because he stopped it himself, without seeking help from a group, or a doctor, she'd always managed to play it down. 'I think your brother may be drinking again,' she finishes quietly.

'That's what Lisa said.'

'When did you see her?' she asks, definitely surprised this time.

'A few days ago. He sent me a text message. It was an apology. I haven't spoken to him since he called me after the accident. Even at Ellie's funeral he couldn't talk to me. He just disappeared, after the service. Never returned my calls. Until the other day, like I say, I got a message and...' The feelings of anger and hurt come rushing back. 'I don't know, Mum. It's ridiculous. He drove the car that killed my wife and he can't even talk to me about it? I don't even know what I want him to say, what we'd talk about, but I just feel like we *should* fucking well talk.'

Mum purses her lips at my swearing.

'It's such a weak thing to do. A fucking text? It's so… insignificant. So, I went round to see him. I wanted to stand in front of him. I wanted… I wanted…'

Mum waits, expectantly, for me to finish.

'I wanted to know he was sorry, I guess.' I'm unravelling, but this time, unlike with Rachel, Mum's steel seems to push it back. It's facts that I want to share with her, not emotion. 'I wanted to shout at him. I wanted to be angry, even for just a moment. Surely that's understandable? Surely I'm allowed a moment of anger, a moment of baseline human response to all this?'

The look on Mum's face suggests she isn't sure, but I don't need her validation on that one. I've read the grief pamphlets. I know anger's a legitimate thing, a part of the grieving process. Even if Simon hadn't dumped his car in a ditch, I could be angry. Given that he did do just that, my anger can be directed at him without apology. 'You know what, Mum, I wanted to make him hurt as much as I was. As I still am.'

'Edward, your brother does hurt,' begins Mum, and I'm taken aback. Where she has sat for the last five minutes, apparently letting words and emotions wash over her, there is sudden engagement. There's animation in her face. She's defending him like she used to when we fell out as kids, one of us tormenting the other. 'Of course he hurts, that's why…' But the moment passes and she sighs, trailing off. She concertinas her scarf neatly on her lap, drifting back to characteristic coolness. 'That's why, it would appear, he's been drinking himself into oblivion.' She smooths the concertina back out, places her hands on her lap and looks at me. 'This isn't easy for any of us, Edward. I wish I had words to say that would make it better for you both, but I don't know what I can say, or do… I'm not…' She stops herself with a swallow of words. 'I haven't seen your brother for weeks. I get the occasional phone call, usually from a phone box somewhere, I think. He rambles about what happened, about how he feels. He tells me things aren't good with Lisa. It's as if he releases a stream of consciousness that he then packages back up again. He is lost, Edward. He is…' She searches for the right word to sum it all up. 'He's devastated.'

'Devastated.'

'Yes, and I am sure that sounds like a tiny portion of what you feel. There are no words to express how this affects any of us, but I wish I could reach him, Edward. I wish I could make him understand that the way he is dealing with his pain is harmful, dangerous even. But I don't know where to begin.'

I drop into the chair beside her and she reaches her hand out towards mine. She pauses before we connect, as if she can't quite manage it. I'm not sure how I feel about the fact that she seems to force herself to touch me in any case. Particularly as her hand is unfamiliar, her skin paper-thin. 'He is killing himself, Edward. And I don't know how to help him.'

I see that her eyes are glassy, her stiff upper lip is not so in control. Is this the first time I'll see her cry?

'Edward, I don't know how to help either of you.'

'Mum…' I drop my head to the table, no idea how to answer, no strength to carry her emotions as well as my own.

When I look up again, Mum looks down at her watch, the tiny gold timepiece she got as a present from Dad on a wedding anniversary, years ago. 'I should get back, Edward. The gardener needs paying before he leaves.'

'Okay.' It's easier for both of us that I don't argue with her desire to escape.

She looks around, reaches for her handbag and pulls out a piece of paper along with a clunky mobile phone. 'I bought one of these, for emergencies. I'll leave it in my handbag. This is the number.' She slides the paper across the table as she stands. 'I am not very good at any of this, Edward, I do realise that, but if there is anything I *can* do – care for Oli, help you with anything – please do call me. If I'm not at home, I'll make sure this phone is on.'

I get up from the table and she moves towards me, waiting for me to kiss her cheek as usual, which duty has long taught me to do without question, then I follow her as she leaves.

The door closes behind her and my body drowns in all of the feelings I've been suppressing while she was here. Rachel was wrong. I am in this alone. Whatever Mum says, however eager to help Rachel may be, it's me and Oli against the world. Simple as that.

I go upstairs to check on him, then head to my room. I don't bother undressing, just climb into bed, wishing – as I do every night – that this night might be the night I sleep.

Floyd returns, jumping up to settle at the bottom of the bed with a purr.

'You ruined her scarf, you scabby cat,' I say, reaching for his tail, which he flicks out of reach.

I pick up Ellie's phone from her bedside table, dragged back out of her memory box, weeks ago. I put headphones in my ears, as I've done each night now, for weeks. I stop before pressing 'play', though, something making me open her text messages. I flick the messages up and down the screen and names of friends and family appear. Colleagues she'd occasionally talk to, and updates from her phone provider about offers and services she'd never need.

And then I see a message from Simon. It says: *I don't even know where to start, but okay, I'll see you there. X*

I read hers before it: *Meet me in the usual place. We need to work out how we're going to tell them, before it's all out of our hands. X*

As I stare at the bubbles of conversation, my blood runs cold.

What is this? What does this mean? Who do you need to tell? And what?

Chapter Seventeen

Rachel

When I eventually got back, Mo was all keen to chat more about work and uni and future plans. I mumbled something about needing a bit of space, scooped up a pile of Mum's magazines from the coffee table and retreated to the relative safety of my bedroom. I say relative safety; looking at the collection of discarded mugs that are hothousing all kinds of furry, green stuff, perhaps my safety can't be guaranteed. Either way, unlike the rest of our flat, my room is exactly that: my room. I haven't decorated as such, but there are photos Blutacked to the walls: school friends, me, my brother Rich, Dad, my mum. There are thank-you cards from parents and pictures painted by favourite babies. (I know, I'm not supposed to have favourites. Tell that to a judge.) Pink, fluffy fairy lights wrap around my cream metal bed head and, in the corner, there's a wardrobe for my clothes, because Mo's perpetual rotation of 'floor to body to washing machine to floor' just never works for me.

I tuck myself into my bed, cross-legged with the pile of magazines on my lap. There are the history magazines I haven't looked at and, bizarrely, a journal about the art of teaching. Mo would call that serendipitous; I'd call it downright bloody freaky! There's also the lone copy of *Elle* from 1985, the year I was born. The woman on the cover is bright-red-lipped and sharp-shoulder-suited. I briefly ponder the era's ill-advised penchant for a double-breasted cut before flicking through the pages. Sometimes, when looking through her magazines, it's easy to imagine what Mum was reading. The pages she'd pore over versus the ones she'd flick past. Did she wonder if that suit would have worked for her body shape? Did she try a red lipstick? My memory is of her in some kind of polyester trousers that rustled as she walked. Sometimes she'd kiss me and the static would make me jump. She had a white shirt that she'd tuck into her trousers, the back slightly ruched, giving her a bulge at the waist. That was her self-styled uniform for work. I don't really remember what she wore on a weekend. Was she bothered about fashion? Maybe so, given this magazine, but I don't know. Those last few months, she wore nothing other than a nightie and a look of distant resignation. Like the final pages of her life were inevitable. I don't want to dwell on the look on her face in those final days, or the sense of sadness that lined her room.

An article about women and work, the opportunities, or lack thereof, makes me tut. The next page is smothered in bikini-body tips and I wonder if anything has really changed. Maybe only a vague shift in what shape the body should be. I come across the horoscopes and, despite not normally reading them (Aquarius by birth, cynic by scientific upbringing), curiosity makes me look.

This is the month for big decisions and letting go.

Oh, for fuck's sake. This month and every month, *Elle*. I flip the magazine shut and sling it onto the floor, adding to the piles that I've read and kept, because what else can I do with them?

I shuffle down into my bed, hands behind my head, eyes to the ceiling. *Did you really want to be a teacher?* I ask her. *Why didn't you think you could do it?*

Why aren't you here to tell me what I should do with my life?

There's a knock on my bedroom door. Mo pokes her head around. 'Get to sleep. I've just decided we are going out tomorrow. Glad rags are required. As is an equipped liver and some staying power. Right?'

I groan, pulling the duvet over my head.

'Don't you even, Rachel Fletcher. We're a long time dead, buck your ideas up. We're starting at Broadway and ending at Oceana. I can't confirm the in-between but it will include cocktails and flirting. This is all part of my new plan to get you up and out and on with your life. Hopefully it will spark a new-found motivation to take control. Brace yourself!' She blows me a kiss then pulls the door shut, padding off down the hallway to her own room.

I groan again, quietly so as not to be heard. *I guess if you're not here, there's always Mo!* I think, flicking the switch on my fairy lights and staring at the illuminated constellations from a plastic star kit Mo bought me years back. As the stars and planets reveal themselves in the dark, I wonder if aeronautics is an option after all. Then I remember I hate flying.

Chapter Eighteen

Ed

I've been calling Simon's number for over a week. I've sent messages that have bounced back. I've spent my lunchtimes at the Arboretum, wandering the paths in search of him. I took the tram to and from a park-and-ride so I could check The Forest tram stop. I called their house, getting through to the answering machine each and every time. The questions are getting louder, and rational explanation is almost silent.

Yet, despite the stress from my real life, the important side of it, the stuff I really need to be dealing with, I'm here, in a nightclub. With colleagues. And it is, without doubt, the last thing I really want. I'm expected to get hammered and have fun, as if those two things are inextricably linked any more.

'Drink up, mate, you're lagging behind. Some of us are on our sixth!' shouts Dave, the office manager.

I attempt a smile in his direction, but really I just want to remind him that Oli will wake me before most of the younger members of our team have even got home, and getting up at that time with a hangover is ill-advised at best. 'This part of our job is more appealing before children, don't you think?'

'I dunno, Janet has always got up to ours anyway,' he gloats, too drunk to consider his response may be a little tactless. 'Besides, we're team building. Get pissed or get fired. You know the rules.'

While it would struggle to stand up in court, the mentality hasn't really improved with the evolution of employee rights, and that is the one and only reason I'm in this club, with colleagues and clients, celebrating a new business deal for them that means more work for us. Dave sauntered over with a grin yesterday afternoon while I was trying Simon for the twelfth time, his mobile number still dead. He slapped me on the back, dropping the client file on my desk. 'Merry Christmas!' he declared. 'Capital One. This will get you back on your feet!'

So, I'm here, in Oceana nightclub, surrounded by a group of people I've little or nothing in common with, all of whom are three sheets to the wind. Greg has disappeared.

With no alternative option, I had to ask Mum to babysit. Which means when I do get home, I have to make small talk until she leaves, or – God forbid – decides to go to bed in the spare room. She hadn't decided when I left – probably because she didn't want to admit that she just wanted to go home – but there's a worry in the back of my mind that she'll choose now to make more of an effort.

'Look, Dave, it's been a great night,' I lie. 'But, if it's all the same to you, I should probably make a move.' I'm in close to his ear so as to be heard over the music. 'That lot won't notice I'm gone now.' I nod in the direction of our clients, sat in a corner of the club, surrounded by bottles of wine; ties loose, shirts untucked like stockbrokers on the late Tube home. 'I really need to get back to Oli.'

A shots girl saunters past, swinging tequila bottles in Dave's direction, and he drags her back by the belt, much to her understandable disgust. I nudge his hand away and she gives me a grateful look.

'One shot, then you can leave!' he shouts, handing me a tiny glass and a piece of lime. He licks his hand, nodding me to do the same, so the girl can pour salt on the patch. The rest of the team are loaded up with the same and I consider losing the lot over my shoulder.

'Three, two, one!' Dave shouts over the beat, and we lick our hands, knock the drinks back, then suck on the tiny piece of citrus. Alcohol strips my tongue and burns my throat on the trickle down to my stomach. I just about cough out a 'Fuck me' before Dave whips the offending glass out of my hand, trying to get it refilled.

'Just a little extra to get you in the mood,' he insists, but I put my hand up to make it clear I'm not getting drawn in. Dave shrugs, then turns his back on me, which means I can push my way through the crowd. I get caught in a queue to the dance floor and am knocked sideways by someone's overzealous dancing. I spin round to glare, only to see Rachel.

'Shit, sorry! Did I knock you? Oh…!' she says. 'Ed!'

I am as surprised to see her as it's clear she is to see me; I nod a hello in her direction.

'I didn't have you down as much of a clubber,' she shouts into my ear, vibrating my eardrum with her volume.

'No, a work do,' I shout back, pointing to the crowd of noisy office workers behind us. She looks, then nods, a neon straw placed in the corner of her mouth. She says something else that I can't hear, straw still in mouth. 'Pardon?' I shout, cupping my hand to my ear like a granddad.

'I said "I see" and "fancy seeing you here".' She comes in close to my ear again, her hair tickling my neck, the drone of music making her proximity absolutely necessary… but more than a little uncomfortable.

'It's awkward bumping into parents when you're out on the piss,' she shouts, not sounding awkward at all. 'How can I present the very model of a childcare specialist when you've seen me falling over drunk?' She looks at me as if this is a genuine, important question.

'Don't worry about it!' I shout. 'I was just leaving anyway.'

'Awww, no, don't go!' she wails. 'Stay, have a drink, have a dance! I've been dumped by my mate who is lost in the club, probably twerking with some bloke she just met.' She takes another sip of her drink then says, 'That's me walking home on my own!' She eye-rolls as though this is a regular occurrence. The smell of her drink, a sort of bubblegum sweetness, mixes with her perfume, producing sickly tones that take up residence in my nostrils.

'You can't walk home on your own,' I say.

'Of course I can!' she replies, as if I'm an idiot.

'Look, let me help you find her before I go. I'm trying to find my mate anyway.' Rachel nods, taking hold of my hand, leading me through the crowds. Her hand is unfamiliar in mine. I want to let go, but she's clasping it tightly. After three laps of the dance floor, she stops and points. 'There!' she nods in the direction of a girl whose arse grinds dangerously close to her partner's crotch. Her partner, it turns out, being Greg, who looks a combination of terrified and like all his birthdays have come at once. He attempts to dance around with her, into the crowd, and, thankfully, I lose sight of them both. I won't say I know him; too many questions when it all goes pear-shaped.

'Look at that. Disappearing into a sea of drunkards. Literally the last I'll see of her tonight.' Rachel stands on tiptoes, craning between revellers to see where Greg and her friend have gone. 'Oh well, bonus is it's an early night for me then,' she shouts, draining her bottle and dumping it on a table beside us. 'I'll no doubt see you at work,' she says, wandering off, unstably, through the crowds.

'Wait!' I shout, doing my best to catch her up. 'Seriously, how are you getting home?'

'I've already said! I'll walk.'

'I'd really rather you didn't!' I shout, but the music volume is waning as we get further away from the dance floor, making me sound louder than I needed to be.

Rachel shakes her head as we take the steps out into the night, brightly lit with street lights, cars' headlamps and the club lights that pool on the pavement. 'It's fine. I only live around the corner.' She points over the road towards Hockley. 'Five minutes max,' she says.

'Well…' I sigh, frustrated. 'Let me walk you there,' I offer, because I can't bear the thought of any woman taking the streets alone.

'Whatever.' She sighs. 'I'd be fine, though.'

She slips her arm through mine with an overfamiliar squeeze, tottering a few steps before kicking off her shoes and carrying them by the heels in her spare hand. 'Stupid things, can't walk in them anyway. I'm more of a flat shoe kind of girl, really.'

'Why do you bother, then?' I ask, desperate for easy conversation to fill the awkwardness, keeping my eye on the path for broken glass she might need to avoid.

'Dunno really. Always feel I'm supposed to when I go out. Stupid really.'

I nod in agreement as we head down Broad Street, where a projection of some dancers shines on the face of the buildings, giving me something to focus on until we've passed it. Rachel babbles on about the night out being due to her best friend's decision to take control of her life and not because she actually wanted to be there. She hates clubs. Always has. Apparently. I keep nodding, politely, whenever it seems appropriate. By the time we reach the end of the road, she gets a whiff of kebab and I'm dragged down the hill to join a queue of revellers looking for sustenance.

The cold night air has woken me up, or maybe it's the tinnitus that now rings around my head. 'I used to love clubbing,' I say, rubbing my fingers in my ears. 'Ellie and I would go, back in the early days, and we'd just dance all night. Not even drink!' The rubbing does not dislodge the ringing. 'I think I'm getting too old for it now.'

'Nonsense,' she says, trying to see past the queue for a glimpse at the menu. 'That's not getting old, that's just recognising the severe damage to your hearing that overexposure to really bad dance music can have!' Moving up the line, she stumbles and I catch her.

'Shit, sorry!' she says, smoothing her skirt down. 'God, fresh air and alcohol. Do you know fresh air is scientifically proven to advance the effects? I was stone cold sober in the club...' I raise my eyebrows suggesting otherwise, but she doesn't seem to notice. 'Now though? Hurtling towards hammered on a runaway speed train! Oooh... pizza!' She slips from my grasp, leaning against the counter to place her order, fumbling with her cash, counting out what's left.

The town clock chimes eleven thirty and I panic that I'll be late for Mum. That she'll want to stay. That we'll have an awkward morning conversation about how I am. About if I've spoken to Simon yet. About anything and everything.

'Look, Rach, I need to get back for Oli.'

'Oh, of course, who has him?'

'Mum,' I say with a groan.

'You know, if you ever need it, I can help with stuff like that,' she says, picking up the pizza that has just been placed down before her. 'Any time. We're allowed to, if you wanted. It just helps sometimes; we know the baby and vice versa.'

Part of me wishes I'd known that before. 'Thanks, I appreciate that.'

She reaches over the counter for a pen, grabbing hold of my hand. She holds it across her stomach – which feels uncomfortably personal – scrawling her number on it, with a smiley face at the end. 'There,' she declares. 'No excuses now. Any time, Ed, okay?'

'Okay.' I nod, stuffing my hands in my pockets, finding the photo of Ellie I put in one of them before coming out. I hold it between thumb and forefinger as I follow Rachel up the hill, through identical streets that feel like a city-centre secret of magical red bricks and years and years of history. It's not a part of the city I've walked before. Quickly, we reach a nondescript door to another red-bricked building.

'This is me,' she says, nodding up to the building.

'Great.' I wait for her to get her keys out, take the steps to unlock the door and leave me to run for a cab. Instead, she pauses, fixing me with an intense look.

'You're doing an incredible job. With Oli, I mean.' I drop my head, not quite sure how to respond to the compliment, desperate to get away. 'He is lucky to have you,' she says, taking my hand to steady her tiptoed stance as she gently kisses me on the cheek. 'Thanks for walking me home.' She smiles, unlocks the building, and then disappears behind the door.

I look down at my hand and reach up to my cheek. 'He's lucky to have you too,' I say to the building, realising in that moment that I'm lucky as well. Lucky to have someone who understands, says what she thinks, and requires nothing of me in return.

A light switches on in one of the flats. The shadow of its occupant moves across the ceiling as they look out of the window. I turn the corner without seeing if it's actually her, grateful for this new-found friendship, but relieved the encounter is over.

Chapter Nineteen

Rachel

I make an ill-advised attempt to lift my head from the pillow, somehow hoping it won't hurt, vast experience to the contrary momentarily passing me by. The weight of my unexpected hangover – I really didn't think I'd had that much – forces me back into the secure folds of my bed. 'Life hates me,' I groan.

I reach out to the side of my mattress, using it as a pulley across the bed, blindly trying to turn my clock to face me… there's an empty wine bottle there instead. Oh. Well, that makes more sense. I push it to one side, blinking a blur away from the only eye I can open, desperately trying to focus on the time. My laptop whirs to life from its position among the covers on my bed; a website page thanking me for my purchase comes to light, and I hope to God I haven't spent my rent on clothes I'll never wear. Again.

There's an overwhelming stench of pizza clinging to the air, making my stomach lurch, bile threatening. Dead-weight legs fall off the edge of the bed, landing heavily on discarded clothes and the remains of my aforementioned pizza below. I stand, then sit back down, woozy. Deep breath, try again. Standing. *I'm standing!* Gingerly, I move from bed to door, down the corridor, past the closed bathroom door and into the kitchen.

I pour water, take a sip, then sling the rest of it down the sink before feeling my way for the lounge, only to find Mo drinking tea, reading a magazine and, irritatingly, looking as though she stopped in last night.

'Guess what I've done!' I say, falling into the chair opposite.

'Blown your rent on clothes?' she asks, as if she knows me better than I know myself.

'I'll send them back. It's fine. Urgh. Where am I? What day is it? Who am I?'

Mo sniggers. 'Relax, I keep telling you I don't need your money anyway.'

'Yes, well. You know that's not how I want it to be.'

'You might have to live rent free when you go back to university.' She winks.

'Who says I'm going back?'

'Time, Rach. Time says you're going. And it's only a matter of.' I groan, head in hands. Head pounding. Actually, head all over the place. 'It's okay, Rach. I can wait. Keep the clothes... unless you've bought open-toed slingbacks again. Those you can send back. Now, where did you slope off to last night?'

'Me?' I shout, then rub my temples because of the ache. 'How was *your* night, more like? Was it worth dumping me for a fumble in the toilets?'

'A fumble in the toilets! How very dare you.' She grins. 'Actually, Rachel, I didn't dump you, and I didn't have a fumble in the toilets. Not that there would be any shame if I had!'

'No. Because nothing says sexy like empty toilet-roll dispensers and the gentle aroma of boy wee. Here then? Do I need to wipe down the sofa? Has he been booted out already? Actually, no, it can't have been here, you're too fresh-faced to have brought him back. Besides, I seem to recollect you saying something about finding a husband when we were out last night, and as you've told me many times before, a man you deem appropriate after overindulging the snakebite and black could not a husband make.'

'Snakebite and black?! Excuse me, bartender, the 1990s want their drink back.'

'I dunno, snakebite, tequila, disgusting but ever-so-sippable alcopops, whatever.'

'I didn't dump you, you walked out on me! I watched you chuff off with some bloke, grabbing his hand and leading him out. You were on a mission and I partly wanted to high five you because he was hot. Not your usual type at all. Much more of a man. Like a proper man. With the ability to grow facial hair and everything. What went wrong? How did you get to the point where you were at home, spending money on clothes you'll never wear?'

'I might wear them,' I say sulkily, nicking one of Mo's cleansing wipes out of the packet left on the table. Its coolness takes the red sting of embarrassment out of my cheeks as a vague picture of Ed delivering me to our door comes back to my mind. 'Anyway, how on earth you noticed I was leaving, with or without some bloke, I'm not sure. The last I saw, you were gyrating by some bloke's nethers! And, as it happens, "the guy" just wanted to make sure I got home okay.'

'I bet he did!' She laughed. 'And?'

'And nothing. As it happens.'

Mo looks at me as if I've just fed her the biggest load of ol' shite she's ever heard, and I leap to his defence. 'It was one of the dads from work, as it goes. The one I've told you about.'

'The one with the dead wife?'

I wince at Mo's bluntness. 'Yes, that's the one,' I say, through the face wipe.

'Fair enough, but I did see you chatting to him, all hair fixing and seductive leaning in.'

'The music was loud.'

'You didn't have to keep touching him though, did you? "Oooh, you're so funny." And "Oooh, tell me that again".' She flicks her hair and taps my arm by way of, frankly, a very bad impression of me. I work hard to resist flinching as the recollection of my being a little over-affectionate starts to appear in the fuzz of memory. The holding his hand, the walking home arm in arm. The kiss on his cheek. *Oh God, the kiss on his cheek.* The pit of my grumbling stomach drops to the soles of my feet. I wonder if I should let him know I was drunk and unaware of socially accepted behaviour towards a widower.

'Greg says—'

'Greg! Who the chuff is Greg?' I ask, just as the bathroom door opens, a cloud of steam escaping into the cold.

'Somebody mention my name?' says the guy Mo was dancing with last night. He strolls down our corridor, half dressed, with T-shirt in hand. I try not to notice his well-toned abs and incredible biceps… but fail.

'We were just talking about your mate,' explains Mo.

'Ah, Ed. Yes. Complicated.' Greg ruffles his hair with a towel, then drops it over a chair. 'Hope you don't mind, but I borrowed some shampoo.' He pulls on a tight, white T-shirt like some kind of reverse Diet Coke break, and I find something on the floor very interesting.

'Course not,' Mo says, standing. 'Coffee?' she asks.

'Why don't we go out for breakfast,' he says, taking a step towards her. Mo gives him a coquettish smile and I wonder what on earth has happened overnight. Between my drunken-ness and her standing here – about to go for breakfast with a man she brought home but did not have sex with, something she has *never* done before – it's like I've woken up in a parallel universe. And not a good one.

'Breakfast sounds great,' she flutters. 'Let me change. I'll be out in a minute.'

'No rush,' he says, watching her walk away. Out of earshot, he turns to me. 'Wow, your friend!'

'Yes?'

'She's…' He stares down the corridor displaying signs of smitten that I've rarely seen in a bloke associated with my long-time, happily single best friend.

'She's pretty cool, yes, so, you know… watch yourself.' I don't know why I get all big sister on him. Mo doesn't need it and I'm too hungover to follow anything through anyway. 'So, how do you know Ed?'

'Work colleagues really, but he's a good bloke. We've been out a few times. More before…' He stops himself.

'Before his wife?' I say, making it clear that I know.

'Yeah.' Greg pulls a chair from the dining table. 'How did you know? Did he mention it?'

'I look after Oli. At the nursery.'

'Oh, right. Cool.' He nods. 'You know, I don't think he's ready for…' Greg pauses, then apparently decides to just go for it. 'He's not ready for a relationship, you know… I don't know if you two…' He waves his hand in the air, suggestively.

'Oh shit, God no! *No!* I wasn't… we weren't… He's… I…'

'Oh, right. Okay, sorry. It's just, Mo said she saw you—'

'Ha! Mo says a lot of things but no… God. I'm just… I sort of know what he's going through.' Greg looks confused. 'My mum died, when I was a kid.'

'Right.'

'Yeah, no. I wasn't trying to, eurgh, weird. I mean, not weird-weird. I'm not saying there's anything *wrong* with him. No, far from it.' *Stop talking, Rach.* 'In any other circumstance…'

'Sure.'

Oh God. 'Yeah.' I pin my lips together. I swallow. I wish the ground would do the same to my entire body. God, I'm an idiot. 'Well, anyway. I'm just going for a shower so…'

'Sure. Okay. Nice to meet you.'

'Yeah. Enjoy breakfast.'

I walk down the hall, eyes half closed in pain at how bad that all just came across. Entirely confused as to why.

Chapter Twenty

Ed

Rachel wasn't there when I dropped Oli off this morning. I saw her briefly as I picked him up, but she was in one of the other rooms. She threw me a wave, and I don't know why, but I pretended I hadn't seen her. Then I felt bad and tried to look out for her as I left, but she was nowhere to be seen.

Actually, I do know why. I know exactly why. Saturday night's kiss on the cheek still bothers me. I know it was perfectly innocent, that there was no agenda behind it, but it sits there, lingering on my skin. Replacing all the times Ellie kissed me on the cheek. The touch of Rachel's hand as she led me through the club, my arm across her stomach – drink fuelling overfamiliarity on her part – as she wrote her number on my hand. Each touch still felt. Touch I've been immune to since the day Ellie died. I built a wall, I felt nothing from that day onwards. Except now I can feel Rachel on my hand, my arm, my cheek. And with it, I feel guilt.

I place Oli's bag on the kitchen side, unpacking and repacking what's needed for tomorrow. But, as I pick each item out, I realise Oli's bear is missing. The bear Ellie bought for him that he has had in his cot since the day he was born. He can't sleep without it, or maybe I don't want him to. What if it's lost? My heart trips up. That bear is a piece of her that he needs, that we both need.

It's 6.30 p.m. I try calling the nursery but the number rings out until an answering machine kicks in. I leave a garbled message, just in case anyone picks up, but they don't. Shit. Shit!

I stuff everything back in the bag, checking again as I do, desperate that I missed it. Then pull it all back out again, one last time. Spare clothes, spent bottles, nappies and wipes are all scattered on the floor. His bag is now empty and there's no bear in sight.

The house phone rings and I leap on it in the hope it's the nursery calling back. 'Hello?' I stuff Oli's things back in the bag.

'Ed. It's Lisa.' I freeze, which can be all that stops me from just hanging up. 'Have you seen Simon?'

'Why would I have?'

'Because when he left the house this morning, he told me he was coming to find you. So, given that he isn't home, and not in any of his usual pissed-up haunts, I thought that maybe he'd actually grown some balls to face you.' Her voice is flat, as if she's severed connection between feelings and words. 'Well, that's that then.'

'That's what then?'

'I told him this morning that unless he came to talk to you, unless he was able to admit the truth to us all, I was not prepared to put up with his behaviour any more. I packed a bag of his stuff this afternoon. I have no choice but to sling it out onto the street.'

'You've threatened this before. You never leave. He never leaves. It's a pointless conversation and one I don't need to be having. Goodbye.'

'They were having an affair, Edward!' she shouts down the phone.

My heart rate quickens, forcing all air out of my chest, igniting a fire in my belly. 'Who was?' I ask.

'Oh, Edward. Simon and Ellie. It's so obvious. Why can't you see it?'

I steady myself. I won't let her get away with this. 'How *dare* you talk about my wife that way,' I hiss, my voice low, guttural. 'You have no idea, do you, of the damage you're causing, the destruction to lives already at rock bottom.'

Oli murmurs, in the next room, then he begins crying. I move through to the lounge, picking him up with my free arm.

'It's all clear now, Lisa. Every picture makes up the story. The years you and Simon have been together… it was always awkward, clumsy. We could never quite get to the bottom of who you were, but I see it now. I see it.' I pull Oli in close to me. 'Suggesting something like this is the single most spiteful, horrendous, vicious thing anyone could say to a grieving man. I don't understand the kind of person that would do such a thing.' My sneer, my hatred towards her, increases with every word.

'I didn't expect you to believe me, Ed,' she starts.

'Why would I? It's not true.'

'How do you know?'

'Because I knew my wife, Lisa. And she would never, NEVER, do something like that.' I kiss Oli on the forehead as he starts to cry again.

'You can believe what you like, Ed. As the grieving husband you're entitled to be confused, to be in denial. I don't know why I put up with him, with his behaviour over the years. Except that I loved him and I forgave him every time.'

Despite a sickness in my belly – a creeping sense of fear – I find I can't hang up.

'He is a shit, always has been. Ellie was no better. You might as well face it.'

'You can think what you like of my brother,' I hiss, 'but I knew my wife.' My voice is clipped and controlled; it's in contrast with how I feel, but I won't have her lambaste my wife. There is nothing I can do for Ellie now except protect her memory, and I will do that – I have to – until I take my dying breath. *Till death us do part.*

On the other side of the kitchen window, Ellie's next project, our garden, is wild and rambling – much like me now, in her absence. I seek out the last of the wild bluebells for strength. 'Don't call me again,' I say.

'She was empty, Ed. So empty, she couldn't even be bothered with small talk. Me and your brother weren't worth her time or effort, that's how it felt, every time we saw her.'

I should just hang up, yet I can't move. I'm rigid with anger or fear, or a need, maybe; a need to hear what else Lisa has to say so that I can put it all together and discount it in one go. So I can process her words and see how much she makes up. So I can distinguish this fear that is wrapping itself around my heart. I do have to protect Ellie, I know I do.

Yet... I have questions.

'Ellie always thought we were beneath her,' she sneers.

'If you were beneath her, why would she fuck my brother?' I sneer back.

'You know what? I can't imagine. It's not even like he's any good. If he was, maybe that would explain it.' Bile rises. 'All I do know is that I don't trust the kind of person who can drop the need to be liked so quickly after we first met her. I knew something didn't ring true with her. That the Ellie she showed us wasn't her full story.'

I can see Lisa's face in my mind. Distorted, spiteful, hateful. The corners of her mouth curling with every vile word spoken. 'Of course they were having an affair, Ed,' she says, low and firm. 'She was in his car, days after giving birth. The signs are all there. What sort of woman isn't at home, days after giving birth? And it wasn't the first time. They had little meetings you know, little chats. They'd been meeting up for months, from what I can tell. I'm surprised you haven't been asking questions yourself.'

'Really? Months? And you know that how?'

Lisa doesn't respond.

'Ellie being in Simon's car that day proves nothing. Maybe I do have questions, who wouldn't? You can think and feel what you like about Simon, but I know what I think and feel about Ellie, and I know what I know. She was my wife, she loved me. The person you describe is not the person I lived with... the kind of person who tried to fit in, who tried to be accepted... the reservation you saw in Ellie, the holding back, that was fear. That was nerves. That was being desperate to be liked and getting the distinct impression that she wasn't.' I take a deep breath, focus returning. 'That's self-preservation... and you know something? So is this.' I slam the phone down, desperate to unhear everything Lisa's just said. Desperate to unfeel every doubt, question or fear I've harboured since Lisa started planting these seeds. Annoyed I didn't hang up sooner. Oli wriggles in my arms and I pull him closer, taking a breath of him in the hope it will revitalise me.

Then there's a knock at the door. I don't move. Has Simon come to see me? Like Lisa said? If it's him... if it's him... If it's him, I can clear up every lie she's fed me and move on with my life, my grief.

He knocks again. I go to answer the door, but as the glass panel comes into view, I see it's not him at all.

Chapter Twenty-One

Rachel

Ed opens the door.

'Don't panic! The cavalry is here!' I hold up Oli's bear in *Lion King* fashion, dropping to a kneel at the front door, before looking up with a wide grin. 'Admittedly, I'm minus a chestplate and sword, but, you know, the principle's the same. Oh—'

Ed's face is ghost-white, his eyes red-rimmed.

'Sorry, is this a bad time? I just—' I try to get up too quickly, but stand on my coat, which throws me into his arms, making a suddenly unfunny situation irritatingly slapstick. 'Shit. Sorry,' I say, breaking free from his grasp.

He takes the bear from my hands. 'Thank God, thank you,' he says nestling it into the space between Oli and his own chest. 'God, I...' He steps back into the hallway, dropping onto the staircase, holding the bannister to steady his fall.

'Ed, are you okay? Shit, Ed, what's happened? Is it the bear? I figured you might worry, that's why I came round,' I explain. 'I hope you don't mind that I got your address from our files. I just thought you might have been worried. Though, really, Ed, it's fine. The bear's back. You can relax.' I reach out to place my hand on his shoulder, but before I do, he's shaking his head, and I can see this is not to do with the bear.

'You did the right thing.' He looks up to me, glassy-eyed.

'Oh, Ed, are you okay?'

He swallows, nodding, but I can see that's not the case.

I push the door closed behind me, then crouch down beside him. 'What's happened?' I ask. 'Do you need to talk?'

Oli starts wriggling and murmuring, a noise that fast builds to a cry. I offer my arms up to take him. As Ed passes him to me, I can smell the problem – with Oli at least – so look around for evidence of somewhere to change his nappy. The door to the lounge is open, giving a glimpse of a beautiful, immaculate room, like something out of *Elle Decoration*. 'He needs changing, would you like me to…' Ed lets out a sigh. It's deep – like he's attempting a regeneration. New air, new strength. 'Upstairs?' I ask, seeing for myself that he needs to gather himself. He needs space. He points behind him, up the stairs, leaning to one side to make way for me to go past.

Having changed Oli and put him back to bed, I come back downstairs to find Ed in his kitchen, his hand on the kettle, two mugs on the side. 'Tea?' he asks, pouring water.

I stand on the threshold of kitchen and hallway, and possibly an unexpected evening. 'I… I don't want to intrude,' I say, looking back at the front door. There's something in the pit of my belly that makes me want to leave, and something in my heart that says Ed needs someone to stay. In the absence of any other candidates, leaving would be a bit shit.

'You're not intruding. I could do without being left alone with the noise of my thoughts, to be honest.' He sounds exhausted, his shoulders are slumped. 'In fact, fuck it, I'm going for something stronger. You want some?' He pulls a bottle of wine from a rack and holds it up.

'No, thanks. The tea is fine.' In truth, I'd give my eye teeth for a glass of wine, but that doesn't feel right either.

'You don't mind if I do?' Ed isn't waiting for my answer; instead he's pumping the handle of an immaculate *Sunday Times* wine gadget and pouring. Heavy red liquid circles up the sides of a wide-brimmed glass as he fills it full. He lifts the glass and takes a long drink, before topping it up. He turns to face me, a realisation dawning. 'Oh, I don't normally… not with Oli…'

'I'm not judging,' I say, hands up, reaching for my tea. 'So… do you need to talk about it?' I ask, before having chance to stop myself. 'Oh God, sorry. You don't have to. I can just drink this and then go.'

Ed stares into his glass. 'How do you find the truth? When the one person you trust is no longer here to give it?'

I wait, not sure if he's really asking me for my opinion, not sure what the right thing to say is.

'You know what, don't worry about it. Ignore me.' He takes another glug of wine before pushing the glass and the bottle to the back of the worktop. He rubs his face with the heel of his hands. 'Would you excuse me a moment?'

He walks out of the kitchen, down the hallway and up the stairs. A door closes and I'm left in his house, alone. Wishing I knew what to say. Wishing I had the tools to do the right thing. Wishing I could leave. *Come on Rach, what's wrong with you?* I shake off the feeling that I'm in the wrong place, or doing the wrong thing.

Photos take up wall space all across the kitchen. There are notes on the fridge, each one written in neat, curly writing. A sketch, too: a pair of red heeled shoes and a rainbow. There's a familiar mobile number scribbled on a scrap of paper, which I realise is mine. He must have written it down from the other night. Is that a good thing?

That he thinks I can help? I feel a split-second swell of pride, a spark of confidence, which is quickly replaced with uncertainty again. *Don't be a dick, Rachel. You CAN help. You've been here. He wouldn't keep your number if he didn't think so.*

I look around for something to occupy my time until he returns, something to make me useful. Pots line the side, ready to be washed. I open cupboards searching for a dishwasher to load up. If I do a few jobs, I can excuse myself and leave. I pull open a few cupboards before eventually finding it, rammed full of clean pots. The walls are lined with more cupboards, which I open and close, trying to find homes for the clean stuff. When Ed finally reappears, I'm on tiptoes placing the last cup on a too-high shelf.

'Oh, sorry, Rachel, you didn't need to…' He moves over to me, taking it from my hands. Our fingers brush, making me blush.

'Thought I'd make myself useful.' I smile shyly.

'Thanks. Sorry. I just…' He sighs heavily. 'I was talking to my sister-in-law just before you arrived.'

'Oh, that's good, to have people on your side, I mean.'

'She's not really on my side. Nor on my brother Simon's, for that matter. Which is part of the problem. She keeps making… accusations. About Ellie. About Simon. About… about why they were in the car together, the day of Ellie's accident.'

I sit down slowly.

'And you know, I don't believe it. I don't, but… I keep thinking about it. I can't stop thinking about it. My brother won't talk to me, Ellie's not here. I don't know how to get rid of these thoughts, this spite. I don't want to think about it, I want my memory of Ellie to be the woman I knew. The one I loved.'

'Of course you do,' I say.

Ed stares at me, his face colouring. 'Oh God, Rachel. I'm sorry, I didn't mean to… that's not appropriate. Sorry for offloading all this. I realise my problems aren't in your job description.'

'Hey, it's fine, don't worry.'

'No. It's not. I think—'

'Please. Don't worry. Really, Ed. It's fine. We all need to talk sometimes. It's no problem.' I can see he's unconvinced. 'Look, I should go anyway.' I look at my watch. 'I've got some… stuff that needs doing so…' *Sure. Stuff!*

'Of course. Sorry, I didn't mean to keep you. Thanks for bringing Oli's bear back. I really appreciate it.'

'You're welcome.' I pause, seeing a broken man before me, but not feeling comfortable enough to throw my arms around him and bear hug it all away. 'See you tomorrow, little man,' I call up to Oli, before heading to the front door. A photo on the side catches my eye and I pause to take a closer look. 'She was beautiful.'

Ed takes a deep breath, sadness swirling around him as he gives a tired, shallow nod. 'She was. The love of my life. Someone who made me the best version of myself, every single day that we shared.'

I bite my lip, feeling a hunger for that same sensation someday. 'You're lucky you found each other.' I smile, then realise how clumsy that must sound to a man in mourning. 'Look, I don't know if I ever said it, but I'm sorry for your loss.' He tries to smile at me. 'And your question, about the truth, we can never know,' I say, and he drops his eyes to the floor. 'But we can feel, and that has to be good enough, for everyone's sake.' The look on his face helps me, in that second, to make a decision.

I pull open the door, a cold rush of air inviting me to leave. 'It's going to take time, Ed. You know that, I'm sure, but if you need anything, to talk or whatever, my help doesn't just have to be with Oli. I can be here for you too.'

'Thanks,' he says, his voice breaking. And I know that I categorically mean it. Nobody needs to fight something like this on their own. That's what Dad tried to do and it fractured him. It fractured us all.

Ed, Oli, they deserve better than that. Just like me and my brother did. Just like Dad did. But what does that mean for me? For this new future Dad and Mo are pushing me towards? Is it what *I* want? Or what they want for me?

Chapter Twenty-Two

Rachel

Confused about this newly emerging dichotomy, I take the long way home, pulling up outside Dad's. The SOLD sign swings slightly in the wind, a sort of in-your-face reminder of my own, personal, bigger picture.

The house lights are off, Dad's car isn't on the drive. Because it's Bridge Night Monday. I'm glad he still goes. He spent so long hiding himself away, pretending all he needed was me and Richard, when we both knew we could never be enough. He needed friends. He needed to talk. He needed to focus on his own journey through life, just as much as he had to support us through ours. Which, I guess, is what Ed needs to do. That Dad never took that time for himself must have made those later years – when Richard and I started to go out more, leaving him on his own – so hard on him. Could it have been avoided?

And that's when I realise that, for the first time since Mum died, I'm thinking about Dad as a man, a human being in his own right. A husband. A lover. A confidant. Someone Mum could share her innermost thoughts with, as he could with her. I remember how they'd laugh, even towards the end. Little in-jokes they'd share; little looks. We didn't just lose our mother, Dad lost his best friend. How could it have taken this long for me to realise that?

My throat constricts and my heart beats harder as I recall the nights I'd hear him cry. The funeral, as he held our hands tight. I always thought that was to comfort us, but maybe it was the other way around. He dedicated a life to me and Richard, pressing pause on his own until he thought we were sorted. And now, because he saw I wasn't sorted, long before I noticed that I wasn't, he's making changes in his life that can help me achieve a dream I didn't know I wanted. Didn't know I needed. And sure, he needs to sell up for his own reasons, for his own life. But he saw how much it could help me, too, and he continues to make the sacrifices of a man raising children, albeit grown-up ones, entirely on his own.

A journey Ed has barely started, which stretches out for years to come.

And I want to help. I do. But for how long? How long do I commit to being at work just in case this man, who I barely know, needs me? Does he have other people he can lean on? I can't be the only one, can I?

I zigzag the back roads from Wollaton to Stoney Street and back home. When I do finally pull into the car park opposite our building, I spot Mo, teetering on the top step as she hugs her dressing gown around her – arms crossed, leaning into Greg's chest as they kiss goodbye. His arms surround her, swaddle and protect her. I don't know what that feels like. Can Dad remember? Can Ed, even? How long before the memories of touch fade? How does that shape your belief in, and your knowledge of, the person you loved?

I lock up and jog across the road.

'Go on, you go. I've got work to do. And Rach's back,' Mo says to Greg.

'Don't go on my account,' I say to him.

'It's fine, Greg was leaving anyway. I'm up to my eyes in a press storm and he is just a distraction.' She grins at me, happy, glowing.

And from nowhere, this rush of feelings and emotions suffocate me. Without even feeling or seeing the tears coming, I find myself standing in the middle of our street, sobbing.

'Oh, Rach, what's the matter? What's happened?'

'I'll leave you two to it,' Greg says delicately.

Mo pulls me inside. 'I'll call you,' she says after him, shutting the door behind us.

We get upstairs, me sniffing, her pushing me up, telling me it's all going to be okay. As we get into the flat, she swings me round for a cuddle. 'Tea or wine?' she asks, and I shake my head, wanting neither. 'Oh, Rach! What's happened? Come on.' I'm dragged through to the lounge and pulled onto the sofa, Mo's hands clasping mine until she reaches for a tissue to wipe my face. She drops the box in my lap. 'Talk to me,' she instructs.

'It's nothing, really, it's...'

Mo gives me one of her looks. I sigh, knowing I'm going to have to explain everything, even though I'm only just working through it myself.

'Oli didn't have his bear when he went home today. I was in a different room, didn't see Oli or Ed. Phoebe didn't pack it and when I checked the room before I left, I found it.'

'Right...' says Mo slowly.

'Oli's mum bought the bear for him. It's special. I didn't want Ed to be worrying that he'd lost it.'

'So you went round,' Mo guesses. I nod. 'Okay. But why the tears? I don't understand... oh... Oh, no, Rach.' I look up at her through my fringe. 'You've got feelings for him.'

'No.' I sniff, wiping tears from my cheeks. 'Don't be stupid. It's not that, I just...'

Mo sits back, taking up the position she usually uses when she's trying to analyse what I'm saying, so that she can work out what I actually mean.

'I don't. I don't have feelings for him. I just… I was there, in his home, and this penny dropped, you know, about Dad. Ed's there, trying to hold things together for Oli. He's trying to survive each day. A tiny thing like the bear can tip him over the edge, and it just makes you realise, made *me* realise, he has to do this all alone. Just like Dad did. Like Dad is still doing, because I'm not grown-up enough to work out what I want in life, or how to achieve it.'

'Well, you need to believe you can, first.'

'I do…' I trail off, realising that she's right, that that is part of the problem too.

'I sometimes wonder if you've stayed where you are because it's easier that way,' Mo says. 'Don't rock the boat, then you can't expose yourself to anything that might challenge you. Anything that might be hard.'

I pick at a piece of tissue.

'Not because you're lazy or anything, Rach, but because you're frightened. Intimidated, maybe.'

More often than not, Mo's right, but I'm not sure if it's that or something else. I make a noise in frustration. 'I don't know. I really think Ed needs someone. What's to say it wasn't serendipity that brought us together? Maybe I'm supposed to help him and, in so doing, I'll learn about myself, about Dad.'

'Do you think?'

'I don't know.' I sigh. 'I am so confused about everything.'

'You don't have to help Ed. He will be okay, one way or another. You don't have to apply such pressure on yourself.'

'I know, Mo. I know I don't have to…' Which is when I realise that I want to. Because the idea of not helping him, of not knowing him, makes me feel… alone. And that invites more tears.

Mo strokes my head, moving salty, wet hair from my forehead. 'Are you absolutely sure that, without realising it, your sympathy for him isn't… evolving?' I look at her, eyes wide. 'I'd understand,' she adds. 'I really would.'

'I don't know, Mo. I don't think so, but… I don't know.'

'Because, if so, we may need to revisit the online dating idea. There's a new one now, for people in uniform. You could bag yourself an officer, or a pilot, or… ooooh, a fireman!'

'I'd end up with a lollipop man!'

'There is a lot to be said for a hi-vis vest and a long stick, my friend.'

We fall into silence, Mo sitting patiently with her hands on my knee. Letting me know she's there, without sticking her oar in and pushing any further.

Eventually I say, 'He asked me a question when I was there.' I move position, tucking my feet beneath some cushions. 'He asked if it was possible to know the truth if the person to tell it isn't there.' Mo cocks her head to one side. 'Like, he's questioning something, you know? Like he's losing faith. I told him he had to believe in how he feels. He knew his wife better than anyone.'

'Wise words.'

'Yes? But how? How does he do that?'

Mo shakes her head. 'I don't know, chuck.'

'No. Me neither. It just seems so… unfair.'

'Life is,' says Mo. 'Men get better-looking with age, women are scrutinised to look younger every day. Men get paid better. Women are expected to conform to some ridiculous notion of perfection created, usually, by men. Pizza, burgers and Cadbury Creme Eggs are significantly more calorific than celery. Life just isn't fair!'

I laugh a bit of a snot-cry-laugh at her last suggestion. 'Yeah, and jeggings – despite being supremely more comfortable than a jean,' I sniff, 'are the single most inappropriate item of clothing in my wardrobe.'

'No, Rach. That's not life being unfair, that's just fact. Avoid jeggings at all cost. No good can come from them.'

We share a giggle and I wipe my face, silently thanking the universe that Mo is in my life.

'Look, I've got an early start tomorrow. I'm on the crack of a sparrow's train to old London Town. Pitching to a PR firm in Soho. May exploit my credit card while I'm there, so I need to get to bed. Liberty top to bottom requires stamina.' She smiles. 'You gonna be okay?'

'I am.' I sniff.

'Just… go steady, will you?' she says, bending down to plant a kiss on the top of my head.

'I will.'

Back in my room, I think about how it must feel to question the very person you have lost, knowing you might never get to the truth. How can you live a life and manage your grief with that? I pick up the photo of Mum that sits on my bedside table. *What's the answer to this one, then, Mum?* But her face drops out of focus, and instead my own stares back, reflected by the glass: a woman in her late twenties with a niggle in the back of her heart. One she hadn't seen taking hold, and one she can't afford to embrace. But she also can't walk away…

I fear the question is no longer, *How do you trust someone who's no longer here?* But, *How do you help someone find the answer… without losing control of your heart?*

Chapter Twenty-Three

Rachel

Ed called the office this morning and told Vicky that Oli wouldn't be in today. When she passed the message on, my first thought was to text him to make sure everything was okay. Then I remembered he's just the dad of one of our kids. I wouldn't do that with anyone else, so there's no need to do that with him, whether I want to check he's okay or not. I'm his child's key worker, that's it.

In fact, being back at work, with only the babies and Phoebe to talk to, has given me some breathing space. I think Mo is wrong; this *is* empathy. It is about self-reflection, too; learning about myself and my own response to life, to losing Mum, to Dad. It's also about the fact that, despite having had them for the better part of eighteen years, I am always surprised by the hormones my period flushes me with. I'm clearly being hormonally irrational. That's all. Which is why, with new-found clarity, it feels nice to pull up at Dad's for tea now. Tea and chat. No specific reason, just to spend time with him. After work. Before I go home.

I knock on the door as I push it open. 'Hiya!' I shout.

'Come in love, hi.' The familiar smell of coffee wafts through again, just as it always does, irrespective of the time of day. 'I've got the pot on, you want one?'

I head into the kitchen to find him surrounded by half-open cardboard boxes, each one with a scrawl of contents on the side, and bubble wrap on any available work surface. 'Wow, Dad. You're getting stuck in. When did these cupboards last get emptied?' I say, picking up an old, faded orange sippy cup that brings memories of being three or maybe four years old. I'd sit in front of the telly on Mum's days off, watching *The Shoe People* and *Wizbit* as she made lunch for me. We'd go to the park, or the shops. Or down to the library to sit in corners reading *Meg and Mog* books in hushed tones. I smile.

'Coffee?' Dad asks again.

'Nah, I'd not sleep, Dad. And nor will you. Caffeine's not good this late in the day.'

'Only ever drink decaff now anyway. You want one?'

I pick a mug up off the side and thrust it beneath the coffee pot. 'Go on then.'

'You want that?' he asks, nodding in the direction of the sippy cup.

'You know what, yeah. I think I do.' I smile, shoving it into my bag. 'It'll probably end up in the back of the cupboard, but... I dunno. Memories, you know?'

'Certainly is funny the things we attach sentimental value to. That old tea set me and your mum got for our wedding... it's mostly chipped and your mum hated it, so I'm not fussed about keeping it. That tablespoon, though? It's the one she always used when she had a go at baking. Was her grandma's. I just can't bear to part with it.'

I feel the weight of it in my hand. The patina of discoloured silver makes me smile, before I carefully wrap it in paper and place it into one of the open boxes.

'So, tell me, what have you been up to? How's Mo? Have you heard from your brother? I haven't since last week, but there's probably not much in the way of Internet signal in the Annapurna Mountains.'

'You can get it pretty much anywhere these days, can't you?' I say.

'Oh, I don't know. He posted something the other day saying that it was a brief link to the world, while they had the Internet. Did you see the photos?'

'Ahh… no. I must have missed them. I'll have to have a look.'

'Yes, you must. The photos are quite breathtaking.'

'He always did have an eye for that sort of thing.'

'Yes,' says Dad, looking over at a photo of Mum. Once upon a time he'd have told me Rich got that from her. He stopped comparing either of us to her after a while. I don't know if it was because it was too much for him, or too much for us. Will Ed have that with Oli? I guess it depends on nature versus nurture, Ellie not having been around long enough to influence him.

Dad moves into the lounge, where more boxes are stacked high, covering most of the patio doors, which haven't been opened in years. 'Sorry about the mess,' he says, shifting some tape and paper from the sofa. 'Thirty years,' he says, looking around. 'Some of it's not been looked at since we moved in.'

I remember that Rich and I got used to living in a slightly chaotic environment after Mum died. I'd bring friends round to begin with, when we were old enough to have them for sleepovers or whatever. After a while, all of them – except Mo – stopped coming, our house apparently being too messy; somewhere to poke fun at, not to go to. Ed's house isn't like that, not yet at least.

In one corner sits Dad's collection of academic journals. Stuff he wrote when he worked at the university; stuff he had published; findings on research he'd done. 'What're you gonna do with all that?' I ask.

'I don't know. I wondered about recycling the lot, to be honest. It's all in the archives at work anyway. I don't need copies.'

'You can't just bin it all!'

'What else do I want with it? I can't take 'em with me.'

'You could build some shelving or storage for them in the new place.'

'It's a caravan, love, there's no room for anything I don't need. And, besides, I meant when I die.'

'Oh.'

Dad started to talk like this a few years ago, as if by acknowledging it would happen at some point down the line it might lessen the blow for me and Rich.

'Anyway, enough of that. I'm living and breathing the packing, I'd welcome some distraction. How are you? What's going on?'

I think for a minute. 'I'm alright.'

'And once again, but with more conviction!' He smiles.

'No, I am. I'm fine. I'm just… tired. Probably tired and hormonal. A combination of the two. Has your neighbour been baking again? I could do with some cake.'

'No, I've got a garibaldi in the biscuit tin though.' He looks around. 'If I can find the biscuit tin.'

'Don't worry, I should probably wait for my tea anyway. It's Mo's night to cook and she hates it if I don't clear my plate.'

Dad smiles knowingly. 'Is she okay then?'

'Yeah, she's great. In fact, we went out on Saturday and she's met someone that she seems quite taken by.'

'Has she? Blimey! Is he prepared for his life to be turned upside down?'

'Ha! I reckon. It's nice to see. She's not been interested in anyone for years.'

'Quite right too, a distraction to her own life, all these relationships.'

'Maybe so. He's a mate of one of the dads from work, actually.' As the words come out, I feel a hint of colour in my cheeks and try to hide behind my mug, taking a long swig of my drink.

'Ah, work. I'm a few weeks off completing on the house now, you know, so that money will be ready.'

'I don't know, Dad.'

'There's no excuses. Your brother's having some to extend his travelling. There are more places he wants to go so he's opted for the university of international travel. What's your course of choice?'

'University of "blow it all on clothes and handbags"?'

Dad looks at me in the way only dads can.

'Okay, alright. I don't know.' I pause and, again, like only Dad can do, he waits for me to continue. 'So, Mo suggested I train to be a teacher.'

'Oh, Rachel!' He claps his hands together. 'That would be perfect. I can totally see you doing that, and your mother...' He trails off, no doubt aware that mentioning how much she would have loved it is bordering on emotional blackmail. 'You'd be brilliant at that.'

'She suggested I study science as my specialist subject.'

Dad's face breaks into the beam of a man for whom pride has just exploded in his heart.

'What do you reckon? Could I be a science teacher?'

'Only the best science teacher them kids would ever have.'

I shift my gaze out of the window.

'What?' he asks. 'What's up?'

I get up, stepping towards the old 1970s sideboard, which has school photos on it. There's one from when I was in the junior school. I remember the day, with my hand-me-down clothes from the family over the road. I smiled a gappy grin at the camera and Mum loved the result. Then there's one from years later, me and Rich together, after Mum had died.

'I never understood why you bought that one,' I say, taking a closer look, the frame cold to my touch. 'We look so sad, empty almost.'

Dad comes over, taking it from me. 'Because your mother would have,' he explains, simply. 'Just like she'd have ordered every school photo you'd ever have taken. How could I not? I'd have been able to hear her berate me the second I missed the deadline!'

'Do you still hear her?' I ask.

Dad smiles, turning away to pack up the photo in bubble wrap, placing it in a box marked 'Keep'. 'I hear something,' he says. 'Time distorts the voice, though. I'm not sure she sounds like she did back then: a faint lisp and the rounded vowels of Nottingham born-and-bred, I think. She's with me. I can still hear, see and smell her. But maybe I have to try a little harder. And maybe it's photos I see, rather than her actual face, you know?' He places a hand on his heart, smiling sadly, sitting back down with a creak and a groan. He seems older than his sixty-three years.

'What do you think she'd say about all of this?' I ask, pointing to the boxes around us.

'I know she'd say I had to do what I felt was right. And that I had to get rid of some of this stuff... and to go easy on my knees and back.' He smiles. 'Too many years not looking after myself; I'm beginning to feel an age. Not mine, necessarily. But one older than I should be, probably.'

'Did you have help, Dad?' I ask. He looks at me, and through the grey beard and messy hair I can just about see the science lecturer within. 'Someone to talk to? To help you through it.'

'I had you and your brother.'

'Yes, but someone for you, I mean. Someone you could talk to about the loss of your wife. About the pain you were feeling.'

He shakes his head, throwing away my comment. 'It wasn't like that back then. They didn't have all the advice people get these days. You'd get sympathy all around, but people didn't expect you to do anything other than manage your feelings in the privacy of your own home. I never wanted you and your brother to see me not coping.'

'I know.'

We fall back into silence, giving me a chance to look around the room. The paintings Mum hung, the curtains she made, the cut-glass lampshade she'd clean in the sink each spring. Probably not cleaned since the spring before she got ill.

'So, you complete in two weeks?' I ask quietly.

'Fingers crossed.' He gives me one of those smiles that parents give when they know you're pretending to be okay with something and, really, you're screaming inside. 'It's a young family, they've had a bit of trouble getting the mortgage, but I think it's sorted now.'

'Good.'

'Yes.' He looks about. 'It'll be nice for a family to breath some life into the place again.'

'Is that how it feels?' I ask, without thinking. 'As if there's no life here any more?'

Dad sighs. 'It's felt like that for a long time, love. I was never any good as a homemaker. Look around you. I've basically piled years on years on years into corners, cupboards and rooms I don't use. That wallpaper's been up since 1986 and God knows when I last washed the curtains.'

'You're supposed to wash them?'

'Apparently!'

'Wow! Who knew?'

'Your mother would have,' he answers with a sad smile. 'Which is the other job that needs doing: all of your mother's magazines.'

'I can help,' I say, wishing more than anything that he'd tell me I don't have to.

'That might be nice, thanks for the offer. Maybe something there would come in handy for the teacher training. Like I said before, she wanted to do it herself someday. There's bound to be something in there.'

'I don't think teaching now is like teaching in the 1980s.'

'Thank God for that!'

'Hmm.' I check my watch, not feeling up to talking about this any more. 'I should go, you know. I've got a few things to do at home.' I take my cup through to the kitchen, weaving my way through the boxes. 'Shall I come round over the weekend to help?'

'That would be great, if you have time?'

'Of course, Dad. No problem.'

He walks me to the door, giving me a cuddle when I turn around to face him. 'You'd make a brilliant teacher, Rachel. And your mother would be so very proud, as would I. But make the choice because that's what you want, not because you think it's a good thing to do in her memory.'

'That's not why I'm stalling, Dad,' I say. He looks at me, waiting for me to expand, but I can't. 'There's just… a lot to think about.'

'Of course there is. No rush,' he adds. But we both know that life can change in a second and stalling could result in nothing ever changing, or worse, an opportunity missed.

Chapter Twenty-Four

Ed

'Thanks for coming over, mate.' Greg takes the new bottle I pass him.

'No worries.' He leans forward to grab a slice of the pizza he brought round, expertly flinging stringy cheese into his mouth before it drops on the carpet. 'Having said that, whatever's keeping you from the office better not be catching! I could do without a week off work; I'm well behind on this month's target.'

'Nothing catching. Just a severe case of I-really-can't-be-bothered that I have allowed myself to succumb to.' It's a better excuse for taking the rest of the week off than, *I am not coping on a day-to day-basis with this torrent of pain and family-related shit.* 'It was that night out on Saturday... it made me realise how much I don't want to do this job any more. And how shit my life is.' Oli grumbles over the monitor, as if he can hear or understand what I'm saying. 'Oli excepted.'

'You been looking for another job, then? What would you do?'

'The only reason I get out of bed in the morning is because Oli cries to be changed and Floyd stamps on my head until I feed him.' I ruffle his back as he purrs on my lap. 'I just needed to buy myself a bit of time, really.' I reach for a slice of pizza myself, not hungry, just not wishing to look impolite.

Greg nods in appreciation of a shot on the snooker we're half watching on the television. Ellie used to love snooker; she'd purposely book business meetings in Sheffield around May so she could hang around and catch games at The Crucible.

'What do you reckon, then, Maguire or Carter for the final?' he asks.

'Carter surely. O'Sullivan'll beat him though.'

'Probably.' Greg nods. 'And buy time for what?'

'To work out my life. Work out how to deal with it when the shit hits the fan. When you're out in a club and feel guilty for not being at home on your own, mourning. How you cope when your sister-in-law accuses your brother of fucking your wife.'

'Woah, wait, what?'

I groan, because as flippantly as I've just reeled all that off, I feel sick every time I think about it. I've stopped calling the house because I don't want to risk having to talk with Lisa again. But every day I try Simon's mobile.

'It's all bullshit though, right? I mean, Ellie wouldn't have... would she?'

'No! Of course she wouldn't,' I say, because I can't admit that, as time goes on, as Ellie's voice in my head shifts and changes, as the clarity of her comes and goes... I can't admit that I feel as though I'm certain of nothing. 'I keep looking around the house, though; it feels... vast. Vacuous. It feels hollow and empty without her in it.'

'You can't move, though, not yet.'

I shrug.

'You can't, mate! You can't make rash decisions like that so soon after... you might regret it. I mean, you know, that's just my opinion—'

'When I want your opinion, I'll give it to you!' I joke, feeling the least funny I've felt in months, as the weight of life pushes down on my heart, on my spirit. 'It's just not getting any easier, that's all.' *Will it ever?* That's what I want to know, or need to know. The house, work, they both feel alien; as alien as life does right now. *Will I ever learn to live with it?*

'You've got good people around you, though,' Greg reasons, draining his bottle of beer. I pass him another. 'I'm always on the end of the phone if you need anything; your mum, she must be about. And I met the girl who looks after Oli; that's got to be reassuring, hasn't it?'

'You've met Rachel?' I check.

'Yeah, she shares a flat with Mo.'

'And Mo is…?' I feign ignorance.

'This girl I met. Last weekend. She's… I dunno. Amazing. We've only been out a couple of times this week. But…'

'A couple of times this week? Blimey! That's intense.'

'Yeah…' He drifts off to a memory and I feel jealousy creep in.

The early stages of my relationship with Ellie were fast, exciting, like an out-of-control roller coaster that was heading in the perfect direction. I can still feel it. She might be fading in and out now, but I can pull myself back to those first few dates. When the fear of commitment was quickly replaced with the fear of losing her. Of messing it up. Of losing out to someone better, someone more worthy of Ellie than me.

'She's… she's amazing!' Greg grins, back in the room.

'Nice one, mate, that's great. I'm happy for you.' And although I try to mean it, the jealousy has taken over, making me feel shit for me, and shit for being a crap friend who can't just celebrate his happiness. I hide it all behind a giant swig of my beer as I reach for another bottle.

For the rest of the evening, Greg chats about the snooker and I fight the need to ask him to leave. When all the beer has gone and the last bits of pizza have congealed, he stretches out. 'Right, I'd better shoot.'

'Good to see you, thanks for coming round.'

'No worries. Just… you know, go steady. It's bound to take time, all of this. It's only been…' He looks to me for the answer, realising he isn't keeping track.

'Nearly four months,' I say.

'God, is that all?' Which is the opposite of what I feel, because it's like my entire life has been hoovered up by the last few months and I can't remember a time before Oli, or what it really felt like having Ellie beside me, day in day out. All I know is that it was right, and it… she… made life worth living.

Greg drops his empty bottles in the kitchen and notices a scribbled sketch of Oli that I did. 'Who did this?' he says, twisting it around for a better look.

'Me.' I take it from him, flinging it onto a pile on the side. It's the first thing I've sketched in months.

'You're good!'

'Cheers, I used to do them a lot, but not so much any more.'

'Maybe you should…' he says, standing on the top step, hand out to shake mine. 'Maybe that's a job you could do,' he suggests, as if it was that easy.

Pretending I'm okay in the sanctuary of my own home is exhausting. Ten minutes later, as I fall into bed, I look over at Ellie's wardrobe. Behind that door is the box of sketches she collected over the years. All the little doodles I'd do for her, from our early days right up until her last. She kept every single one of them along with little memory prompters: cinema tickets from our third date – *Capote*, chosen purely because she'd always loved Philip Seymour Hoffman; the venue receipt from the wedding; the tinfoil ring I put on her finger, just after I'd proposed. All sorts of bits and bobs from our life together.

I get up and stand before her wardrobe with new-found determination. The need to smell her, to have her clothes close to me; her memories, her treasures. When I open the door, her smell hits me full force like holiday sun when you step off a plane. It's suffocating. Shoe boxes are neatly stacked one on top of the next. A photo of what's inside each box is stuck to the front, reminding me how organised she was, how on top of things.

At the bottom right-hand corner sits the candy-striped box I packed away, this one without a photo. I move it out and sit for a moment. I don't go through her stuff normally, I just stand and rest my hands on her clothes. It feels intrusive, somehow, to open boxes and dig around. I guess the time will come when I have to sort it all out... I lift the lid on the box and the parcel and letters she hadn't opened slip out, showing little sketches on scrap paper below. Each one drawn in my hand, the date and my initials in the corner. A kiss. A heart. Sometimes both. I lift a few out, staring at them, not quite connecting with the Ed I was when I drew them.

On the top, there's a drawing of me carrying a wedding-dressed Ellie over the threshold to our home. Complete with veil, bouquet and caption: *Here's to us, Mr and Mrs Moran.* There's one of her singing into a microphone; I drew it for the first anniversary of our first date. I place it on the floor, grasping more in my hand.

A text message from Mum interrupts my thoughts: *Your brother's back at his house. Thought you'd want to know.*

The news stops me in my tracks; pictures are scattered around me. Our past, on paper. A past I thought I knew precisely.

I need to talk to Simon.

I have to have the strength to believe. In her. In our marriage. But I can't do that without his version of events.

I look at my watch. It's 10.20 p.m.

Chapter Twenty-Five

Rachel

'Rachel? It's Ed. I'm sorry to call so late, but...'

I fling one of Mum's old *Marie Claire*s on my bed, sitting up. 'Are you okay? Is Oli?'

'We're fine, I just... I need a favour. It's huge, I'm sorry to call you so late.'

'It's okay, don't worry. What can I do for you?'

'I need someone to sit with Oli, I have to go out.'

'I can do that.' I reach for my diary, lid in mouth, pen poised to write. 'When?'

'I need you to come over now?'

The phone crackles slightly. 'Now?' I check, spitting the lid out.

'I know, I'm sorry it's short notice.'

'Ed, are you sure you're okay?' He sounds hurried, he's rushed and breathless. Whatever his answer, he doesn't sound alright. My heart now makes a slow but determined journey from chest to throat. There's something wrong. I can tell.

'I just... I need to go and see someone... my brother... it can't wait. I'll pay you, of course. Double for getting you out so late. Are you sure you don't mind? I wouldn't ask if—'

'Don't worry.' I put the lid back on the pen and throw the duvet back, jumping out to reach for my clothes. 'Give me ten minutes.'

'Okay. Thanks, Rachel, I really appreciate it.'

'It's fine. I said I wanted to help and I meant it. See you in ten.'

I hang up, lifting my nightshirt over my head and replacing it with a sweater and jeans. I ram odd-socked feet into my trainers, throw my book and phone into my bag, pull on my coat and lift my keys from the hall table. Mo's telly seeps through a crack in her bedroom door. 'I'm just popping out,' I shout up the hallway, moving quickly before she has chance to follow and ask me where.

When I open the front door, Greg is standing there, about to knock on it. 'Greg!'

'Hi. Mo asked me to…' He pulls at his neck, his face taking on a gentle pink hue. 'You're off out late.'

'Yeah. Quick job to do. Erm… Mo's in her room.' I hold the door open for him to take it, then take the stairs three at a time. Greg watches me leave. 'Tell her I'll be back in a bit,' I shout back up the stairwell before darting out of the building.

A passing car lights up my way as I jog over to the car park, coat pulled over my head to hide from the downpour that has been on and off all day. I jump over the puddles, surprising myself with uncharacteristic agility. Amazing what you can do when the adrenaline kicks in.

Ten minutes later, just as promised, I pull into his street. His house, in the middle of the grand terrace, is all lit up. Every single light on except for the tiny window upstairs at the front, which, if memory serves, is Oli's room. Ed stands in the lounge, looking out, so I flash my car lights to let him know it's me. He disappears from the lounge and, seconds later, the front door opens.

'Thank you so much for this.' He stands back for me to come in.

'It's no problem, I'm glad you called me.'

I peel my wet coat off, shaking it out on the top step before hanging it on a vintage hat stand beside the door. I brush myself down and ruffle my hair to refresh it from the weather, while trying to catch my breath. There's a nervousness in the air and I don't know if it is him, me, or both of us. Nor do I know why it's there. 'Phew! Right. Is there anything I need to know before you go?'

'Oli went down at seven, I don't think you'll hear from him now. I made you a tea, it's in the lounge. But there's coffee in the cupboard, if you'd prefer it, or wine on the side. Just help yourself to whichever you want.' He takes a deep breath. 'I don't know how long I'll be. I...' He drops his head.

'It's fine, take your time.'

'Simon is at home. He disappeared for a while. I just... I need to ask him about the accident. About what happened. About the things Lisa is saying, I need to know they weren't—'

'You don't have to tell me, Ed. It's fine. Go on. Do what you need to do.'

He stares at me, seemingly gathering breath and strength. 'I need to know the truth about Simon and Ellie.' He stuffs his hands in his pockets, change rattling as he pulls his keys out. 'Before he disappears again.'

'Of course you do. I understand. And I'm sure he will too, when you talk.' I resist the temptation to reach out and reassure him before he leaves the house. Not least because there's nothing I can say to help, not really.

From the back of his lounge, I see him jump into his car, pause, then start the engine up and race up the street. A window in the lounge is open, making the sound of rain bouncing off the pavements even louder. I'm taken back to the days when Mum was in her bed, not able to move. If it rained, I'd climb in with her, having first opened the windows so we could hear it fall. We'd cuddle, listening, smelling the air that flooded in through the open bay. She always told me to look out for the rainbow. I have always looked for the rainbows ever since.

Those are the little things you miss. Things that Oli will never know. Whatever truth Ed needs to find, without it, years down the line, he can't help Oli see the magic in memories he had no time to collect. He can't give him thoughts and feelings and magic that she might have created, were she still here. They both need that, desperately.

I look around, feeling out of place in the room. A gentle, flameless glow from the fireplace teases the room with half-hearted heat. Mum loved our open fire. If this was home, Dad would have complained at the heat in early May and Mum would have told him it was just a little bit, because she loved the process of fire-lighting, of keeping it going. Of watching the flames. Is that why Ed has it lit now?

I stoke the embers, trying to revive it for him. On the hearth, beside the stoker, there's a gilt metal-framed picture of Ed and Ellie. It's heavy, ornate; it's beautiful. As with the photo by the front door, which I noticed the first time I was here, hers is not the face of someone in love with anyone else but him. Their bodies are in sync, their heads tilt at the same angle. Their smiles are mirrored and their fingers intertwine. She loves him. Whatever Ed is questioning, it can't be this. Surely? It's here, plain to see. It's in the house, in the walls. Beyond the sadness, there's a history of home, of love. Can he not sense that any more? Could he ever?

Lights on Oli's monitor, which sits on the coffee table beside my tea, suddenly spark into life and distract me, green gathers pace to orange, hinting at red until all the lights flash as a piercing cry comes over the speaker. I take the stairs two at a time. 'Sshhhhh, shhhhhh,' I say, entering Oli's room. He pulls at his ear, his cheeks ruddy red. He grumbles and fidgets as I pick him up, crying into my neck. 'Hey, sssshhhhhh...' I hold him out to take a good look. Too early for teething, surely? Earache? Medicine and a clean syringe sit in a small wicker basket on a shelf above his cot. 'Do you need medicine, little man?' I ask, propping him on my hip as I reach for the bottle, syringing some sugary syrup into his mouth. Almost instantly he calms, enough for me to lie him down. Sporadic fits of movement pass and after five minutes of head stroking and soothing, he's sleeping again, his breath heavy and content.

I tiptoe away and hover outside on the landing, just to be sure. There's a door, wide open, lights on. Is it Ed's room? I fight the urge to look, to peep inside his room, so I look down to the floor until I'm satisfied that Oli is fully settled. But I'm drawn back to the open door, which, I see now, leads to an open box beside an open wardrobe. What looks like drawings are scattered around the box and its lid. A tiny step is all it takes from landing to beyond the threshold; my racing heart stops sharply as a floorboard squeaks. I hold my breath as silence returns. I rest against the wardrobe to steady myself. Unmade bed, curtains drawn tight shut, his switched-on bedside lamp is drowned by the strength of the main light, spotlighting the box and its contents.

I peer. Pictures, drawn in the same hand as the one on the fridge. The initials 'EM' are written neatly in the corner of each one. Ellie or Ed? Whoever, there are loads. Tiny scribbles, bigger illustrations. I bend over, taking a closer look. Most are of Ellie, some with them both. A car, a house, a beach. A babe in the arms of its mother or its father. Who's drawn them? I lift them up to see the detail. Beautifully drawn hearts hold messages inside. Messages, it's clear, from him to her. There are cartoons of conversations between the main protagonists.

These are cherished. Ed drew them for Ellie and she has kept them because they're precious. Yet again, his answer is here, in front of him. This is it. And as I reach, absent-mindedly, to drop the pictures back inside the box, beneath her hanging clothes, I see something else at the back of the wardrobe.

Books.

Pulling the sleeves of my jumper down over itching hands, I sink into the thick cream carpet. Large-petalled lilac and cream flowers cover the bedroom walls, reducing the size of the room to boudoir cosy. The sight of these books before me, and the urge to take a closer look, make the room all the smaller.

Lines of colour-ordered clothes hang above, neatly packed shelves of folded cashmere jumpers, pure cotton T-shirts and scarves line one side. Stacked beneath it all are more boxes, each, apparently, with a photo of its contents. And there, behind those, I see book spines. Glimpses of numbers that make up years: 2001, 2002, 200... something I can't quite read... 2004... all the way up to this year.

I reach out, hovering above them, my fingers tingling. Does Ed know these diaries are here? Surely, he must. But what if he doesn't? What if he doesn't and the truth lies within these books? The truth he's so desperate to prove so he can lay Ellie's ghost to rest? For him to read it in her own hand would solve everything, wouldn't it?

Chapter Twenty-Six

Ed

A neighbour's curtain twitches before I've turned the engine off. Simon's house is lit by an orange glow. At the end of the path, by the front door, their box of recycling now leans up against the step, seemingly empty. Was that only last week? The week before? I've lost track of time, it seems so much longer ago.

Lime-green light on the dashboard flips to 11.15 p.m. and second thoughts begin to creep in. Why am I doing this now? Why am I doing this to Ellie? Have I forgotten so much that the memory of her words and her touch have altered? Have they changed into the words and touch of a woman who lied? There's a burning sensation in my pocket where her picture rests. I see her; for the first time in days I can see her clearly. I close my eyes and I can smell her, sweet, strong, evocative. I can feel her holding my hand and kissing my face. I can hear her: '*I love you, Ed. It's me, you and him against the rest of the world.*' That's what she told me when Oli was born; she was exhausted but bursting with love. Our heads touched as he lay naked on her chest, skin to skin, and we morphed into one that day. Before he arrived it was me and her; in that moment it changed to us. *Us.*

So I know Lisa's lying, I do really. I don't need to talk to Simon…

Except that I don't know *why* Lisa is lying, and I need it to stop. For Oli's sake; for mine. For Ellie's.

A deep breath lifts my head, rejuvenates my will and launches me out of the car, up to the front door. Their too-loud TV blares through the windows, but I try knocking anyway. The single-glazed glass flexes, my reflection warps, but nobody comes. I grasp the cold, wet door handle and push the door open. Inside, the blistering temperature of too-high heating hits me in the face with the same force as Ellie's perfume from her wardrobe. I catch my breath.

Standing in their hallway for a second, the kitchen is up ahead of me. To one side, a frosted-glass door to their lounge is closed, but hazy colours from the TV reflect on the gloss-painted staircase. Gritting my teeth, I open the lounge door, which scuffs against the carpet, to see Simon, slumped, bottle in one hand, empty glass in another.

I swallow a soreness that rests in the back of my throat. My heart pounds.

'Simon?'

Nothing.

'Simon?' I try, louder.

Still nothing. I can feel irritation grow, anger. The invisible straps of my constraint tighten as I walk towards him, then press 'mute' on his remote before leaning into him. The smell of stale alcohol itches my nose. 'SIMON!'

His eyelids lift stickily, his head shifting back slightly to focus on my face.

'S'Ed,' he slurs, his eyelids shutting again.

'Where've you been?' I ask him, his head lolling down, chin to chest. 'Simon!' I try, shaking him, his head falling back in the chair.

'S'Ed,' he repeats, eyes still shut. He doesn't look like my brother. His face is grey, his hair thin. He looks like he's not eaten in weeks. He stinks of alcohol and BO, and his fingernails are filthy, what hasn't been bitten quick-short.

'What's been going on, Simon?' I ask. 'Where've you been? Why are you…' I look down at the empty bottle: whisky. He always hated whisky. And the wine bottle on the other side of the chair is red, not his usual white. 'Where's Lisa?' I demand. 'Where've you been?' But there's nothing, no chance of sense from the state he's in.

Do I leave? Do I move him? Do I wait until he's sobered up? He slurs something undetectable and I feel compelled to shift him upstairs. To put him to bed until the morning, when I can come back and try to talk to him before he disappears again.

I pull him up from the floor and try to get him to stand, but his legs give way and I have to catch him by the waist, pulling him back up. With his arm around one of mine, and my other arm around his waist, he leans against me as we take the stairs. The bedroom door opens with my kick, darkness stretching out before us. The bedroom light bulb blows as I manage to flick the switch on, leaving me to wait until my eyes adjust to the darkness.

Leaning Simon up against a wall, he slides down to the floor, floppy and completely out of it. Getting the landing light on gives me enough light to see the way to the bed, and I drag him over to it. A phone falls from his pocket, so I put it into one of my pockets to avoid standing on it. When I've tucked him in the bed, I pull him onto his side, just in case he's sick, then go back downstairs for water.

The kitchen is a mess. Filthy plates, empty milk cartons, half-eaten food all over. Is this Lisa's doing? Is this how she's been living in his absence? I open the cupboard for a clean glass, finding nothing. I search for a mug that hasn't grown mould, eventually finding one that I can just about rinse out. I fill it with tap water, then take it upstairs for him.

'Here, for when you wake up,' I say, though he won't hear me over the snoring. I study his face in the half-light, anger fizzling out to be replaced with sadness. How did he get like this? How did we let him get like this? 'What happened, Si?' I ask, crouching down beside him. 'What are you doing? How long have you been like this?'

Then I remember his phone and put a hand into my pocket, finding it inside. Which makes me wonder...

I flip it open to find it just surviving on the last of its battery juice. I click open his text messages but the folder is empty. Not a single one. Deleted on purpose? I tap my finger on the screen, thinking, which opens up his voicemail folder.

My heart stops. There's a message from Ellie. Her voice. The sound of her. Will it be how I remember it? The way she'd inflect certain words, the lilt of her Northumberland accent, the softness?

My hands shake as I press 'play', and she speaks. *It's like she's here. Like nothing has changed.* 'Simon, it's me,' she says, then pauses.

I cough all air from my lungs. *If I can hear her, why can't I touch her?*

'I think I've worked out what we say. It's going to hurt, of course it is, but I think we can do this. And in the long term... it will be better this way, I promise.'

What is, Ellie? What will be better? And what way?

The sound of her hanging up, the end of her message, makes me sink to the floor. I press 'play' again, desperate to hear her voice, my eyes tight shut with the pain of hearing her hurting almost as much as her words confuse me. *Tell us what?*

'Tell us what!' I shout out. Simon mumbles something before turning over. 'What's going on, Simon?' I pull at him. 'Why was my wife in your car? What the FUCK was going on?' I shout, my hands now pulling Simon up, his head lolling back. 'What did you do?'

'Edward!'

Mum, wrapped up in her coat, rushes into the room. She pulls me off Simon, who falls back on the bed, groaning. 'What on earth are you doing?' she says, looking down at Simon, checking, in what light we have, to see I haven't hurt him.

'What am I doing?' I spit. 'I'm trying to find out what the hell *he* was doing the day he killed my wife. I'm trying to find out what on earth they were doing together on that day, when she should have been at home, with me. I'm trying to—'

'Well, it's a good job I came when I did. I think perhaps you should leave,' she says sternly. 'You're clearly in no state to help, and he's in no state to listen. I didn't tell you he was back for this to happen, Edward. I told you because I thought you'd want to know that he was okay, that he was alive. I thought I'd check in on him myself, and thank goodness I did.'

'Yeah? Well, I was glad you told me. And I did come to check he was okay, but I have questions, Mum, and I've every right to the answers.'

'Of course you do, but he can't answer them in this state, can he?'

'I didn't know he'd be in this state when I came around. All I want is the truth, Mum. It's not much to ask, just the truth. Something I can't ask my wife because she's dead.' My breath is heavy with more, more I want to say but can't because I don't know where to start.

'What truth is there to know, Edward? What on earth are you talking about?'

Mum stands before me, her own breath now heavy. Nerves in her voice. Despite the half-light, I can clearly see she's frail, thin. Shadows form in the hollow of her cheeks. She looks old, older than I remember.

Is this a new thing? Is the stress of all this ageing her, or had I just not noticed before?

She looks between me and Simon, her sons at war, and I realise I can't answer her question. I can't tell the woman who gives us a cheek to kiss, who hovers in the background of our lives, because showing affection or love is more than she can cope with. I can't tell her anything because she's already broken enough. What would she do with any of this information I have? Defend him? I can't hear it. Explain it? How could she?

'Mum, Ellie was in Simon's car,' I say, breathless. 'I don't understand why. I don't know if he was drinking then—'

'Of course he wasn't.'

'How do we *know* that?'

'The police would have breathalysed him, Edward. They'd have to. At the scene.'

I fall silent, because I realise she's right about that much. The idea he was drinking has poisoned my perception of events; a suggestion that's lingered from the second Lisa told me he was back on the booze. But even if he was sober, it still doesn't answer everything. The text message, the voicemail. Lisa's accusations. Something was going on, no question about it. And standing before Mum, her chest heavy with the rise and fall of split loyalties, I feel the most alone I've felt since leaving hospital on the day of the accident, carrying Oli's car seat out into a winter sun that blinded me, strapping him into the car, clumsy with disbelief.

I'm on my own. It's as simple as that.

'Whatever questions you may have, now is not the time to seek answers. You're my sons, the two most...' She trails off, turning her back. She tucks Edward into his sheets, silence replacing the end of that sentence. 'Get some sleep. Calm down. Let's talk about this in the morning. God willing, your brother will be sober.' She moves to usher me out of his room. 'You only have half the story, Edward. You cannot assume the ending.'

'I know the ending,' I say, my voice low.

'You know part of it.' She goes to reach for my arm, but stops short. 'I wish I could take that pain away, Edward, but I can't.'

I look at the woman who gave me life. Do I remember her being so cold? As a child? Was she always aloof? Is that even the right word? It's not so much that she doesn't want to engage, as she can't. I learnt that many years ago. She taught me everything I do not want to be myself as a parent, especially now, in circumstances like this.

When I became a father, my perspective changed in an instant. My priorities and what I would do to protect, nurture and love my son. I don't understand my mother's position, her thoughts. I don't understand her approach. I came to get answers, I leave with more questions. And I've nobody to talk to about any of it.

Chapter Twenty-Seven

Rachel

I run my finger down the Liberty print book. Two thousand and twelve is cleaner than the others. No real breaks in the spine, but then I guess she didn't get a chance to use it like the others. I'm curious as to the contents; religiously kept daily commentary, or meetings and birthdays? Who'd keep so many notebooks? And among memories and drawings, too? The box before me is full of tickets, receipts, sketches and the brochure to this house, which is barely recognisable.

I rub at my chest, now tight. Nerves make my fingers stiffen. Is there something here that can help? Something to show him she was true? Has he read the diaries? Should I?

5 January 2012
Dear Diary,
He's here. And I know I said I'd stop writing, but how could I finish this journey anywhere but with his arrival? Ten years of diaries, written almost daily. I have to finish on a positive note.

I look up, my heart racing, aware that I'm crossing a line so bold, so clear. A line you cannot uncross, and yet, as my eyes drift back downwards, I can't quite tear myself away. It's for him, it's to help…

He's perfect. My beautiful, perfect, gorgeous boy, he completes me. As I look into his eyes, my own stare right back at me: my nose, my lips, my heart and my soul. I cannot tell you how that makes me feel. My home is full and my life has promise. Whatever challenges life may throw in the coming weeks, months or years, we will get through them, as a family. That's the promise I make to my boy. Xx

The fabric cover catches on the roughness of my hand as I close the book. Has Ed seen this? Surely, if he had, it would be all the information he needs? But what if he hasn't? What if he respects her privacy in a way I've totally ignored? What if he is missing out on the opportunity to lay to rest all these questions? He needs to believe, he has a right to see that he *can* trust her, doesn't he?

But, how can I tell him? To do so means I'd have to admit to sitting here, in his room, their room. With her private diaries.

I feel faint. I feel sick. What have I done? I'm sat here, looking through a dead wife's diaries. *Oh God. Oh shit. What was I thinking?* I fumble to close the diary, my hands itching. I toss it onto the wardrobe floor, burnt by guilt. What right did I have to read this? How could I kid myself this was okay? I feel as though I know more than Ed does at exactly the time he should have all the ammunition he needs to protect her memory, to protect their love.

Maybe I could leave the notebook out for him to see? Except that he'd know then, he'd know what I'd done, wouldn't he? He'd see things weren't as he left them. Maybe that doesn't matter. He might forgive the intrusion if it gives him the truth he needs?

Would I? Would I forgive me?

I'm not so sure.

I reach for the box, pulling it towards me. I'll put it all back, I'll get out of here, I'll give myself some time to think about how I might be able to sort this out constructively. I could do more harm than good just throwing it all at him.

What if he finds out and is so angry that he takes Oli from nursery? He doesn't speak to me again?

Would it matter? He's just a parent from work, that's all. Oli's dad. Nothing more...

I think...

Ignoring where my thoughts lead, I shake it all off and push the diary back in place, but something's in the way.

A packet slips down, its contents tumble out: a DNA test.

Then I hear the front door opening. Ed has returned.

My body turns to stone, the weight of what sits in my lap, plus the sound of his return, all combine to push me down, my knees heavy in the thick pile of his bedroom carpet. Oxygen abandons my body and my blood runs ice cold. Ed calls out, his voice moving from hallway to kitchen and I know that I have about four seconds to shove the test into the envelope, get everything that should be in the box back where I found it, then get out.

My hands shake as I let the wardrobe door slip shut and take three long, tiptoed steps out of his room. I hold my breath a second until I know I'm out and his bedroom door is closed behind me. *Adopt calm. Adopt cool. Buy yourself time to think.* If only I had time to go back and take out that envelope, hide it about my person. He doesn't need to see that. I wipe clammy hands down my jeans, tiptoeing back downstairs.

'You're back sooner than I was expecting.' I try to keep my voice light, but look over my shoulder in a not altogether innocent fashion. I wonder if I sound as guilty as I feel. *I was trying to help. I've gone too far.*

Ed bustles towards me and we meet awkwardly at the bottom of the stairs, my position on the last step bringing me perfectly up to his height, eye to eye, nowhere to hide.

'You were upstairs, is Oli okay?' He flings his coat on the bannister, looking past me. His eyes search for a potential problem, his voice is constricted.

'He's fine – I just… I heard a murmur, that's all. He was a bit unsettled, teething I think. I gave him some Calpol, I hope that's okay?' An itch and heat has spread across my chest. I reach to my neck, placing my hand at the bottom of my neck as a fear grows. Did I shut Ed's bedroom door? Have I changed anything in his room from how it was? Was the box in or out of the wardrobe? Was the door to the wardrobe open? How did I find any of it?

I can't picture how things were when I found them. I need to leave before he goes up there. I can't stand in front of him, trying to find a lie that fits with what he might find. So I push past him, more forcefully than I intend, apologising as I collect the still full mug of now cold tea from the lounge and busy myself through to the kitchen. Mug rinsed out and put on the drainer. 'Must have got distracted,' I explain about the tea. I straighten out the tea towels on the cooker handle. I fuss.

'It's okay,' he says, dropping into a kitchen chair.

I keep my back to him, wiping down the crumbless worktops. 'The fire was a treat, we used to have one at home.' *Is it still lit?* 'Dad used to hate how often Mum had it on, but she just loved it. She'd keep it burning for as long as she could get away with it. Well past spring, given the chance.' I ramble my way around a few jobs, then look around to make sure I've not missed anything. Searching for my handbag.

Ed sits with his head in his hands. I daren't ask if he's okay, or what's wrong. At any other time I would have done.

'Oh, now then, what time is it?' I check a watch I'm not wearing, tapping my arm then pulling my jumper sleeve down. 'I'll make a quick bottle before I go. If you dream feed him, you might get a longer sleep.' Ed doesn't move, he doesn't even acknowledge what I'm saying. He gets up, then drops back down again. 'Ed... is everything...?'

But before I can leave, or ask him the question, he's lost all control. I watch as he sobs into the kitchen table. I can't move, I can't speak. I can't do anything until he's ready.

I'm not sure how much time passes until he's got enough control to acknowledge I'm still here. 'I'm sorry, Rachel. Sorry this...' He reaches for the kitchen roll, pulling off sheets and burying his face into them. He wipes his eyes, red-rimmed and bloodshot. 'I just... I tried to... I'm sorry, I...'

But as he breaks again, so do I. Rational thought has left the building and I move to cradle him, his head pulled into my chest, holding him close to try and fix him. And this – despite being more for me than for him – takes down his guard. The sound of his grief breaks through and as he loses total control of his tears, I'm unable to hold back my own. Tears for what I have just found; tears of anger and self-hatred for looking; tears for abusing his trust; and tears for Ed and this moment. His whole body shakes, he tightens his grasp of my arm, and his fingers dig into my clothes as if he's desperate for something to cling on to, something to steady him in the moment. I haven't heard the sound of a man suffering debilitating heartache like this since my dad. But the memory of a sound I've blocked out returns louder in my heart than ever before. Dad, in his own room, crying into his bed in the hope it might swallow the sound. It didn't.

One of Ed's hands grips on to my arm. The other pushes against the kitchen table, forcing him closer into my chest. Everything about this moment makes me want to stay and leave in equal measure. It's too personal. Too close. Too painful to hear when I know what sits in his wardrobe upstairs. I stroke his hair, holding him tight into my chest and I realise how completely and selfishly I am hurting too. Gradually, eventually, the sound of Ed's grief starts to lessen. His hold loosens enough for me to stand back. Beyond the sound of our breathing, and the hum of the fridge, there is a silence; I wait until he is ready to break it.

'I'm so sorry, Rachel. God, I am so...' He trails off, still not able to look at me, shaking his head, his fists clenched on top of the table. 'I'm so sorry.'

'It's okay, Ed. It's okay.'

Does he feel guilt at the closeness we've just shared? I know I do. I step back further, then return to making up a bottle. Guilt scratches at my conscience.

'Tea?' I offer, my last words before I'll take his silence as my cue to leave.

'I'd prefer something a bit stronger,' he says.

'That's exactly why I am offering tea.'

He smiles, sadly, and the cycle is broken. 'I saw Simon, my brother.' *He's talking. He's talking to me.* I swallow back the urge to go straight to him, instead planting my feet firmly at this distance, my hands palm down on the worktop. 'And?'

'We haven't talked, since...' I don't need him to explain. 'He fell off the radar, disappeared. Started drinking. His wife... well, she said stuff. Made accusations.' He shakes his head. 'They're poisoning my mind, Rachel. My memories. They're splintering my heart and I need it to stop. I can't go on thinking the most...'

'What stuff?' I ask, carefully.

He shakes his head. 'I feel like I don't know who she is any more.'

'Who?' I whisper.

'Ellie. I feel like I don't know Ellie any more. Like she's a stranger to me. Can you imagine that? How that feels? To be faced with the loss of your wife and at that very moment question the validity of your marriage, your relationship? Everything that was supposedly stable, secure and future-proof is in pieces around me. Things don't add up, Rachel. They don't add up and he's so pissed he can't answer and she's... not here.' He takes a breath, a pause, regaining control. 'I'm frightened, Rachel.'

I wish I could tell him he shouldn't be, but now I don't know if that's true. 'I'm sure it's... I mean, I don't...' I can't. I can't say anything because I don't know the truth either.

He gets up, reaching for a bottle of whisky before pausing, putting it back and sitting down. 'I arrived at the hospital that afternoon... you know... I remember the smell... they have a particular smell, hospitals, don't they? Like clean is trying to cover up death or something. I was distracted, though. People talk about living a nightmare, but it really did feel like that. Like I was in the worst possible dream. All noise seemed muffled, somehow... None of it was real. I don't remember the specific details of what anyone said to me that day – conversations seemed to leave me as soon as I'd had them – yet I remember the strangest, smallest details of the little things around me.'

'I remember that,' I say, pulling a chair up. 'Sitting in our lounge as Dad tried to explain what had happened. My schoolteacher was there – Mr Roberts – he brought me home from school when it happened. He sat in the background, out of place, and I remember wondering who was taking class if Sir was round at ours.'

'When I think about the minutiae of it all, the random little details of open doors that should have been closed, or litter in the corridor. The very things that distracted me at the time are now the things that draw it all back and, suddenly, the muffled, cotton-wool sounds return.' He pauses halfway through a breath, a memory interrupted. 'As I walked down that corridor, to the room Ellie was in, I tried my hardest not to see, hear or feel anything going on around me. If I didn't engage, none of it could be true. But the memories, the image, it's crystal clear. I engaged. It came true.'

This time I can't not take his hand, and yet, as he holds mine back with both of his, I wish he wouldn't, I wish I hadn't.

'As I got closer, I noticed an old guy. Dirty, scruffy, he had cuts to his face, his arm was in a sling strapped up to his collarbone. As he was wheeled towards me, I made way to step aside and let him pass. Then I realised he wasn't old, or dishevelled. He was Simon. It didn't look like him, he looked... I don't know. Maybe it was just the fact I was about to identify Ellie; maybe it was the situation that made him look this way; but he looked strange. Different.'

He holds my hand tighter and I wonder if he knows he's doing it.

'When I saw him... the look on his face... time ground to a halt. As did I. And I knew, I just knew. He'd called me when it happened. The ambulance crew took the phone from him as he shouted down it, as he screamed out in pain. It wasn't until I got to the hospital that

I realised the pain he screamed was the realisation he was responsible. He was guilty.'

'Oh, Ed.'

He takes one hand away, rubbing the side of his face. 'That same night, back home, my jaw ached from teeth clenched all afternoon, trying to stay strong, failing. I was fighting this urge, a sort of animal instinct, to hate him, to lash out.'

He rubs his nose, then his face, one hand first, then both, leaving mine free to retreat to the safety of my jumper sleeve. I could tell him that things like that fade; that the memories of the pain are replaced with love. But I still remember it all too. It never goes.

'I try to fight it sometimes. I don't want to remember. It hurts and it won't go, Rachel. It won't go.' He swallows, eyes focused on mine, until he stares back into middle-distant memories. 'They gave me back Oli, you know – after. They said that he was fine. That Simon had managed to get him out of the car. And I remember thinking at the time, the last person to touch Oli wasn't her.'

I hug myself, the trace of her diaries still laced on my fingers.

'Lisa thinks they were having an affair.'

I stare at him.

'I needed to know.' His voice is low, controlled.

'And?' I say carefully.

He shakes his head. 'I don't know. I don't know. I don't know. And it's killing me, Rachel.'

And here comes the guilt, a great tidal rush of it coursing through my veins. *Do I know? Do I know the truth? Should I tell him, despite what that ultimately means?* The baby monitor flickers and the kitchen grows cold.

I can't tell him. Because I don't know either. Not really. I'd be making assumptions, too, like he is. Like Lisa may have.

'You need to try to sleep, Ed. You can't face this, you can't fight it, exhausted.'

'How can I sleep?' he asks. 'When every time I close my eyes her body lies before me. Cold. Cut. Lifeless. Every time I close my eyes I can smell the diesel from her clothes, and the blood. That sticky, metallic smell that days before had been new life, a smell shared with Oli, and in that moment... it was death.'

'Ed...' We stare at one another for a beat, before he nods, letting his head drop to the table.

'I think you should go,' he says. 'If that's okay.'

'Of course,' I say, jumping up to grab my bag, relieved for a chance to get away. 'I'm so sorry, Ed,' I say, wishing I could explain what I was sorry for.

Ed gets up to follow me down the hallway. 'I'll see myself out,' I say, but he's there, right behind me. My skin tingles as he reaches beyond me for the door, his arm brushing against mine.

'Ed. You're all that matters to that little boy now. It's important you remember that. Bitterness and anger, it changes nothing but our hearts. It makes us ill. Acceptance and learning to cope, to manage, to find a way to put on the face of someone who's dealing with it on the days when you aren't. That's what you need to find. You won't get over this, having someone to blame or not. You will just get on with it. Because you have to. We all do.'

He nods.

'Look in her eyes,' I say, pointing at the wedding photo by the door. 'That look is what you have to hold on to.'

I pick up my coat from the stand as Ed fumbles in his pocket, pulling out a ten pound note. 'Please, I can't. I'm just glad I could help.' I say, guilt coating my words.

I leave him staring at the photo of the day they thought the rest of their lives would be for each other. At least, I hope that's what was in her mind. *Please, God, don't let that envelope have had anything to do with Ellie. Please, God, don't let him realise what I've done.*

I couldn't bear it if he hated me.

Chapter Twenty-Eight

Ed

One heavy foot in front of the other, the stairs are mountainous, the whole house overwhelming. It's too large and too full to be so empty and cold, but it's just that. Without Ellie, it's empty. Cold. It's not home.

I push open our bedroom door.

I make my way to our bed and drop into it; duck-down cushions my fall. I don't change. I don't wash. I've no energy to think. I'm done. This is the turning point. I can't fool myself into thinking that clarity can ever come. Rachel's right about acceptance.

I lift myself enough to climb under the covers, wrapping up on Ellie's side of the bed. Her perfume sits on the bedside table, residue on her pillow from the last time I sprayed it. I lie there, eyes closed.

And then I realise: I never close our bedroom door.

Because of Oli.

I haven't closed it in months.

I open my eyes. There's a dress, trapped in the wardrobe door.

If I was cold before, I'm colder now. And breathless, because I wouldn't do that, I'd notice. I make sure Ellie's clothes aren't trapped when I shut those doors. Just as she always, meticulously, did. I search the room for signs of anything out of place. Nothing obvious, except the dress. And the door.

Her box is still there, on the floor beside the wardrobe. Have any papers moved? I jump out of bed, kneeling, packing everything back in with no thought to order or form. I check the wardrobe and the floor for more papers strewn and, as I do, I see Ellie's diaries: things I never knew she kept until the day I came to find a dress, something perfect for her rest in peace. That's when I found them. I knelt before them, running a finger along each spine, but the pain of reading Ellie's words, by her hand, was too much. And, besides, they're private. Each time since, when I've reached out to them, yearning to be drunk on her, on her memories, I've always stopped, my hand hovering just above them, as if they're surrounded by some kind of opposite magnetic force field that stops me from making a connection.

So why are they out of order?

Why does 2012 sit before 2011?

I move it back. Because she'd have hated that more than the idea of my touching them. She liked order, form, conformity, albeit on her terms. I check the rest, chronologically packed right back to 2006. The year we met. I inhale deeply as, against everything I've believed in before, I open it up to read.

10th January 2006

Dear Diary,

Today I met my future husband. I don't know his surname. We haven't been on a date. And if it turns out he has annoying habits like mouth-open-chewing or not-really-snoring snoring, I reserve the right to revoke my proclamation. But all things considered thus far, he's the one.

It's also the day I bought the most incredible pair of boots. Literally the best you've ever seen. Delicious, pillar-box red, suede wedges and fifty per cent off! Who cares it's minus three degrees and snow is imminent, the God of January Sales smiles down on me. I'm not sure which I am more excited about... husband or boots? Probably, digging deep, it would be the husband... but it's close.

So, here's the scene: department store escalators – I know, right, heady with the glamour – I'm going up one side and he's going down the other. It's been a good morning at work, a couple of quick wins. The boss is unusually chipper and we've a happy client so I deserve a treat, right? Post-Christmas retail reward for hard work and dedication. (Actually, it wasn't so hard. It pays to ply PRs with gin cocktails and exclusives... I digress.) So, I'm moving from fragrance to footwear and there he is: Morning Guy. Meet me at the traffic lights guy. My goodness I like your Alfa Romeo Spider guy. That one. And, just like every morning for the last few months, when we arrive at the traffic lights at the same time on our independent commute to work, he has a sort of naughty glint in his eye.

Today, minus cars and in the flesh, our paths cross. He's headphoned up, tapping the handrail as he makes his way in the opposite direction. It's pleasing to find that someone whose head and shoulders have caused such a stir, can back it up with equally exciting rest-of-himself. A mid-grey, three-piece suit and polished brogues; office immaculate. He looks posh cufflinks away from a catalogue model, one of the really hot ones. In a top-end catalogue (oxymoron?). Dark eyes that search you out of the menswear pages. All brooding. The sort of catalogue model with a hint of stubble and a look that says: stand by the Xerox, things are gonna get steamy.

At the risk of sounding a bit Richard Curtis film (not that there's anything wrong with that, per se!) our eyes meet and my heart does that flippy thing, where for a split second you think you've stopped breathing. He offers a smile, I reciprocate, stumble over a mouthed hello and – despite our entirely innocent and completely silent exchange (maybe we don't need words?) – my aforementioned heart takes residence in my mouth. As I get to the top, I see him walk away without looking back and, laughing at my own stupidity, I invest all newly found energy in the boots (the boots!), which stand proud at the top of the escalator, patiently waiting my arrival.

Shoes off. First boot on, Morning Guy reappears. Breathe. Remember to breathe.

'Hi. I'm Ed.' It's funny, he does look like an Ed. 'So…' He pauses, before starting to talk, but I'm not sure what he says as I'm trying to act cool, standing with one foot in boot, the other be-socked and throwing me off balance. He steadies me until I hold my hover to the same height as the boot, by which time he's asked me out. I giggle a yes, give him my number, and tell him to text me when and where.

Which he did. Ten minutes later. I don't mind admitting, I swooned. I never swoon. I've outgrown swooning.

So now I'm in my bedroom, surrounded by discarded clothes, having finally settled on black mini skirt, polo neck, opaques and the boots. Because maybe they're good luck. My hands are shaking too much to perfect my usual 1960s eyeliner, and the butterflies in my stomach tempt me to back out, except backing out is no way to start things with your future husband. I might not tell him that bit. Wouldn't want to scare him off.

And I'm terrified. Because although I didn't set out to bag a man today, and although the above makes me sound more high maintenance than I actually am, I think I could really like him. There's just something about him.

If the sales gods are up there, can you have a word with the ones in charge of romance? Please don't let me come across as a dick!
Xx

My palms are sweaty and my heart beats heavy. I flick through more pages: the first time we went to Mum and Dad's and I introduced her to everyone, the memory tainted with Lisa's suggestion that Ellie gave up trying to impress them. I remember now, it was a disagreement about a newspaper article. Dad had read out something from the *Daily Mail* and before she'd had chance to think, Ellie had given her very strong opinion on that particular newspaper. She was shut down. So she shut down too.

There was the time we came to view this house: '*Oh my God, this is a forever home, Ed.*' We weren't married, but I remember thinking this was where I'd propose. And a few months later I did. She was in the bathroom, trying to get warm because the heating had broken but the electric shower still worked. She stood beneath it, letting the steaming water thaw her out and I said it before I'd even realised I was about to.

'*Will you marry me?*'

'*In a heartbeat.*'

'In a heartbeat.' I place 2006 back, running my finger along to 2011. Opening it up, a picture falls out. Me, Ellie and our friends, taken on a timer the night we conceived Oli. We lay in bed that night, wrapped up in each other and love and home and the future. '*Anything is possible now we have each other, Ed.*' She traced a heart with her finger on my chest. Every inch of me tingled.

That was the woman I knew and loved and that is the woman I want to remember. The mother of my child, the woman who planned our endless possibilities. The woman who would be heartbroken if she knew I was questioning any of this.

Fuck, I'm even questioning one of the few people who has helped me. Rachel wouldn't snoop around. I know she wouldn't. She's not that type of person, she understands what's going on. Whatever brought us together – circumstance, serendipity, Ellie – she is on our side.

Frantically, I gather up the diaries, cradling them in my arms as I go downstairs and out into our rain-soaked garden. Threatening clouds hover, adding fuel to my urgency. I lift the lid on the incinerator, dumping them inside as I yank it free of the undergrowth. I roll it up onto the patio. I grab newspaper and firelighters, then lighter fluid to combat any damp in the air. I let a match flame kiss the air above the diaries and, instantly, high flames dance into the sky, grey smoke twists up and into the night as I watch the paper curl; Ellie's writing disintegrates against the heat.

I have the truth in my heart and that is what I'll take to my grave. I'm sorry I questioned you, Ellie.

Chapter Twenty-Nine

Rachel

The flat is silent when I trudge in, defeated. What I want is to be looked after while I work out how to deal with all of this, but instead there's nothing. No radio, no talking. No Mo to save the day. Though on second thoughts, it's probably for the best.

Our Ikea trip fairy lights are finally in place, stretching across our fireplace, emitting a warm white light, but even the arrival of magical, tiny night lights can't ease the suffocating fear and hatred in my heart. Mostly hatred, in truth. How could I have done that to him? How could I have done it full stop? What possessed me?

And how do I say something? Should I even?

I check the door for signs that Greg is still here, his shoes, his coat. Anything. I don't want to interrupt them, but I need Mo. I need to work out what the hell I do next. Our usual solution of damage limitation over a burger and a beer is not an option. My relationship with Ed is beyond saturated fats and alcohol. What am I even talking about? I'm his child's nursery nurse. That's it. There is no relationship, nor should there ever be. That I even think that, after what I've just done, proves what an abhorrent individual I am.

I read his dead wife's diaries, for fuck's sake.

Whatever moment I'd like to think we had back then, it was circumstance, not need. Not desire. He didn't need me, specifically. He needed anything, anyone, someone to hold him. And I can still picture the moment: his eyes sodden with grief and loss, his body deflated, beaten, trampled. Lost.

I took advantage.

The door to Mo's room opens and my best friend pads out. I resist running up to her and taking her down with a massive hug. It's tempting to hold on to her until this has all blown over, but I don't suppose that's much good for her newly emerging relationship. Sleepily, she rubs her eyes and smooths out her hair. 'Hey, you,' she whispers. 'I heard you come in. You okay? It's late.'

'I know.' I nod, trying to hold back the wobble in my voice, the tears, but I fail. 'Shit, Mo, I've done something awful.'

'What? What do you mean? What have you done?' She pulls me close then leans back to check my face. 'What's happened?' I shake my head, unable to speak. 'Rachel, hey, come on now. Breathe, take a deep breath. Calm down. Come on, come in the lounge.' As she pulls me through, my body judders as the last couple of months – of what, I'm not quite sure – finally catch up with me; the last couple of hours being the ones to finally break me.

'I'm awful, Mo,' I stutter. 'I'm a horrible human being.'

She reaches for tissues, wiping my eyes. 'No, Rach. Don't be silly.' She lifts my head, my eyes meeting hers, no escape. 'What on earth has happened?'

'I did the worst thing you can possibly imagine, Mo. I am shit and vile and shouldn't be trusted.' My breath spikes as I try to get back in control.

'Rachel, is this…' She pulls me down onto the sofa then sits back slightly. 'Is this to do with Ed?' But I know she knows the answer.

I nod miserably. 'He called,' I hiccup. 'He asked me to help with Oli. He wanted to go to see his brother and I'd offered to help out any time he needed me.' Mo nods knowingly, and I have to look away. 'So he went, and I was at his house. Oli cried and after I'd settled him, I stood on their landing and noticed something. In his room.'

'Oh, Rach.' Mo cradles her face in her hands. She's smart, she'll be piecing the evidence together as I tell her. I may not even have to say it all.

'I went into his room,' I whisper.

'Okay...'

'There was this box, full of stuff. I don't know what... memories, drawings... that sort of thing.' She waits. I know that she'll have worked it out, but she's going to make me say it after all. 'I don't know why? I just...' I reach for some tissue, picking at the ply for something to do with my fingers. 'I found diaries, too.' I look everywhere but at Mo now. I can feel her studying my face as if trying to work out who I am. We both know a woman's diary is sacred. 'Everything he thinks he knows is under question, Mo. He's doubting his wife; his sister-in-law has been saying some awful things; he's trying to work on his grief but he has questions. There are loose ends, you know?' I try to justify myself. 'I just thought—'

'That if you looked, you could find something to help.'

I bury my head in my hands. 'Oh God.'

'And?'

I look up at her, tears spilling down my cheeks, dropping from my chin to the tissue on my lap. I sniff hard, shaking my head, sickness swelling in my belly. 'I don't think it's okay.'

'Of course it's not okay, Rach,' says Mo.

'No. I mean, I don't think "it's" okay.' Mo crosses her legs in front of her, waiting for me to continue. The lounge is cold. The air feels thin, as though we're ascending a mountain with each word I utter, oxygen supply depleting. 'I thought something in her diary might help, so I was scanning the pages, nothing inside suggested a problem. She stopped writing it when she had Oli, but that didn't mean anything. I mean, who has time with a newborn?'

'Exactly.'

'Then he came back.'

'And found you?'

'No, but he came back suddenly, so I tried to put the diary back, but it wouldn't go in. Something was in the way. An envelope.'

'And? What was in it?'

'A paternity test.' Mo's eyes widen. 'Why would you have one if there wasn't some reasonable doubt? For what purpose?' I ask, genuinely hoping she might have a good answer. One I'd not been able to come up with while wracking my brains for the entire drive home.

'Rachel, I don't know. But you're right. This isn't good, and you can't get involved. You need to step back, you need to put some distance between you both.'

'I need to tell him, though, don't I? Surely!'

'What good would that do?'

'He'd have the chance to work out for himself how he wants to deal with it.'

'And he'd also know you'd been snooping around his room, around his dead wife's belongings. Why would you do that to him? To yourself? Backing off means you don't have to rock what's already unstable in his world. You don't have to make things worse. You can just quietly, gently, extricate yourself from whatever grasp he has over you.'

'It's not a "grasp", Mo. I thought I could help.'

'You like him, don't you?' she says simply.

'What? No!'

'Rachel…' She fixes me with that look. The one she always uses when she's being the grown-up in our relationship. 'You like him.'

I shake my head. 'I don't. I can't. I…' I bite my lip. *Shit… Do I?*

'You need to step back. You need to walk away from all of this. This isn't good. It's not your place, Rachel.'

'How can I do that without walking away from Oli too? He's already lost one person in his tiny life—'

'He's months old, Rach. He won't know.' Mo's observation cuts deep, but I know she's right. 'And if you really care about Oli, maybe it's best if you do step back.'

'How? How has this happened? I don't want to feel it.' I pick at my chest, my heart, trying to pull out and throw away whatever feelings have crept up and swallowed rational thought. Whatever feelings make me kid myself that I'm doing something for someone else's benefit instead of… instead of… 'Oh God, Mo. This had nothing to do with him, did it? This wasn't me trying to help him, this was me trying to help me. Save the day. Be the one to make it alright. I was trying to be Wonder Woman but I turned into Catwoman.'

'It's an obscure reference, my love, but, yes, I think you did.'

I reach for a cushion, pressing it into my face with a groan. 'Oh God, how can I love one of the dads from work? That's never happened before! And I've met some *really* hot ones!'

'You *love* him now?'

'Shit, I don't know, Mo. No… yes… probably not. I don't know. I didn't even realise I had any feelings until forty-three seconds ago!'

I look to the ceiling, my head dropping away from Mo's gaze. I'm trying to lighten the mood because that's easier than facing the reality of what's going on here. Thank God Mo understands that my flippancy is deflection.

I get up to stretch my legs and pace out a plan of action. On the mantelpiece, lit by the fairy lights, is a photo I hadn't noticed before. It's Mo and Greg, surrounded by trees in full lime-green bloom. A late-evening sun shines from behind the camera, lighting up their faces. Greg stands behind Mo, his arms wrapped around her chest, his face nestled next to hers. She holds on to him, one hand clasped to his arm – her other outstretched to take the photo. There's a building behind them, red-bricked ruins.

'Our second date. We went to Rufford Abbey,' she explains. 'We walked around the lake, we sat watching the squirrels. We shared chips in the café. We took this.' She reaches to pass it to me. 'He brought it over tonight as a gift, asking if we could officially be boyfriend and girlfriend.' She smiles, dreamily. 'It was... so lovely!'

I feel a twang in my heart, a hideous kind of jealousy. I want that. I want that sense of hope and new-love excitement. Those butterflies with the calls and texts, the excitement of first dates, the togetherness you feel when you realise your dates are turning into long walks and lazy days because all you want is to sink into the comfort of one another, no third parties needed.

'I'm really happy for you, Mo.' I place it back on the mantelpiece, the photo of my best friend blooming as much as the trees around her. 'He seems like a good guy.'

'He is.'

I'm hurtling towards a change of life. I can feel it. A change in the comfort of my routine, of mine and Mo's. And not just because she has a new man in her life, but because I need to make some changes. A new job, maybe. Or a new focus, a new interest. Anything to put some distance between me and Ed or Oli, or both. Except I'm rubbish with uncertainty, with new normals that I don't yet know or understand.

So not only do I intensely dislike myself right now, I am also deeply terrified. I can't see the light in this particular tunnel.

Mo stands behind me as I stare out of the lounge window. 'Rach, this was just a mistake. You haven't got a bad bone in your body.'

I hold myself tightly. 'So what do I do now?'

She moves to stand beside me, nudging me gently with her hip. 'I don't know. But I do know you'll be okay,' she says. 'I promise you that. But you need time, you need a plan. You've got to work this out for yourself.'

I nod. We fall silent. Mo tries to stifle a yawn. 'Go to bed,' I instruct.

'It's okay, I—' The stifled yawn returns to interrupt her.

'Go on, go. I'll just sit here for a while. Is Greg here?' I ask.

Mo nods.

'Go on. Climb into bed and curl up to him. Tuck cold feet into the crook of his leg, it's an official girlfriend privilege.'

She squeezes me, with a kiss on the cheek, then heads back into her room, slowly closing the door behind her.

I'm alone. I'm cold. My mind is in overdrive as I stare at the wall, my life running through my mind. The job I took to pay bills, which is okay, but not great. The home I share with my friend, who's moving on without me – as she should – could soon become too cosy for three. The child I care for and the father for whom, it would appear, I have feelings. In the space of a few hours, all the things I would hang my sense of self upon are shifting. I need to find the strength to shift with them, or be left behind forever.

It's just a matter of working out how. And when. And where…

Chapter Thirty

Ed

I wake up with a start, my body turning to ice as I remember what I did last night. Her diaries… the smoke… the hope of truth swallowed in flame. Oli's link to his mother's words, now dust and ash in the base of an old metal dustbin. I get out of bed, step across to the window and peer out, down, the fire now nothing more than a slumbering glow of Ellie's innermost thoughts.

Oli stirs, pulling me away from the sight of last night's rash behaviour, but the guilt I feel as I pull him close remains. It's not that I think he'd want to read them necessarily, or that that's even a good idea, but just to have them; a piece of his mother, her hand, her writing, her choice of words and her dedication to recording her life. And I've burnt the lot.

But then I remember the message, the voicemail. Her voice, as if she was still here. Something that could have lifted me instead pushed me darker, deeper into despair and distrust.

I lie Oli down in his bouncy chair, down in the kitchen, before heading to the window to look up to the sky, uselessly searching for answers. The only thing I know with certainty is that it's time Oli and I moved on. If we're to find any strength in our futures, we need to rest our past in peace. We can't do that by living it every day. By living here.

This house, her home. Ours while she was here, of course, but hers now. Her memories, her plans, her vision. I can't stay in a place where every photo of us, every piece of artwork she chose, stares back at me. Where every conversation we ever had about curtains and colours and the future can be heard, if I listen hard enough. Her laughter in the walls, our love in every corner; it's all overshadowed with new second guesses about what she meant when she said 'forever', about what she felt when we held each other close.

Easy memories of rows appear. The bickering when we were tired, or teasy. Like the day she turned away from kissing me after I told her she railroaded me with her home-making. Or when we argued over where we should have spent Christmas because she was belly full of Oli and wanted us to be on our own here. Did she turn away those times because she was cross, or because she'd had enough of pretending that she loved me? The deep sigh, when we got back home with Oli that first day... was that exhaustion or a realisation that we were forever connected, when maybe she no longer wanted to be?

When she left Simon that message, did she intend to break my heart?

And if so, how much longer did I have? Did we have?

And why can I remember the few dark times more clearly now than the good, the happy, the joyous ones?

The doorbell rings out, making me jump. I wipe my face clear of fear to find Mum on the top step, looking tired, wrung out. 'May I?' she asks, stepping in before I answer.

'Of course.' I close the door behind her, pausing to take a deep breath and dig for whatever strength I might be able to find. When I get into the kitchen, she's standing above Oli, looking at him as if he's about to perform for her entertainment. Has she kissed him and I missed it? Has she touched him? Does he realise she's anything to him? A grandma is supposed to be fun, loving, someone to cuddle and bake with. Someone who dotes on you. Does she have that in her? Does she wish she could be that way?

'You look tired,' she says. I resist telling her the same thing as she stands on ceremony in the middle of the room, dressed in the same clothes as last night, but make-up free. I don't remember the last time I saw her without it.

'Have you been home?' I ask.

She shakes her head.

'Would you like a drink? Anything to eat?'

'No. Thank you. I'll get something when I get home.' She pulls a chair out. The scrape of the legs leaves a mark on the floor.

'How is Simon?'

Mum takes a heavy breath. 'Barely sober, even this morning. I've left your father with him while I came here.'

'Right.'

Mum reaches into her handbag, pulling an envelope out. 'The paperwork came back from the investigation.' Her hands shake as she unfolds it. 'Simon's solicitor called this morning to tell us that he is to be charged.' I look up. 'Driving without due care and attention. The fatality... obviously that adds a complication.'

'A "complication"?'

'I don't know how else to describe it, Edward,' she says, her stiff upper lip failing to hide the tremor in her voice. 'I don't know whether to mention her name. I don't know how to broach this subject. We've all tiptoed around it for so many months now. How do you get it right?'

'Sorry.'

'Please… don't. Don't apologise. We're all hurting here, Edward. My sons are breaking and I'm not equipped to deal with it. I don't know where to begin. I don't…' She grits her teeth, adjusting her posture, repainting the game face. 'Your brother faces a custodial sentence.'

She passes me the paperwork, but blurred vision prevents me from reading all the words. 'I don't understand. What does this mean? "Due care and attention", what was he doing or not doing?'

'A witness, who came forward, says your brother was tailgating at high speed.' My stomach turns. 'Which is why they're charging him.'

I jump from my seat to the sink, retching into the Belfast sink Ellie bought at a car-boot sale. '*It was a bargain, Ed. Don't you just love it?*' I hear, as I throw up.

I spit into the basin, running water to splash my face. 'Why?' I say, rubbing my eyes. 'Why!' I spin round to face Mum. 'Why did this happen? What is wrong with Simon? What the fuck is wrong with him?'

'Edward, he wouldn't have done this to Ellie on purpose. He didn't set out to kill her. It was an accident. I don't know why he was driving that way, or what was going through his mind. He must have been upset or stressed about something. He would never have intentionally hurt her. He loved her.' Mum's voice is now shrill, out of control. For the first time in my life I see emotion in her eyes.

'What did you say?'

'She was your wife,' she stutters. 'You're his brother. She was family. Even if she hadn't been, he wouldn't have put himself at risk like that. He was lucky to survive, Edward.'

'He had my wife in the car, Mum. He had my son!'

'I know, Edward. I know!'

I run the cold tap again, this time shoving my head beneath it, letting ice-cold water take my breath away until my heart pounds with an urgency to breathe.

'It's why he's drinking, it has to be. He can't forgive himself. He's tortured.'

'He's tortured? *He's* fucking tortured, Mum?'

'I know. I know. I don't know what to say, I don't know how to deal with this. It was an accident.'

'It was avoidable.'

'It was…' Mum doesn't bother finishing her sentence. I sink to the ground, and she steps towards me. I study her shoes, tidy, black court shoes with a low heel, the same kind of shoes she's worn since I was a kid. Presentable. Giving the right impression.

She crouches before me, her knees clicking. 'Simon is killing himself with the pain of what happened. He needs to know…' She stops herself, gathering strength for what's about to come. 'He needs to know that you can forgive him, Edward.'

'I don't know if I ever can,' I say, cradling my forehead in intertwined hands. I press my thumbs into my temples; the pressure gives brief respite from the ache. Mum's hands touch mine. They're cold, but soft. She doesn't hold me, more rests her hands on mine, but it's enough to make us see each other again. To look at each other with new light. 'How can I forgive him when I don't know what I'm meant to forgive?'

'He made a bad choice, he was distracted. He wouldn't be the first person or the last to drive recklessly. It's just that in this instance, the outcome was… devastating.'

'But it's not just that.'

'What do you mean?'

'There was a message, Mum. On his phone, from Ellie. There was a text from him on her phone. It isn't just that he could have avoided this, that he could have driven more safely, been more aware of the road, of other cars around him; it's the messages that make me question why they were together in the first place.' Mum shakes her head, not understanding. 'What if they were having an affair?'

'An affair? Edward... why? Why would you think that?'

'Why would he be so distracted, enough to cause an accident, if it wasn't something major? Why would Lisa say so if they weren't?'

'What did Lisa say?'

'That it wouldn't surprise her. That she never knew where he was any more. That their marriage was over. You put it all together, it's hard not to question it.'

'Oh, Edward. It can't be. Surely. He wouldn't do something like that. Ellie wouldn't have. You know that.'

'Sometimes I do. Sometimes I believe I knew the very bones of her and at other times I find myself staring into blackness, wishing everything would be over.' My skin prickles.

'It seems to me that Lisa is the problem. Your brother, he's different. He's changed. He's quieter. Weaker, maybe. Simon was never the strong one, that was always you. He never had total confidence in himself, in his worth. But she's... I don't know... whittled away what confidence he had over the years. She'd say anything to hurt him. I believe that more than I believe her accusation.'

A text message comes through to her phone, the volume of the alert splitting through our conversation. It sends a bolt from her bag to her hand, making her withdraw from me as if we were never connected at all. 'Your brother's awake. I should go.'

Mum picks her bag up, slipping the strap over a bony shoulder. Her eyes are tired and sad but she holds her head up high. 'We have to meet with his solicitor this morning. He's going to advise us on what happens next.'

'Okay.'

I pull myself up and Mum catches sight of a look I've tried to hide. 'I am pulled in both directions, son. You both need us, but maybe… maybe Simon needs us more right now. You have strength, you have Oli. He has nothing.'

I grit my teeth as I watch her leave. Because I feel anything but strong right now.

Chapter Thirty-One

Rachel

'Vicky, I'm due some time off, I wondered if I could book it?' I'm hovering at the top of the stairs leading to the mezzanine office in the main entrance hall. I lean against the wooden stairgate between us.

Vicky peers over her glasses, reaching for the diary. 'When did you have in mind?'

'Um, this week?' I offer, hopefully.

'This week! Rachel, you can't waltz in here on a Monday morning and ask for time off. I have ratios to meet, quotas.'

'Okay, okay.' I didn't really expect it to be that easy. 'So, when then? When's the earliest you could spare me?'

Vicky stares at me suspiciously. 'If you've got a job interview, I'd rather you just told me.'

'No! I don't. I just…' I pick at a splinter on the gate, peeling it off, which lifts more of the wood and makes the splinter worse. Vicky stares at me, lips thin, unimpressed. I try to stick the splinter back down. 'I just feel I've left it too long for a break. I'm… tired.'

She chews on her pen, checking the diary, muttering as she flicks weeks and days back and forth. 'I suppose next week could work. If you absolutely must.'

'Next week? But—'

'The week after?' she offers, making a point.

'Okay, okay. Next week. Yes. Thank you.' I take a holiday application form from the tray, leaning across the gate to her desk so I can complete the form and get it signed before she changes her mind. She scribbles on it, slipping it into her in tray before turning back to her computer.

I hover.

'Yes?' She sighs. 'What else?'

I swallow. 'I'd like to request a room change.' She stops typing. 'To the pre-schoolers. I've given it a lot of thought,' I lie. 'I think I'd be better suited to the older children. I realise that may mean a pay cut, I know Julia may not want to swap as a manager. I'm happy to work as her junior. However, it works best for the team, really. I'm in this for the long haul,' I lie again, 'and I'm prepared to make the relevant sacrifices to get to where I want to be.' I am so full of shit it's making me squirm.

'It works best for the team if you stop in your room, the one you are qualified to manage – training paid for by us, if I remember rightly – thereby leaving everyone else where they are, too.' I bite my lip. 'Do you want to tell me what's going on?' Vicky asks, putting her pen down and swivelling her chair around to talk to me properly.

I cough a frog clear from my throat, lowering my voice. 'I just… I think I'd be good at it. I'm really not enjoying the baby room any more. I haven't for a while.' The bell goes for the front door, a parent arriving to drop off. I hold my breath. *Please don't let it be Ed.*

'It doesn't work like that, Rachel. Moving rooms takes planning.'

'Moving rooms?' says a voice. 'Rachel? You can't!'

Maisie's mum looks up at me, arms full with Maisie, change bag and home-made cakes; reminding me Maisie is one today. 'The birthday girl!' I deflect. 'Take her on through, I'll be there in a second.'

When I turn back, Vicky is leaning back in her chair, peering at me. 'You see, the parents like you in there. The babies too. Why this sudden change of heart?'

'I can't explain.' Well, I could, but I suspect I'd get fired.

'What's going on? You stand there, looking like your world has crashed at your feet. You ask for an out-of-the-blue holiday, swiftly followed by a room swap. Now, why would you think I'd be suspicious of all of that?'

Well, when she puts it like that.

The phone rings, my interrogation interrupted. I snatch to answer, relieved to have something else to do. 'Good morning, Little Toes nursery, Rachel speaking, how can I help?'

'Rachel. It's Ed.'

'Ed.' *Shit.* 'Good morning!' I turn my back on Vicky as my cheeks flush. 'Are you okay?'

'No. Oli won't be in today. He's… I'm… he won't be in.'

His voice is flat, disconnected. Oh God, does he know? Has he worked it all out? Is this an excuse before he just stops bringing Oli in altogether?

'We probably won't be in all week. Maybe two. I'm not sure how long. I'll let you know.'

'Is everything okay, Ed?' I ask, my voice low as I try to take a step further away from Vicky so she has less chance of hearing his response. 'Can I do anything? What's happened?'

'No, no, Rachel. You've done enough.' I've done enough? What does he mean?

'I'll let you know when he's coming back. Bye.'

'Okay, bye,' I answer, but he's already hung up. Oh God. Oh no. He's worked it all out and he now, totally and understandably, hates me. He's going to take Oli elsewhere and I won't ever see either of them again.

Maybe that should be okay. Maybe it's for the best.

Oh God, what have I done?

'Rachel?' Vicky is standing beside me. 'What's going on?'

'Nothing, Vicky. Nothing at all. Ed Moran was just calling to say that Oli is going to be off for at least a week.' I fight back the urge to cry. 'I don't know… he's obviously poorly. I'm not sure. Anyway, that's fine. I'll make a note in the diary. Thanks for the holiday approval.' I fumble my way back down the stairs. 'I'd better get on.'

Jogging up the corridor, passing the 'No Running' sign, I hide in the safety of my room, leaning against the door to click it shut, my eyes closed.

'Rachel! Why do you want to change rooms? You can't change rooms, the babies love you! Unless it's to stay with Maisie?' She winks, sitting down on the playmat beside her little one. Maisie giggles and kicks her legs in glee. 'I mean, I'd understand, look at that face, after all.'

'You're right! She is cute. And at least at this age they can't answer back!'

'Exactly.' She smiles up at me. 'You okay?'

'Yup. Thanks.'

I turn away, fussing with bags and pegs. Maisie's mum covers Maisie in kisses, apologising for being at work on her big day. Any other time I'd have reassured her that Maisie is fine, that her life won't be ruined by her mother's return to work. That guilt is sadly one of those things parents have to get used to. Like I've any idea what I'm talking about. This time, though. This time I'm desperately trying to work out how I can go on holiday on Friday and never come back.

Chapter Thirty-Two

Ed

I put the phone down ten minutes ago, yet I've been sat here staring at it. Twice, I picked it up to call him, both times hanging up before dialling.

Part of me wants to talk to him, part of me never wants to see him again. Part of me wants to get me and Oli in the car and just drive. Far away from here. From everyone and everything. From reality. From anyone who knows us. The pitying looks when I walk down the street. The side glances at work from everyone but Greg.

Even the cashier down at Tesco Express makes me want to kill myself every time I go in.

It's the look on her face when she asks if I'm managing. *Of course I'm not!* I want to scream, but I always smile politely and nod. That's what I want to run away from: all the people that keep me in this state of grief. A state I don't need to be kept in because I live and breathe it every day. It's not going anywhere. It will always be with me. But I need to run, drive, walk. I need to stare at the sea just like she would. I need anonymity and a never-ending horizon to work out what the fuck I'm going to do next.

'*Skeg Vegas, Ed!*' Ellie would shout every time life got bigger than she could handle. She'd drape herself around me... '*I want to feel sick on candy floss, doughnuts and cockles. I want fish and chips for tea and a full English for breakfast. I want to push penny and ride the roller coaster. I want to stand with the wind in my hair and stare out to sea.*'

That's what I need to do. Stare out to sea. Resist the urge to Reginald Perrin it into the water, but get some perspective. The idea is giving me motivation for the first time since Mum left.

Grabbing our old weekend bag from beneath the stairs, I ram it full of clean clothes from the radiator. Wipes, bottles, powdered milk, ones books, toys. Charging cables and tech. The bag bursts at the seams and there's no chance it'll zip, but I hulk it from door to car anyway. I top Floyd's bowl up with food and clean water, ignoring the guilt pang that I've not arranged his usual top-notch cat hotel for the duration of our break.

I strap Oli into his car seat, swinging him over the table and into the crook of my arm, grabbing keys, wallet and phone from the kitchen side. If I leave now, I can be there by lunch. I'll find us somewhere to stay and tonight we will stand on the beach and watch the sun go down.

Locking the house up makes me pause. It's the first time since Ellie died that I won't have come home to our bed... to drift off with her smell. That I can walk away like this, lock up and step back, tells me something. The lights have gone out on the home she sprinkled stardust over. Its vastness is no longer a potential to be filled, but a burden of what should have been. I step back slowly, looking up to its grand front: new sash windows, front door painted and polished and perfect, the brass knocker she bought from a thrift shop.

'*You can carry me out in a box, Ed. I'm never leaving this place.*'

She didn't have to. I did. And now that she's gone, I don't want to stay.

I dial the office. I need to let them know I won't be in. 'Dave, it's Ed. Look, I know I've got meetings in for today but I won't be coming in. I need to take some time. Sorry to let you down, but… it's important.'

'Ed, Capital One are coming in. You've got your strategy meeting. This isn't—'

'Ideal, I know it's not. But it's what I need to do. Give them to Greg, give them to anyone. I don't care.' As soon as the words come out I realise how true they are. How fundamentally I feel them. How they sum up my exact level of interest at the moment. 'You know what, Dave? I don't care. And I should. But this isn't going to work. I resign. I'll be taking my four weeks' gardening leave from now and would appreciate it if you and the team could give me some space.' I hang up, switch off the company phone and post it through the letter box. It's me and Oli now, and that's how it should be until I know what needs to happen next.

Chapter Thirty-Three

Rachel

I knock on Dad's door, ready to hold up the Marks & Spencer meal deal I picked up for our tea, but I'm disappointed when there's no answer. I was trying to surprise him. His car is on the drive so he should be in. I'm leaning against the window frame, trying to peer into the lounge, when Dad looks up from a laptop that rests on a packing box before him. Seeing me, he breaks into a warm smile and my heart lifts a little as he summons me in.

'Hello, love! Look who it is!' he calls as I wander into the lounge. Dad twists the laptop around for me to see my brother's face taking up most of the screen, a tiny picture of me, blurred from the back light, in the corner.

'Bloody hell, Richard!' I dump the meal deal on the table. 'Look at that beard. You beauty!' I tease, tickling an imaginary beard of my own. 'That's…'

'Impressive?' He laughs.

'I was going to say, that's the kind of facial hair a fisherman would be proud of, but, yeah, whatever.' His eyes are crinkled, so wide is his grin. His face is sun-kissed and I just know that he'll have tiny freckles across his nose, where he's always had them when the sun comes out, ever since he was a kid. 'Well, big brother!' I say, perching on the chair that Dad has vacated for me. 'Look at you!'

'Sofia says it makes me look manly.'

'It makes you look something,' I tease. 'And who is Sofia?'

'Hello!' says a voice, and this beautiful woman with thick, dark hair and Disney-wide eyes leans in from his left. 'Nice to meet you,' she says, her accent rich with Italian vowels. 'Richard has told me so much about you,' she continues, looking up at my brother like someone who loves him. *How did he manage that one?*

'Your brother wanted to introduce me to his girlfriend,' Dad explains.

'My fiancée, Dad,' Rich corrects.

'Oh my God!' I shriek. 'You've only been away a few months; how did you manage that?'

Rich grins, pulling Sofia in for a kiss. 'I know, right! And I didn't even have to pay her!' She playfully slaps his arm. 'And she's way smarter than me, too.'

'A goldfish is smarter than you,' I taunt, enjoying the distraction that comes with sibling banter. It's like he's never been away.

'She's a doctor of philosophy, cockwomble! Take that and shove it up your common. What do you think she likes best about me? My sparkling wit or my massive—'

'NOPE!' I shout, fingers in ears. 'Do not even...'

Dad pulls up another chair, and I shift over so we can both see and be seen. 'Rich is changing his travel plans, isn't that right?' says Dad. 'He's heading over to Italy now to meet Sofia's family.'

'Yeah, well, that's the other thing. Rach, since you're here, we can tell you both. We're planning to marry in Sofia's village. Just a small do. We'd love it if you could come and visit but we totally understand if you can't for whatever reason. I know the house move and stuff might make it difficult, Dad.'

Dad sniffs, wiping away a tear.

'Oh, Dad, I hope you're not…'

Dad shakes his hand in the air, taking a moment to compose himself. 'No, no, I'm not. I'm just…' I put my hand on his knee, Rich waits, watching. Sofia gives him a concerned look. 'It's fine, Richard, Sofia. I couldn't be happier for you both, truly. You know, your mum and I always dreamed of doing something like that. Jetting off to a warmer place, marrying in a remote village somewhere, living happily ever after, away from the ups and downs of our families.'

'We're not doing it to get away, Dad. It's nothing personal, I promise.'

'I know, son. I know. It's fine, I'm really happy for you, truly.'

Dad drops his hands to mine, squeezing it. I try to disguise the cry that threatens with a cough and he squeezes even harder. He can tell this news is creeping up on my heart.

'Rich, this is brilliant. So… brilliant.' I sniff.

'You getting choked up, little sis, you massive wally?'

'Nah, it's all this house packing, it's kicking up dust. I've got something in my eye!' I smile, the very best one I can muster.

The screen starts to flicker, Rich and Sofia's faces pixelate before the screen goes blank. 'Ah, I wondered how long we'd have,' says Dad, clicking it shut. 'Still, that was probably good timing, wasn't it?' He turns in his chair, taking my hands. 'You need to talk about it?' he asks.

'Oh God, Dad. I don't even know where to start.'

Except, it seems I do, as I pour the story out from the day Ed came to visit the nursery, to the crisis in confidence over life, and a career, to throwing all morals out of the window and showing my true, hideous, boundary-smashing colours from the depths of Ed's wife's wardrobe.

'And the worst thing about it all?'

Dad cocks his head to one side.

'I've got this awful feeling I'm… developing feelings for him.' I hiccup, sniff, then blow my nose. I daren't look at him now. If I see pity, I'll crumble. If I see disappointment, I'll crumble. If he is about to cut me out of his will for being a hateful woman, I'll understand completely, then crumble and fall. 'So, I booked a week's holiday to give me time to think, picked up dinner to come here and see you, and then Richard announces all of this happy stuff and that reminds me that my life is going well and truly nowhere, and I know, Dad,' I say, breaking off to blow my nose, 'I know this all sounds very self-indulgent and whiny, but I am at a total and utter loss as to what to do next. I mean, what even is the point?'

I do look up at him now; my dad, the man who, without even realising it, I've come to rely on in life. At times, when I thought I was there for him, I've realised he has been quietly, but steadfastly, there for me. The man who tried his very best to raise two children alone. The man who worked hard at his own career, but never quite got where he might have done because his focus was always us. The man I ignored when he tried to get me to concentrate on my exams at school instead of the boy over the road, who showered me with teddies and attention. The man who went out and bought me everything I needed when I started my period, even though I couldn't actually tell him; somehow, he just knew. The man who I was so disappointed in when he told me he needed to sell up. The man who now reaches over to wipe my tears, who takes my hand with a smile, who pulls me in for a hug and then whispers into my ear that he loves me, and he is proud of me, and that at some point in my life, I need to stop being so hard on myself. The man who says, 'That may as well be today.'

I relax into his arms, letting him hold me like the child I used to be. The child I probably still am, in his eyes. I cry softly, my heart aching. Eventually, he leans back and says, 'Let me get this dinner cooked, let's sit down and talk. I've said it before, you can do anything you want in life. What happened to that list? Let's make a new one. Let's work something out and see how we get you there.'

He goes into the kitchen, leaving me to draw an old crocheted throw around me, and I wonder what I'd ever do without him.

Chapter Thirty-Four

Ed

I settle Oli into his travel cot. He lies good-naturedly, lifting his teddy up to his face and sucking on its nose. He gurgles and chatters before drifting off to sleep.

From the pistachio velvet wing-backed chair in the window, Skegness seafront stretches out before me. The Pleasure Beach with its multi-coloured lights that Ellie used to love; the roller coaster; the pitch and putt; the aquarium; the theatre. A town she would immerse herself in from the second we arrived to the moment we'd leave. Bingo, fish and chips, the casino. Right now, this feels noisy and in my face; it feels brash. Or maybe that's just life now; maybe life is brash.

I read the message from Mum again: *Your brother's case will be heard tomorrow at 3 p.m.* The enveloped report lies closed on my lap. A report on one day, four months ago. The contents of which change nothing at all, but I feel as though I should read them. I should know the detail, however painful it might be.

I pour wine into one of the mugs from the tea tray, then rip open the envelope to read. Words like 'icy', 'tailgating' and 'undertaking' jump out, making my stomach lurch as a visual flash of the scene I never saw appears in my mind. That Simon and Oli survived, it would seem, is a miracle. My subconscious explores 'what ifs': what if Simon had died, instead of Ellie? What if they all had, and I was sat here alone; neither husband, nor brother, nor father? What if they could lock him up for the rest of his days to save me the pain of having to talk to the man responsible for 'lack of due care and attention'.

Where understanding and sympathy once hovered, albeit shadowed by anger and hatred, there's the taste of cheap wine and bitterness. How could he? How could Simon be so fucking stupid? So... careless? How could he do this to me? To Oli? To Ellie?

He denied her life, he denied her motherhood. How does he deserve to carry on in life without paying for what he has done? Instead of sitting comatose in his house, feeling sorry for himself, he *should* pay. He *has* to.

Would it make a difference if I was there in court? To him? To the judge and the jury and everyone in between?

Muddy sea rolls, out beyond the string of brightly coloured lights along the road. Grey and cloudy skies have formed across a vast horizon.

If Simon's in court tomorrow, he'll have to be sober. If he goes down, I may not get a chance to confront him for years.

I look over to Oli, who is fast asleep. The room is cold, dull, cheap and uninviting. It's as empty as home feels, but that bareness gives clarity to decisions I've been avoiding.

Oli and I need to go back home.

I need to talk to Simon.

It's time the house went on the market.

It's time to wrap up loose ends, then find a way to move our lives forward. I don't mean moving forward as in away from Ellie – she will always be with me – but forward, with purpose, focus and intention. With the strength our son needs. Tonight, he and I stay here. We'll walk the promenade tomorrow. Early doors. We'll enjoy the sounds of bingo callers and the smell of sweet doughnuts. We'll do the things she'd have wanted to do, having come all this way. We'll do them in her memory.

Then I'll drive the two hour journey home in time to see Simon before the hearing. I have only one question, and I'll know the truth the second he answers, regardless of what he says.

Chapter Thirty-Five

Rachel

In the fifteen minutes it takes for Dad to heat up our three-minute dinners in the microwave, I've been staring out of the window, the clatter of knives, forks and bowls a slightly stressful soundtrack to my mood. How much noise does piercing a piece of film and waiting for the ping need to make?

I groan at my impatience, rubbing my hands across my dry, salty face, trying to eliminate the feeling of dried-up tears that I've really no place to shed. My head falls back in the chair as I take a deep breath – this mood, these tears, it's all so bloody ridiculous. *I* am ridiculous. Twenty-seven and hurtling through life without purpose, without focus.

Dad wanders through with two bowls of steaming curry. 'Here.' He hands me mine. 'Get that down you. We have work to do.'

'Oh, Dad, I don't know. I don't think I'm up to planning. I need some time, I need to take a breather, something I seem to have been incapable of doing for the majority of my adult life.'

'We all throw ourselves into things, you know. Sometimes we don't feel we have an alternative. It's not a sign of weakness, you're not a bad person.'

'You try telling my heart that.'

'I could, but I know your heart all too well; it pays no attention. Just like your head. Not that I'll stop trying, mind.'

We fall silent, both focused on creamy korma and rice for the next few minutes, until I realise I've been daydreaming about Mum, standing up front in a classroom. 'D'you think Mum'd have made a good teacher?' I ask.

Dad scoops up the last of his korma sauce with home-baked bread while thinking about his answer. 'Honestly? I'd have never told her this, but... no. I don't think so.'

'Really?'

'Really. I couldn't see it myself. She loved you and your brother. God, she'd have fought a war for you, if needs be. But she wasn't that maternal, not really. She didn't love all children, like some people do. She wasn't one of those mumsy mums, you know?'

'I *do* know! I remember sometimes wishing she had been, like when friends came to school with home-baked cakes in their pack up.'

'As opposed to a Penguin bar and a curled ham sandwich, you mean?'

The memory is fonder now than it once was. Fond enough for me to feel bad for speaking ill of my mum's own style of maternal instinct. 'Well... yeah, I guess so. God, that sounds awful, doesn't it?'

'Hey, don't worry! I used to get the same pack up. I mean, I loved your mother, but I can't tell you the number of times I'd accidentally forget the Tupperware in the fridge, just so I could indulge in the university canteen instead.'

'Wow!'

He laughs, then sighs, his gaze drifting to a photo of Mum that has always been pinned to the table, beside his chair. 'And you know,' he says sadly, 'I'd eat every single one of those rubbish sandwiches again, if it gave me one more day with your mother.'

I nod. 'Or the undercooked new potatoes, the tasteless fish, the cold soup.'

'Nobody needs cold soup!'

I smile at him trying to lift the mood.

'She wasn't a great cook, your mother. But my God, she was a fine woman.'

His description of her hurts. Because it feels so far from the person I am. So out of reach. Would Mum have been proud of me, were she still here today? Would I be the same person, had she not died? Was my path laid out before me, or did the fork in the road that was her death forever divert my future as she took her last breath?

Even here, having this conversation, these thoughts, the drama still comes through.

'You could teach, though,' Dad says simply.

'Dad!'

'I'm serious. I think Mo was right. You *could* teach! I could never see it in your mother, like I say, but you? You're different.'

Do I want to be different to her?

'How long have you worked at that nursery for? Eight years? It's not the kids you don't like, it's the job. The age group, even. You could totally stand up in front of a class of kids and inspire them. Primary? Secondary, even – you can relate to how hard it is being a teenager.'

'It was hard because of Mum.'

'The reason doesn't matter, it's more real to you than most. It's more raw. You feel it still, I can see that.'

'I couldn't handle teenagers.'

'Primary then. Five, six. The kids just beginning their school life. The kids who are wide- eyed and ready to take on the world. As of next week, the money for this can be in your account.'

'The house sale is going through?'

'It is. And the caravan is ready. The spare cash will be waiting. What better way to refocus your wandering mind than this? You know, you're not a bad person, love. Honestly, you're not. You made a bad choice. Christ, we've all done that. But that doesn't have to dictate the rest of our lives.' He fixes me with that Dad look again. 'You could do this. You've lived life. It's not always been easy. That's what they want, that's appealing.'

'Going back to uni with a load of freshers isn't appealing,' I groan.

'Well, you could keep making excuses for the things you don't want to do, or you could pull your socks up and work out a plan. These are your choices, love. And they're nobody's to make but your own. Now, are you going to help me pack? If I'm going to pay for your university course, this house sale has to go through.'

'I haven't said I'm going yet.'

'No. But if I know you like I think I know you, you'll come to your senses very soon. I just want to be prepared. Tell you what, go home. Talk to Mo, read, scour the Internet. You said you were taking some time off? Go on walks, take some time for yourself. See if you can find the woman I can see sitting before me.'

'The woman?'

'Yes. The woman. She reminds me of someone I once knew. Someone pretty great. When you find her, you'll realise what you want. I've got to hand the keys over at 11 a.m. next Friday. Meet me in town at the Left Lion. Tell me what you have in mind and I'll buy you lunch to celebrate.' I look at him, uncertainly. 'Up you get,' he says, pulling me from the chair. 'I've got stuff to do. And so have you.' He ushers me to the front door. 'See you next Friday.'

Dad stands on the top step of the home that lies in boxes at the very end of its service to us. 'You're going to be fine, you know,' he says, and I realise I have no choice but to believe he might be right.

Chapter Thirty-Six

Ed

Neither Oli nor I slept much last night. He startled me awake at eleven with a cry of pain, his cheeks red-hot, his fingers in his mouth, searching, chewing, grizzly. To be fair, I'm not sure I'd have slept much even had he not been so restless. When I did climb into bed for half an hour's respite here and there, I was restless too. I tossed and turned, mattress springs finding their way into my back, side or leg with each new position. At one point, Oli was in bed with me, his limbs soft and warm, his gentle breath like my own personal lullaby. When he cried out, pulling him in close gave me comfort because I was needed, though it wasn't long before I could hear Ellie's words: *'We could roll on him, Ed. We might suffocate him.'* And *'What if it became the only way to get him to sleep?'* Part of me doesn't mind. Wouldn't mind. Sleeping alone just reminds me what I've lost.

So it's through gritty eyes that I've walked this promenade, up and down, since 8 a.m. I bought tea in a styrofoam cup, its contents hotter than the sun, plus a bacon sandwich that I managed no more than three bites of.

I waited for the bingo hall's first call at nine thirty. *Eighty-eight – two fat ladies; twenty-two – two little ducks; all on its own the number one.*

I bought fresh doughnuts, taking a bite and letting its sugary coating stick to my lips for as long as I could possibly manage without licking it off – just like she would have done. Then I took Oli down to the shoreline, letting ice-cold water tickle his toes. I'd dangle them as the sea crept closer, Oli instinctively bringing his legs up each time. I watched the wind turbines swing round and round in perfect unison, momentarily mesmerised, transfixed, by the spin of the blades.

And now, I stand here by my car. Ten thirty. I can't drag this out any longer. It's time to face Simon, to face Lisa, if she's there. Whatever peace I may be able to find in this new world, I have to embrace it. My survival depends on it.

Travelling out of Skegness and into the Lincolnshire countryside, bright yellow oil-seed rape surrounds us. Despite the murky sky, the yellow brightens the road. Grey and acid yellow stretches out ahead like a backward Yellow Brick Road minus Scarecrow, Lion and the Tin Man. I come to a turning: straight on for Lincoln, then Nottingham, or left for Coningsby and Cranwell. Ellie told me a story once, about a school trip to Tattershall Castle. Then later on, when she was older and driving, she'd come out here on dates with young squaddies. Even after those flings fizzled out, she'd describe Sundays in village pubs with a good book beside an open fire; happy on her own, happy in her skin. Company not essential.

I take the road that leads me past the castle and her memories. Through the villages of Spilsby, East Kirkby and Conningsby; Tattershall itself. '*I love Lincolnshire,*' Ellie said once. '*I love its honesty, its transparency.*' And as I drive the single road through the fields, it's almost as if I can feel her here. As if a place she once talked fondly of has lapped up her love and taken it for its own. Tiny schools, the village stores. The planes overhead from the nearby air base.

The cottage houses with rambling gardens and fields beyond.

Maybe there's a future here. Somewhere smaller. Somewhere that we aren't known, not because I want to leave her behind, but to help us to find our own lives forward. In a place I know she loved.

I daydream the idea all the way back to Nottingham, so that when I hit the ring road, I've made three calls to estate agents, booking in appointments for valuations. I've been so distracted by new-found plans that it's only as I'm about to pull into the car park by the courts that I realise I don't want Oli with me when I do this; I don't want to take him into a place like that. I don't want the energy that spills from the walls to infiltrate his tiny heart.

It's 12.30 p.m. I put my foot down, asking Siri to dial the nursery as I weave through the traffic and out the other side of town. Vicky answers.

'Hi, Vicky, this is Ed, Oli's dad. I know I said he wouldn't be in for a week or two but I need to do something. Can I drop him off, would that be okay?'

'Of course, Mr Moran, no problem at all.'

'Great, thank you.'

When I get to the nursery it's feeding time. The smell of warm baby food permeates the corridors. There's chatter and noise from each room, happy sounds and declarations of 'well done' to the kids who've eaten up. The baby room, by contrast, is much quieter. Rachel sits in a corner, feeding one of the babies. 'Hi,' I whisper, dropping Oli's bag off by his peg.

'Ed!' She looks up, startled. 'I thought—'

'I know, I just… I have to be somewhere, I hope that's okay?'

'Of course.'

She gets up, placing the baby down in a cot, coming over to take Oli from me, her touch clumsy and out of character. 'Are you okay? I wasn't expecting to… is everything alright? Did you…?' Her words trail off and I wait, wondering what she was going to say. She coughs. 'Never mind. What time will you be collecting him?' she asks, her tone suddenly formal.

'I'm not sure, I've got to…' I decide against expanding. I've over-shared enough in recent weeks. 'By six at least.'

'Great, okay.' She smiles awkwardly. 'See you later then.' She takes Oli over to the other baby who has grown cross at being put down halfway through his lunch.

'I'll leave you to it,' I shout over the increasing noise. 'Thanks!'

She waves, her head buried in the cot, Oli in her spare arm.

Twenty minutes later, I've parked up and jogged down to the courts. I stand outside the imposing sandstone building, which is sliced in two by a glass panel that reflects the now bright-blue sky. People come and go but I can't move. My feet are rooted to the pavement as I begin to realise what I'm doing, what I'll hear. This building holds the people and information that will decide the fate of my brother, the future of my family. Information that will pick apart the events leading up to my wife's death, putting them back together piece by piece, the outcome remaining the same. The second I step over that threshold, I cannot turn back. I can't unhear things, I can't unsee them. I can't pretend this isn't a pivotal moment in the story of Ellie's death.

With a deep breath, I push through into the foyer, searching the walls for directions on where to go next.

'Edward?'

I snap around in the direction of the voice to see my mother, cradled by Dad, a suited man in a black gown beside her. She sobs, and Dad guides her to a row of seats.

'Mum? Dad? What happened? What's going on?' I crouch down beside her, the stoic woman I know in tatters before me. 'Mum?' When I look up to Dad, his face is pale, grave. He shakes his head.

'Mr Moran?' asks the man beside us all. I nod, standing to face him. 'Your brother has been given a custodial sentence. Four years. They've just taken him away.'

As his words filter, the world around me begins to blur. His words merge into one another. 'But I thought' – I check my watch – 'he wasn't due in until…'

'They had a no show. Brought the case forward.'

The sound of Mum's sobs fade yet I feel as though everything else around me is louder, larger, more intense than it was before. 'But… I need to talk to him,' I hear myself say. 'I was going to talk to him.'

'I'm afraid you'll have to apply for a visit. And then wait to see if he wishes to see you.'

'But, this can't… no… NO! I need to… you don't understand. Mum, Dad. I need to… I can't… NO!' I shout. 'Fucking NO!'

'Mr Moran!' The man holds his arms up, raising his voice. He tries to shield me from Mum, or her from me, I'm not sure. 'Perhaps you should get some fresh air.'

'I don't want fresh air,' I shout. 'I want to see my brother!'

'Edward!' shouts Dad, his hand on my shoulder. 'Stop!'

I look to him, my breath heavy, his eyes firm, immovable. Just like they always were when he'd step in to take over from something Mum had lost control of. 'Not. Now,' he says.

I stagger back a few steps, turning and pushing my way out of the door and into the afternoon sun. Two blokes push past me as they make their way into the building. The road is noisy, buses and cars racing past. A siren screams out and it feels as though Nottingham spins around me, pushing me into a corner by the building, my stomach heaving, empty. Bile hits the pavement as I retch in pain and dismay. How can this be? How can any of this be?

I drop, slowly, to sit on the low wall that surrounds the courts. Someone takes hold of my shoulders. 'Hey, it's okay. It's all going to be okay, shhhh, shhhhh.' But when I look up, Lisa's face comes into view, forcing me up and away from her. 'Ed, it's okay. I'm here to help. Ed, please,' she says, jogging after me.

'Since when have you wanted to help? Me or anyone?' I shout. 'Since when have you cared about anyone apart from yourself?'

'I'm sorry, I know I haven't helped. I know I've said things. Things that must have hurt!' she shouts after me. 'It's been hard for us all!'

I cross the road before the lights have changed; she dodges cars to follow me.

'Ed, please! Stop!' She pulls me by the arm, swinging me around.

A group of people in a bus stop nearby pretend they aren't watching, burying their heads in phones or books with the occasional side glance in our direction.

'What happened?' she asks. 'In court. What did they say?'

I stop dead. 'You weren't there?' I spit. 'You left him to go through this alone?'

'We were splitting up, I told you…'

I clasp my hands on the top of my head. 'How is this fair, Lisa? How are you here, standing in front of me, after all you've spewed in the last few months. After deserting my brother, probably when he needed you most. How are *you* still here when my wife is six feet under?' I take a step towards her. 'He's just been given a custodial sentence and you wander the streets, still causing upset,' I hiss, spit catching her eye. She wipes it, head down, but doesn't step away.

'We might not be together, Ed, but I still have feelings for him.'

'Really? You didn't just come here to gloat at him? To see him get what you think he deserves?'

'What, and you don't think he deserves it too?'

'I don't know what I think!'

'Well, I do. I think that your wife was killed because your brother was driving like an idiot, fuelled by the fact that they'd got themselves into a mess they couldn't talk their way out of.'

'What mess? What are you talking about?'

'The one where they were going to leave us. Be together. Plunge us all into misery for their own selfish gain. Christ, Oli's probably not even your son, Ed!'

My legs buckle. I fall against the wall, lungs clean empty of breath. From the corner of my eye I see her standing there, watching me, waiting. I stumble, falling towards her. 'Never, *never*,' I repeat, pushing her against the wall, my arm across her chest, 'NEVER speak to me again.'

'Hey, leave her!' shouts a woman from somewhere behind us.

Lisa bites on her lip; she holds my gaze. 'Don't worry,' she whispers. 'I'm gone.' And she pushes herself up off the wall, unsteadily walking away, leaving me alone in Nottingham with words that pierce what is left of my strength to carry on.

Chapter Thirty-Seven

Ed

I don't remember the walk back to the car, or the drive back to the house. I don't remember pulling up, getting out or unlocking the front door. I don't remember anything when I finally realise I'm in our room, pulling clothes out of my wardrobe and throwing them into a suitcase. I can't stay here, *we* can't stay here. Clothes lay messily on top of each other, trainers, underwear, anything I might need for the foreseeable future is shoved in, forced down, zipped away.

I take an empty duvet cover from the airing cupboard on the way to Oli's room, using it to collect blankets and clothes, nappies and wipes in. I get stuff to bathe him with, the baby monitor, the temperature gauge, the mobile that shines stars on the ceiling. Toys and cards given to us on Oli's birth fall to the ground as I pull out things of sentimental value to throw into a bag on the side. I get anything he might need in the future to remind him of the love he had from his mother; the person he has to believe she was. The person I have to believe she was too, even if right now I just don't know.

I throw the bags down the stairs, watching them mark the walls as they tumble to the bottom, coming to rest by the front door. I shut the curtains in all the rooms. I run downstairs, throwing my laptop and chargers into a bag. I shake a black bin bag into the air, letting it blow open for me to throw in days' old wet clothes from the washing machine.

I pause by the fridge. Photos, drawings, notes in Ellie's hand. It's the first thing to slow me down. I pick a letter from beneath a magnet, running my fingers over her handwriting before pulling everything else from the fridge and shoving it into the bag. Magnets scatter as I lift off the bits I want to keep.

Outside, everything is chucked on the back seat of the car, in the boot, in the passenger footwell. I run back up to the house, pulling coats and more shoes from the downstairs loo, along with the cat basket for Floyd. And then I see a photo of us, taken beside the Major Oak in Sherwood Forest on an anniversary one year. On the day, we said we'd take one each year until the day we, or the Major Oak, finally died. We hadn't been back since that day; one of those things that never quite happened when life took over. I lift the photo from the wall, cradling it. Then I collect others: us with friends; the house on the day we bought it; a selfie on the doorstep; us on our wedding day, the framed print that welcomes everyone at the front door.

Gently resting the photos and pictures on the back seat of the car, I layer them with coats to stop glass from breaking until I know where they will be hung next.

Looking back up to the house, the air grows heavy. The lightness of a late-spring blue sky has gone. It's time to leave. It's time to put a key in the back garden, hidden from view. A solicitor can pick it up. A removal firm can put the rest of the house in storage for me. An estate agent can get it on the market so I don't need to come back.

I'll take the last few bits from her wardrobe. The boxes. Then I'm done.

Adrenaline depleting, I'm out of breath by the time I make it upstairs to the bedroom, bracing myself for the scent of Ellie as I open the wardrobe door. I take a deep breath, desperate to imprint the notes of red roses, freesia and tobacco flower from her favourite perfume. I run my hand along the line of clothes, recalling the times she wore a dress or a suit from the collection before me. Floyd weaves between my legs; is he aware something is happening? I kneel and he rubs against my leg before dramatically throwing himself on the floor, purring, inviting me to rub his belly. He is as much a part of her as these clothes, as these memory boxes. I pull the latest one forward, lifting it out. An open envelope behind falls free, spilling its contents onto the floor.

And my heart stops.

My body stiffens. Slowly, I reach out.

No. No. Please, God, no. This can't be, this isn't… sickness returns, thick in the back of my throat. I sweat and shiver in equal measure at the sight of a home test DNA kit.

Someone cries out, shouts. A sound so animalistic, so guttural, that I don't realise at first that the someone is me, in pain, hurting, my chest tight and my heart piercing. It's a pain that knocks me from my knees to the ground, dissolving me into the floor, the DNA test resting in the palm of my hand.

Chapter Thirty-Eight

Rachel

It was gone seven in the evening by the time I decided to take Oli to his house. There was no answer from Ed on the home number, nothing on his mobile. Everyone else had left work and I was sat in the semi-darkness of Vicky's office, waiting. I'd tried the other number we had for Oli – Ed's mother, I think. There was no answer from that either and I suppose I felt I had no choice but to be proactive.

I stuck a note onto the nursery's front door to tell Ed where I was, just in case he came by. I sent him a text message to let him know I'd see him at his, just in case. I left a message on his answering machine at home, again, just in case.

So, to see his car outside his house as I pull up is perplexing. Worrying. More so is the open door to his home. I search for signs of something awful, though I don't really know what signs I should be looking for, or what might have happened, I just know that something feels wrong. Something feels major. I scan the house, and up and down the road, then over to Ed's car as I fumble to release Oli from the back seat of mine. His car seat bumps against my legs as I half jog, half walk, wait, then jog again, up the path.

The sound of my knocking on the open door echoes into the hallway. 'Ed?' I call out, stepping inside, fearfully looking through doors. 'Ed, are you here?' I call again, checking the lounge and kitchen. The signs he's been here are all over: papers strewn, pictures removed, bits of washing falling from the machine, and there are piles of discarded coats on the floor of the downstairs loo. It's as though the house has been burgled except that the TV remains, as does the radio, and Ed's keys are on the side.

Oli's car seat rocks on the dining table as I unbuckle him and scoop him up. 'Shall we see if Daddy's upstairs,' I coo, my voice peppered with nerves. 'Come on, baby. Come on,' I say, pulling him in close.

When I get upstairs, I see Ed's bedroom door is open. I pull Oli in closer to me as I take slow steps that reveal Ed's feet first, then the rest of his body, leaning against the bed. Seeing the shallow rise and fall of his chest gives me relief, and I search for breath from my own empty lungs. 'Ed?' I whisper gently.

His eyes stare into the distance; he doesn't seem to hear me, or notice I'm there, even. I carefully step forward, desperate not to startle him.

'Ed, what's happened?'

But I don't need to ask again; the DNA test rests in his hands. He blinks, slowly.

'Oh, Ed.' I move to crouch beside him with Oli still in my arms. 'You found it, but it doesn't mean… Ed, just because she had this doesn't mean…' His eyes flick up towards me. 'You have to believe in her, Ed. You have to be strong, for Oli. Look, I brought him, I was worried.'

I pass Oli to Ed, who vacantly takes him from me, sitting him out before him as if he's never held a child before. As if he doesn't know who Oli is. Oli wriggles, letting out a gentle cry for his dad. Reaching tiny arms and fingers for his dad's arms, pulling at the skin, gently, for his attention.

'Ed, I wanted to tell you, but I didn't know how. I didn't know what to say. And it proves nothing, Ed. It's just stuff. Who knows why she had it, but Oli is yours. I just know it. Look at him, Ed.' He shifts his eyes to look at me, but it's like he doesn't really see me. 'Look at him,' I repeat.

'You knew it?' he says, his voice breaking.

I swallow. Wishing with every single fibre of my being that I could say no, but I nod, slowly.

'How?' he asks, his eyes now focusing fully, recognising that it's me sat beside him. I look down, wishing I knew how to answer. 'HOW?' he pushes.

I sit back, clutching my knees to my chest. 'That night, when you went to see Simon, I just...' I meet his eyes, certain that I must at least give him the respect of my focus. 'Something wasn't right, Ed. Something about it all. You had questions... I just couldn't believe it. I wanted... I wanted to help. And I can't believe that I would abuse your trust like that. I can't forgive myself for it, but I don't know, I was confused. I was...'

I look away now, realising I can't admit why I was looking. Or where my feelings went from that day onwards. Or that now, sitting here before him, watching him hurt all over again, I just want to pull him into my arms and hold him until he gets his strength back. I can't admit to the fact that I am falling completely and entirely in love with a man who stares back at me with disgust in his eyes.

'Leave,' he says, his feelings made clear.

'Ed, please. Let me explain, let me—'

'GO!'

Tears sting at the back of my eyes, my throat suddenly red raw. 'I'm so sorry, Ed. I'm so sorry. I didn't mean to… I didn't mean anything.' Oli starts crying, still held out from Ed's body. 'He needs you, Ed. You are his father, he needs you… please.' I push Ed's hands, holding Oli, closer to his chest. 'Don't push him away,' I insist, standing. 'No matter what the truth, Ed, Oli is your son. You need each other.' I step back out of the room. 'And I am so very, very sorry.'

'LEAVE!' he spits.

I turn around and do exactly as I'm told.

Chapter Thirty-Nine

Ed

I don't move until I hear the front door shut. I don't go downstairs until I see her car disappear from view. I don't cry until I've buckled Oli up into his car seat, into my car, Floyd in his basket and the memory box placed beside him.

I don't know what I'm going to do, or where I'm going to stay, until I see the B & B in the middle of rural Lincolnshire.

I don't know what my future now holds.

Chapter Forty

Rachel

I didn't go home straight away. I drove out to Wollaton Park, turning up the long drive flanked by trees and dozing deer in the fields beyond. I pulled up in the car park, wrenching the handbrake and stalling the engine. The judder of the car forced my control aside and I sobbed until I had no energy left to cry. Then I waited until it was dark, before driving home.

And here I am. Exhausted, my head pounding, taking the steps to our flat, everything hurting. It hurts to fish keys out of my bag. It hurts to push open the door. It hurts to step inside and find myself alone in the flat. It hurts to realise I'm glad Mo's not here.

I go to my room, falling into my unmade bed. Mum's photo stares at me, setting me off crying all over again. I bury my head in my pillow and don't stop crying until I fall asleep.

The room is dark when I'm woken by the sound of Mo tapping on my bedroom door. 'Are you in there?' she asks, pushing the door open and letting a shaft of light seep through, lighting up my face. 'Rach? What's the matter?' she asks, which makes it clear my face is as puffed up as it feels. My eyes swollen and red. 'Fuck, what's happened?' She comes over to my bed, tapping my bedside light on as she sits down. We're lit by a hazy glow.

'Ed knows I looked through Ellie's stuff and now he hates me.'

'I don't understand, how did that come about?'

'He brought Oli in this afternoon but didn't show up to collect him. I knew something must be wrong so I took Oli home and found Ed with the DNA test in his lap. I told him I was glad he'd found it, that I hadn't known how to tell him it was there, but that it probably didn't mean anything, which, of course, told him enough to know I'd been through her stuff.'

'Oh shit, Rach.'

'He was looking at Oli as though he didn't recognise him.' My voice wobbles, the image of Ed's distance and anger coming back into full view. 'I think he believes Oli's not his son.'

'Oh, no, Rach.'

'And I'm to blame.' I wipe my eyes, annoyed I'm crying again. Annoyed I can't even keep that much in check. 'If I'd hidden the test when I found it, none of this would have happened.'

'Rach.' Mo takes my hands, staring into my eyes. 'That's not the answer. Surely you can see that.'

I bite my lip, closing my eyes until I know I'm back in control. 'I know. I know, I just… I wish I could change it. I want to take his hurt away, I want to take it for him. I keep thinking I should call him, or pop round, maybe.'

'I think you need to give him some space.' She takes her hands back, pulling her cardigan over them.

'I know, but I don't want to.'

'I don't think you can help him right now, Rach. In fact, I think you maybe need to take some time for yourself.' She thinks for a moment. 'Shall I ask Greg to call him? Just to check he's okay. Would that help?'

'Yes. Yes, get Greg to call him. Please. Ask him to say that—'

'Rach, I can't ask him to *say* anything. I can only get him to check everything's alright.' Mo lifts my chin up. 'Seriously, Rachel. You need to step back.' I nod, knowing full well that she's right. 'Give me a minute.'

She goes out of my room and I pull up the duvet to my chin, trapping it down as I hug myself in tight. The room is cold, or maybe that's just me. Either way, I shiver, growing colder the longer Mo's gone. When she comes back in, she brings a steaming mug of tea and a glass of wine. 'I wasn't sure which was more appropriate,' she says.

'What did he say?' I ask, reaching for the tea, clasping my fingers around the mug, the heat burning my skin.

'His phone was switched off. Greg says it must be a work one as it's just ringing out dead. Ed handed his notice in the other day.'

'Right.'

'Greg's trying to get hold of him through Facebook.'

'Okay.'

Mo sighs, climbing beneath the covers, dropping an arm around my shoulders. 'Bloody hell, Rach, you sure know how to dig yourself a hole.' She pulls me in for a squeeze, kissing me on the side of the head. 'What are we going to do with you?' she asks.

'Fuck knows,' I answer.

She reaches for the wine on my bedside table. 'Do you mind if I...?' she asks. The light catches and sparkles something on her finger; a large vintage diamond ring sits on the third finger of her left hand.

'Mo!' I say, reaching out for her hand. She tries to pull her hand back, stuffing it under the covers. 'What's that... Mo!' I put my mug down, shifting to sit up. 'Are you...?'

'I'm so sorry, Rach. I know now's not the time. I was going to tell you when I came in the room, but I could see something wasn't right. It's no big deal, we can talk about it another time.'

'No big deal! Oh my God, Mo!' I reach to pull her hand free so I can study the ring close up. 'It's beautiful,' I say, my eyes filling with more selfish tears. I stare hard, hoping they'll stop, but one escapes and drops on her hand.

'Oh, Rach, no, don't,' she says, wiping my face with her sleeve.

'What,' I sniff, moving back to wipe it for myself. 'Happy tears,' I try. 'I'm really happy for you.' I go to take a deep breath to show I mean it, but fail miserably, letting out a muffled sob instead. 'You deserve it,' I sniff. 'He's great,' I hiccup. 'I am really...' She pulls me in for a hug, holding me so tight I can barely breath. 'Shit,' I mumble into her hair. 'I'm a really shit friend.'

'Sssshhhh.' Mo strokes my hair. 'It's okay,' she hiccups, and I realise that we're both crying. 'Now look what you've started,' she says, half laughing.

'I am happy for you, truly,' I insist.

'I know. I know you are.'

I pick at the bed sheets, twisting them around and around my finger. 'I just...'

'I know.' A knock at the door interrupts the words we don't need to speak, so well do we know each other. 'Come in.'

'Hey.' Greg stands awkwardly at the door and I escape Mo's clutches to get out of bed and go and give him a hug.

'Congratulations,' I sniff into his ear, wiping my nose before I leave snot on his shoulder.

'Erm, thanks,' he answers, uncertainly.

'Have you got hold of him?' Mo asks, crossing her legs beneath my duvet.

'Yeah,' Greg says, taking a step closer to his new fiancée. 'He's gone away. He says he can't stay, that he needs to go where he can work out what to do next. He...' Greg looks to me, then back to Mo. 'He said he doesn't want anyone to get in touch.' I nod, knowing the last bit is for my benefit. 'He said he has to start afresh.'

Mo looks at me, pity all over her face.

'It's okay,' I lie. 'It's fine.' But at that moment, I realise none of it's fine but I have no way of ever making things better. 'Look, you two. I'm tired, I need to sleep. It's been a long day. Congratulations.' I try to smile. 'I'm thrilled. I guess you'll be moving in, Greg. I can move out.'

'No,' he says, 'that's not…'

'It's fine,' I answer, standing as tall as my jelly legs will let me. 'I was going to be moving out anyway.' I go to kiss Mo on the cheek. 'I wasn't sure how to tell you, actually, but now's as good a time as any, Mo. I think I'm going to take your advice. Retrain.'

Mo's eyes widen. 'Teacher?'

I nod and she squeaks. 'The house sale is due to go through and Dad has the cash, so I'm going to go to uni. I was going to be moving out anyway. Maybe head to a new city for the course.'

'Where? Where are you going? When?'

'I'm not sure, maybe Sheffield. Possibly Leeds. But Dad needs help moving out before then, so, you know. He said he didn't need any help, that I had to go off and think about my future, but I reckon I'm clear so I'll go and stay with him for a few days, help pack the last of his stuff up. Then there's Rich. Rich is getting married!'

'What?'

'Yeah.' I laugh a sob, tripping over my words. 'Yeah, so… me and Dad can go to Italy. For the wedding. Rich won't be back for a while, he's—'

'Rachel…' says Mo, reaching out to my arm.

'It's fine.' I half smile, taking her hand. 'I'll go to Dad's tomorrow; I'll let you know about Italy. And when I can empty my room.'

'You don't have to,' repeats Mo.

'No, Rachel,' Greg says. 'You don't have to… we were…' Mo reaches for Greg's hand, giving him a warning glance. It doesn't take a rocket scientist to work out they were probably thinking of buying their own place now anyway. I let Mo think I haven't worked that bit out.

'It's all fine. Life's moving on, as it should. Now, go on, you two. Go and celebrate. But do it quietly. The last thing I need to hear is you two at it in the room next door!' My attempt at humour falls flat. Mo reaches her spare hand to Greg's arm. 'Go on,' I say, ushering them out of my room. 'See you in the morning.'

I lean against the door, clicking it shut behind them, sinking to the ground. I've lost Ed. I'm losing Mo. The family home will soon be gone and there is nothing in my future that offers stability or security. I feel like I need everyone and no one. I feel left behind.

Ed's gone to start afresh. It's time I did too. Maybe distance would be the best thing for all of us. Mo once accused me of pushing her away – I was struggling with something, I don't remember what right now, but she stood in front of me and shouted that she was going nowhere, that I would not force her out of my life. And she was right, she stayed around. But maybe now it's time I found a way to stand on my own two feet. It's not so much pushing her away, as searching for myself.

Chapter Forty-One

Rachel

Dear Ed,

Before you rip this up and throw it away, something you've every right to do, I wanted to write and apologise. I wanted a chance to explain. Explain. Apologise. Words that seem lame now, compared with what I did that night. Offering a reason seems crude and I don't really know what else I can say, except that I feel like I owe you some sort of explanation.

I've spent a lot of years pretending I had no drive, no fight for life. If I didn't push too hard, things couldn't fall away. If I didn't pursue the things I wanted in life, I didn't have to face it when I failed to achieve. I don't know where this came from; a fear of losing, a fear of failure, a fear of experiencing pain? Maybe all of those things.

When I met you, I was approaching a crossroads. I felt there was something missing in my life and the two people who are most important to me both seemed to agree — Dad was offering to pay for me to go back to university, Mo had all these ideas for jobs I could do — but I was passive in the whole process, no confidence to pursue anything, no clue as to what I really wanted in life. Then you arrived, with a story I recognised. Your pain was something I could feel, something I empathised with. It made me think about how Oli might be, growing up without his mum. It made me think about my dad, and what he gave to raise me and my brother without his wife by his side. These thoughts gave me perspective, but also, perhaps – purpose. I wanted to help. An idea that feels embarrassingly self-important now I look back. God, I'm sorry! You taught me things about my own father that I might not have seen before and I… in my twisted stupidity… thought I knew what you might need.

I know that I was wrong. That I abused your trust. I wish – above all else – I wish I could change that. If time travel ever comes into play, I'll be first in the car back to 2012. Maybe that's what I should be studying at university… science and engineering!

If you're still reading, if you've got this far without burning the letter or sticking a pin into a frozen effigy of my face (I've read it works, I wouldn't blame you!), please, Ed, please accept my deepest, most sincere apologies. Don't take my attempt at humour as flippancy, more… embarrassment that I was such a dick when you needed it least.

To you, and to Oli, I am so very sorry.
Yours sincerely,
Rachel x

I fold the letter into an envelope, mark it up with his address, hoping it will find him, wherever he may be. I stick on the stamp I got from Dad, knock back the fresh orange juice and leave enough euros for the drink and a tip.

Dropping the letter into an Italian post box, I look up to the sky. *Right, Mum, your son's getting married and I've got a date with Dad. We know you're shining down on us.*

Head as high as a flawed woman could ever hold it, I head off down the cobbled street, seeking shade from the sandstone buildings that tower either side, waving to Dad as he rounds a corner to meet me.

'Done?' he asks, offering his arm.

'Done,' I say, taking it.

'Come on, then. We have a wedding to attend. Tomorrow, we travel the length and breadth of Italy before you have to go home and get your head down. But today, it's limoncello and wedding cake for us.' He gives me a side squeeze and I cling on tight to him. I *will* stand on my own two feet… I will.

Just as soon as we land back home.

PART THREE
SEPTEMBER 2016

Chapter Forty-Two

Rachel

'You'd never have gone for a tuxedo four years ago, Rach. Not only are you a graduate, but a ballsy one too! I am SO impressed!' says Mo, straightening my leopard-print bow tie like a proud mother. 'You definitely looked the hottest of all the graduates!'

I beam. 'D'you reckon? I wasn't sure if it was a bit, "I'm a feminist, in your face the patriarchy".'

'Well, if it was, yah boo sucks to them. But, no, it just looked like someone in control of their destiny to me. Someone with the shoes of a hooker,' she says, kicking my red stilettos with her own comfy Converse shoes. 'Also, Greg said he definitely would, if he wasn't married to me.'

'Little bit weird,' I say, feeling myself colour.

'It'd save me a job, to be honest,' she grins. 'It's a bit awkward when you get this fat, you know? And also, it's almost five years together. Gets a bit samey after a while.'

'Samey! That's your husband you're dissing.' I bend down to talk to her pregnant belly. 'Don't listen to her,' I instruct my future godchild. 'She loves your daddy very much… even if he does push the boundaries of taste every once in a while.' I give her tummy a pat. 'Now, where's that drink he promised?' I ask, pulling my cap and gown off and dropping it on the seat beside us.

'Here it is,' says Dad, handing me a pint. 'A toast?'

'No, Dad. Don't be embarrassing.'

Greg sits down beside Mo, handing her a Coke and a bag of Quavers. 'Oh, my actual God, I am starving,' she says, shovelling several into her mouth at once.

'You've never looked more ravishing,' says Greg, leaning in to give her an affectionate kiss. 'Doesn't my heavily pregnant wife just make your heart swell,' he says, and I roll my eyes at them. She can pretend she's not up for it any more, but I'm certain it's just the hormones.

'Anyway,' says Mo. 'Yes, a toast.'

Dad raises his glass. 'To my brilliant daughter, a Bachelor of Education and all-round brilliant woman. You have worked so hard for this and I'm so very proud.' He sniffs and drinks.

'Dad, you better not be crying! I cannot handle you crying!' I bite my bottom lip because I made a promise to myself that I would not unfold on this day. 'Tears are for losers.'

'Leave him alone, he's allowed. It's not every day you do something so cool,' Mo teases. 'To his brilliant daughter, a Bachelor of Education… we can only fear for the future of humanity with you in charge of a class.' She winks and we all raise our glasses.

'Could be worse, could've been you going into teaching!' I clink her glass.

'Ha ha, touché!'

'I chuffing well did it, Mo,' I grin, nicking a Quaver from her pack. She glares at me. 'It's only one!'

'You try telling the baby that!' She pulls the bag closer. 'And, yes, you did. I always knew you could. I am almost as proud as your old dad.'

'Less of the old, Maureen!'

'Less of the Sunday name, Pa Fletcher!'

The pair grin at each other, cheers-ing themselves in mutual appreciation. I lean back in my chair, my heart full of friends and family and an overwhelming sense of achievement.

There were times in these last four years that I didn't think I'd make it to here. The day I turned up to a school having put my dress on inside out, not able to turn it back the right way because of that old wives' tale that says you have to roll with it so as not to have bad luck!

The day I turned up at the wrong school altogether and fell out with a receptionist who I thought was gatekeeping, but who was in fact trying to tell me that I was due at a school with a similar name, but in the next village along.

Or even before that, before I started training, when I was packing to move out of Mo's, my heart breaking. Or when Dad and I handed the keys over to the house, the estate agent asked if I was okay, and I fell into his startled arms and sobbed. Poor bloke stood rigid, presumably wishing he'd never asked!

Yet, despite those… and many more embarrassing moments… I did do it. I'm here, I made it. And the only person who's not here to celebrate with me is Rich, who continues to travel the world with his wife. (We don't even know where he is at the moment; probably some commune in darkest Peru.) The point is, it's been such a long time coming, I can't quite believe I'm here.

'So, when do you start?' asks Greg.

'Monday. I get the keys to the house tomorrow and have the weekend to get unpacked and prepared, then straight into it.' My stomach flips with nerves. 'And I'm totally fine, not remotely nervous, or anything. Nope. No way. Everything's going to be fine,' I say.

Mo winks, then grimaces.

'You alright?' I check.

'Yup,' she says in a clipped voice. 'Just those stupid Braxton Hicks things again.' She breathes through whatever is happening to her body and, not for the first time since she got pregnant, I vow not to have children. It's clearly deeply uncomfortable. 'Little fucker has its foot in my ribs too,' she says. 'Which doesn't help.'

'Ha! You're so maternal,' I say, laughing.

'You try feeling maternal when you've got a bowling ball between your legs, not to mention the permanent heartburn. And have you seen my breasts lately?' Dad coughs, embarrassed, and Greg mutters something along the lines of 'he should be so lucky'.

'Bet you forget about it all the second the baby arrives!' I say, the butterflies from work chat being replaced with bubbles of excitement about their pending arrival. 'Oh my God, I can't wait.'

Mo and Greg grin at each other, him pulling her in for another kiss. The part of me that used to feel jealousy at how happy they are isn't so strong now. I don't know if it's because I'm happier these days, more content in my own skin. Or if it's because I'm not desperate to rush into anything. Boyfriends have come and gone in the last four years. I've had fun, but nobody that I could fall in love with. Nobody that matched up to… well, I'm not going to go there again. Somebody will, one day, I imagine.

We sit, chat and laugh about the day. Mo and I reminisce about the times before she met Greg when we first moved into the flat. Before things changed; before life changed me. Before I thought wearing stilettoes for the day was a smart move. What I wouldn't give for Mo's Converse shoes right now!

Shoes kicked off beneath the table, two hours pass and it's time for me to head out into the big wide world on my own.

'Look, I need to make a move, guys.'

Mo's eyes fill.

'Don't!' I instruct. 'I'm only going down the road. Okay? An hour. That's all!' She bites her lip, holding on to Greg's hand, nodding. 'And you can visit any time you need to get away from him!' I say, nodding in Greg's direction. 'This is no different to when I moved out.'

'Except that I wasn't heavily pregnant and irrationally hormonal,' she sniffs.

'Well, yes, that much is true. But, seriously, I'm not going far. And as soon as that baby arrives I'll be back anyway, okay? Just you see if I'm not.'

Mo nods again and I smile at how our roles have briefly switched. Once I'd have been the one in bits and she'd have been pulling me up by my boot straps.

'Now, you look after yourself, and let Greg look after you too. And look after each other for that matter. You're on that bit of a roller coaster where you're being dragged up. The carriage is making that ominous clicking sound all the way to the top and your heart is getting progressively closer to your mouth.' Mo looks at me blankly. 'What I'm trying to say is that when those waters break, prepare for the oblivion drop!'

'I don't think that's helping,' says Mo, no longer able to hold her tears back.

'Oh, shit, sorry. Come here, then.' I get up and put my arms around her, planting kisses on the top of her head. 'You've totally got this, okay? And I'm on the end of the phone whenever you need me.' She nods and sniffs and I give her a squeeze.

'Dad, do you want a lift back?'

'No, love, you're fine. I'm going to take the bus, thanks. It's the wrong direction for you anyway.' He smiles up at me, his face older, but somehow more relaxed over the last few years. 'Gonna pop by and see your mother first, tell her about your day,' he says, nodding to some flowers he's brought to put on her grave. 'She would have been so proud of you, you know. You've done what she only ever dreamed of. And you're going to be brilliant.' He gets up, pulling me into a bear hug. 'Go on, you get off, love. You've got a big week ahead.'

'Okay, alright.' I put my hands on my hips, with Dad's, Mo's and Greg's faces all looking at me. God, where would I be without them? Even Greg, who has taken on the role of annoying big brother since marrying Mo. *I love them. So bloody hard!*

'Thank you, you lot. Even you, Greg. Thank you thank you thank you.' I blow kisses, backing out of the pub. 'Love you!'

'We love you more,' sobs Mo, taking a tissue from Greg to wipe her eyes.

'Look after her,' I instruct him and he salutes his response.

I turn away, my heart flitting as fear sets in. *You're on your own now, kid,* I think, stepping out into Nottingham's bright, late-summer sun. Staying here to attend uni was fun. There was something about knowing the city so well that gave me the confidence to push on through when the young'uns on the course seemed to be steaming on ahead of me. For all my talk of leaving and standing on my own two feet, I guess I realised I needed the support of those who gave a damn, just to get me through it. And they did, they do, and now I'm here. A qualified teacher. About to stand on my own two feet. Finally!

Butterflies go crazy in my belly as I head off to my car, a new chapter about to begin...

Chapter Forty-Three

Ed

Waking up on the extreme edge of my bed, core strength only just saving me from falling, I realise it's time Oli slept in his own bed from time to time. He had an excuse last night, or maybe I did – it will only ever be his first day of school the once. He's growing up.

I slowly turn my head to see his tiny, perfect face, his eyes still flickering dreams. I move myself, careful not to topple out of bed, or wake him. I'm getting pretty good at stealth parenting like this. When he's awake, there is no doubt that he is growing up. His humour, his attitude, his generosity of spirit all shine through. But in this state, he's all baby. All 8lb 6oz of him, but bigger. And older. No longer strapped to my chest, but usually not far from my grasp.

I sneak out of bed, making the most of a chance for quiet. I tiptoe down the stairs, narrowly avoiding the collection of Lego stashed at the very bottom, but in so doing, I'm thrown off balance, making the process of navigating our shoes by the front door all the more difficult. I manage it, but not before almost tripping over the now geriatric cat. Floyd looks up at me with eyes that could sour his own milk, before meowing in disgust. 'You old bugger,' I offer, reaching down to stroke his scrawny back and, despite his obvious disdain, he plods behind me into the kitchen to be fed.

'Daddy, I am so excited I literally cannot breathe.'

His little voice sings through the open plan of our 1970s ex-army home. I turn to see him skipping down the stairs, clapping his hands with glee.

'You *literally* cannot breathe?' I ask him, constantly amazed by his grasp of the English language. 'Mind the Lego!' I add, hearing a thud as he leapfrogs it from the next-to-bottom step.

'I *literally* cannot breathe!' he repeats.

'Right,' I say, nipping past him to brush the offending Lego into a box that I stash beneath the sofa. 'Well, we had better sort that out straight away. You can't go to school if you literally can't breathe now, can you?'

He goes to the cupboard, pulling cereal boxes out while giving me my orders. 'Can I have Weetabix and Coco Pops, can I watch *Curious George* and is it time for me to get dressed yet?' I look at him. 'Pleeease?' I wonder if all four-and-a-half-year-olds – four years and eight months if you were to ask him! – are as excited as this on their first day of school. He has been building up to it, ticking off the days on our two-man family calendar, his squeals of joy getting louder as this day got nearer.

'You can have whatever you like, mate. Breakfast of kings today, in fact.'

'What do kings eat for breakfast, Dad?'

'Weetabix mostly. And Coco Pops. Which is handy.'

'Yes.' He fist pumps the air, before launching himself onto the sofa.

'Kings don't jump on the furniture though!' I shout over my shoulder, as I busy about the kitchen fetching his breakfast. Oli digs out the TV remote from beneath the cat, who has filled himself up on cat biscuits and moved to teeter on the back of a cushion. 'Floyd, I'm trying to put the telly on.'

Floyd meows before heading upstairs to take up his now regular daytime position on my bed, shuffling only to keep up with the shaft of warmth on the duvet cast by the sun through my window. He thinks I haven't realised, but the long black hair is a giveaway. Ellie would have hated it.

'Here you go.' I place Oli's bowl down on the small lap table that he uses in the lounge, sitting at the dinner table in the corner of the room to eat my own breakfast while scanning all the first-day-at-school photos that fill up my Facebook timeline.

'What are you going to do today, Daddy?'

I look at my diary, lift the pages up in my portfolio and blow out a deep breath. 'A bit more colouring in today, mate. The usual,' I say. What I'm actually doing is pitching for a picture-book illustration, a job I'd really love to get, a leg up in the world of children's book illustration, major for me, but Oli has always called it colouring in.

'Daddy?'

'Yes, mate?'

'Do you think that Mummy can see us walking to school? You know, like Santa can?'

I look over to her mini-me. His face shaped like hers, his eyes the same green. 'I am sure she can. Keeping an eye out to make sure that you are good.'

'I'm always good.'

'Of course you are. Now eat your breakfast. School awaits!'

As I eat my own, sifting through the job list and planning out my day, my thoughts are interrupted with moments I'm trying to ignore.

Moments I don't usually have to deal with because life goes on and you find a way to manage. I wonder what it feels like, today. As he sits there overloading his spoon and spilling breakfast everywhere. 'Mind the carpet!' I say. I know how I feel about all of this, life moving on. But what does it feel like for him? To be fair, he's never known any different. She was never there for the big stuff with him. He has no idea how different it could be. I get up, ruffle his hair and collect his now empty bowl. 'You'll get indigestion eating that fast.' But he doesn't hear, because he's already halfway up the stairs.

Twenty minutes later, we leave the house and make our way to school.

'Dad?'

'Yes?'

He reaches his hand into mine; he rarely does that any more. Apparently holding hands is for girls. Ellie would've had something to say about that and I have echoed her thoughts, but he won't budge. 'Will you be picking me up today?'

'Yes, mate. Of course I will.' I pick him up now, give him a kiss and a squeeze before letting him push me away, looking over his shoulder to see if anyone has seen.

'Good,' he says, his nerves a little more visible to me now.

'I am going to do a bit of work from home, then I'll pop to the shops for some tea. Then, I'll come and get you.'

'Can you get me some chocolate and a comic?'

'I'll get you a comic or some chocolate, not both. In fact, neither unless I get a please.'

He slaps his hand to his forehead. '*Pleeease.*'

'Which?'

'Chocolate. No! A comic. No! Please can I have chocolate... please.'

'That's probably enough pleases. Chocolate then. Yes, and I'll pick you up. Easy peasy.'

'Lemon squeezy.'

We carry on walking in silence, but I can see him looking around for his friends. 'James!' he shouts to a little boy over the road. James waves and jumps in mutual excitement. As we arrive at the gates to his school, he pauses for a moment and I prepare myself. 'Dad?'

I kneel – eye-to-eye contact – and smile. 'Yes, mate?'

'I've changed my mind.'

I wondered if this might come. I've been asking around, how do you deal with the sudden backtrack they might take. It's a big day, no wonder. 'Don't worry, Oli, it's fine,' I say, rubbing his hand and squeezing his shoulder. 'By the end of today you'll have wondered what all the fuss was about. I promise. You'll be fine.' I kiss his hand.

'I know, Dad,' he says, frowning. 'I mean I've changed my mind about the chocolate. I want a comic.' And with that, he runs off towards James, and a gaggle of kids suddenly meet in the middle of the playground, shouting and full of life. I'm not alone in being a single parent bringing him to school this morning. I see a few others on their own. But I see more in pairs. Mum and dad here to celebrate their child's first big day. I look to the sky just in case she can see. It's small comfort on a day like today.

Chapter Forty-Four

Rachel

From my car, parked up in the staff car park, I watch the school gates teeming with parents and their children: drop offs for the older ones, parking up and walking hand in hand with the younger ones, some screaming with joy at the sight of long-missed friends; six weeks is apparently a lifetime when you're a kid. The occasional child clutches on to the leg of a parent, and I feel their pain. One cries and his mum tries to cuddle him, while his dad gives him a pep talk over her shoulder. I wouldn't mind one of those – a pep talk – *Man up, Rachel, kids can smell fear.*

Judging by my reflection in the rear-view mirror, the kids will be able to see my fear too. My brow is frozen furrowed, so much so that I can feel craters forming in the lines across my forehead. The telltale signs of a lifelong frowner. Usually I can't help it. Usually it's just the way my face is, but today... well, today I realise that small people are significantly more intimidating than anyone gives them credit for. I hadn't anticipated this when collecting my degree certificate.

Right. Bag over shoulder, butterflies from Friday now massive bats in my stomach, let's do this.

* * *

'Good morning, Miss Fletcher.'

Being called Miss Fletcher makes me want to run away a little bit, as the reality of it all hits. *I am in a real-life, grown-up situation.*

'This is exciting, isn't it? Your first day, their first day. How do you feel?' asks Mrs Clarke, the teacher from the classroom next door. She's putting out the chairs, preparing her classroom for the day's new arrivals.

'Oh, you know. Mildly alarmed. Terrified. Wondering if I can change my mind about it all. Is this normal? Were you terrified on your first morning, Mrs Clarke?'

'Crikey, I can't possibly remember that far back. But probably, yes.' She smiles. 'It is exciting, though.'

'Well, yes, exciting is definitely one of the other words... vomit-inducing, there's another.'

'Oh, love, no need to be frightened, they're barely five years old. What on earth can go wrong?'

'I've just completed four years of teacher training, how many stories do you want me to offer?'

'Ha ha, you'll be fine! I'm here if you need anything. Now, we have a few jobs that need doing before we let them in.'

She delegates a list of things to sort in our respective rooms: drinks on tables, check all pegs for correct labelling, set out the role-play area – today they will be shopkeepers. I busy myself in my new 'office', aware that tiny eyes peer through the glass door as I move around the room. An oversized wall clock with multi-coloured numbers ticks loudly with each passing second, sending me into a much-needed meditative state as it eventually leads us to 8.55 a.m. and the bell rings out to break it.

Deep breath, Rachel. I walk towards the door, about to open it wide and welcome in the new start. A little boy peers through the window, his brilliant green eyes shining, his face happy and bright. I bend down, balancing on the balls of my toes to greet him at his level. He pulls a funny face so, hoping to have found a comrade, I press my nose fast up against the glass, pulling a face in return. He motions behind him for his dad to share the fun as I cross my eyes. His dad bends down too, cupping his hands to the window, glass now the only thing between us, and he sees me. And I see him.

My heart stops. I can't escape.

Ed!

We mirror one another as we slowly stand, eyes locked through the glass.

A clap of excited hands behind me brings me back to now. 'Right, Miss Fletcher, are you ready?' Mrs Clarke peers around the connecting door. 'Time to let them in!' She bustles off to her own door, and the sound of her welcoming students pushes me to unlock my door, despite the overwhelming nausea that has replaced nerves. Gone are the butterflies and bats in my belly, hello herd of elephants stamping through my heart.

'Good morning, in you come, erm... pegs over there... Hi, hello, lovely to see you...' The children file in and I can't work out if all this is really happening. 'Go on, hang your coats up. Oooh,' I say to a small, curly-haired girl, 'what a lovely red coat you have, in you go... yes, mums and dads, you can come in. Just for today, mind you.'

Parents file in too, oversized among the tiny tables and chairs. Ed and Oli are the last to come in, the end of the queue. As they get closer, I lose control over my mouth, tripping over instructions, a sick feeling now in my throat.

'Rachel?' he says, when he finally gets to the door. I don't know why he is asking. We both know it's me. And him. We both know it's him. *It's him. Oh God.*

I cough, attempting to clear the nerves. 'Hi. Well, this is…' He stares at me, studying my face, my eyes. 'This is a surprise.' He's still studying me. I feel scrutinised, vulnerable… I feel sick. He looks a little older, he has some grey to the sides now, his eyes hide behind new thick, black-rimmed glasses. Well, new to me at least. Oh God. Does he notice the tiny details of time in me? Not that it matters. *It doesn't matter.*

'In you go,' he says to Oli, pushing him onwards.

'Yes, go on, Oli. Hang your coat up.'

I try to beam at Oli, but he leans into his dad. 'She already knows my name,' he whispers.

'Yes… she…' Ed's words trail off and I realise he doesn't know what to say any more than I do.

'Come on, let's get you sorted,' he says, taking off Oli's bag – a rucksack as big as he is – then an oversized coat that might see him through until his teens. 'Let's get these hung up.' Ed's eyes are still on me.

I bite my lip, suddenly not trusting myself to handle this the way that Ed might want me to. Should I acknowledge all of this here and now? Should I acknowledge it at all? Or should I act like we don't even know each other? For now… Or should I hand in my resignation at break time and move schools altogether?

A few parents start to leave, children giving big kisses. One seems wobbly and I'm grateful for the diversion. 'Come on, it's okay. We're going to have the best day. Tell me, do you like Lego?' The small girl nods, her chin wobbling. 'Great, can you be my helper with the Lego boxes today then? I want us all to start off by building whatever comes to our minds.' The girl nods, letting her mum kiss her head and leave. 'The boxes are over there, by the carpet. Go and sit down near to it, and when we've all said hello this morning, you can help us to get started.' The little girl nods nervously, but does as she's told, seating herself close to the Lego.

A few more parents leave and the children start to file onto the carpet, sitting in a straggle of crossed legs and tiny school uniforms that wear the children, not the other way around.

Ed was the last to come in and now he's the last to go. I'm still stood by the door as he comes over. I busy myself with the papers for register, fumbling with the pen top and pretending I'm checking I have all I need. Of course I have all I need, I've checked it ten times already this morning.

Ed moves straight past me to the door, and my heart sinks at being ignored. But he stops, turning back around. 'I didn't know you worked here.'

'No.' I cough. 'I, er, I just started today.'

'Right.'

'I… I didn't know you lived here.'

'Yeah. A while now.' He pauses, his eyes fixed firmly on mine, and part of me wants to run a mile and part of me wants him to take me in his arms. This is not good. This is really not good. 'We moved here not long after I last saw you.'

'Oh.' I go hot and cold at the same time. Clammy. 'I see.'

He blows a kiss to Oli, then turns to leave. I reach for the handle to pull the door to, but Ed turns around and moves back towards me again. 'Right, class,' I say, because I can't do this here or now. Ed stop in his tracks, takes a deep breath, then leaves, this time without turning back. And I watch, breath held, unable to turn away.

Chapter Forty-Five

Ed

I don't know how it looked, but I felt as if I was staggering from class to school gate, falling against the black metal railings when out on the pavement, trying to get my thoughts in order. I've been in some kind of weird daze all day. Was it seeing her for the first time in four years that made me feel that way, or the fact my first thought on seeing her was *Rachel! It's Rachel!* Like I was pleased. Like it was good to see her. Like I'd forgotten what she did.

I was supposed to be the one in control today, this morning. I was supposed to be keeping my emotions in check for Oli's sake. Being the grown-up who could lead him through this rite of passage, his first day at school; a day that would be more different for him than the other kids. The ones with two parents, two people to support the change, whether still together or not. But as I crouched down, met familiar eyes through the glass, and had the slow dawning of who it was, my heart lifted; it skipped, even.

I got home and dropped onto the sofa, staring vacantly at the ground, my feelings muted. Then this bizarre motivation set in, where I started doing stuff I haven't felt like doing for weeks. Little jobs. Phone calls I didn't want to make. A new client pitch that had become too big to handle. I took my portfolio down to the library to copy the bits I wanted to send off to another possible new client. Was it all distraction? Did it help to stop me thinking about her? Or am I overthinking it all? Is this mood simply because my boy is experiencing his first day of school and the house is quiet? I'm a bit lost without him here in the afternoon. My wingman has gone.

Maybe this has nothing to do with her.

And yet, as I sit here in my car, clutch pedal depressed, at 2.40 p.m., I realise that as much as I want to see Oli, pick him up and hear about his day, I can't move. I'm paralysed. Rachel was there at the strangest of times, she saw me at my lowest, she held me as I sobbed. She made me feel comfort and discomfort in equal measure. And the hurt, when she told me what she'd done... it was so deep. It was so unexpected.

A tap on the window sends my heart to my throat.

'You alright, dear?'

Glynis, from over the road, feigning concern. She doesn't know I've seen her net curtains twitching each time I leave the house. I try, but fail, to open the window, my car keys still not in the ignition. 'Yes, thanks, Glynis,' I shout, trying to turn the key and press the switch. The window rolls down.

'You've been sat there since quarter past two, love, I thought you'd fell asleep!' she chuckles.

'Oh, yeah, I've just been on the phone.' I motion towards the hands-free kit that obviously hasn't yet connected with my phone, but I don't suppose she'll notice.

She peers into the back of the car. 'No Oli?'

'No.'

She raises her eyebrows as if there is some kind of story to be discovered, forcing me to expand.

'First day of school.'

'Ah, bless him. I remember my Michael's first day of school. Lovely memories. He cried like a baby for the entire morning, wouldn't let me leave. Then, when I did finally go, he got so upset he was sick all over the story carpet and the teachers sent him home.' I stare at her, dismayed. 'Still makes us laugh today. He's such a mummy's boy is our Michael.'

I wonder if the forty-three-year-old that visits her week on week knows that she talks about him this way.

'I bet he looked ever so grown up in that uniform, didn't he?'

'Yeah, he did. It's massive on him. It'll probably do him till sixth form.'

'Oh, I wouldn't think so, dear. They grow ever so fast, you know.'

'Yes. I was… never mind. I'd better go and fetch him.' I smile politely.

'Yes, it wouldn't do to keep him waiting on his first day, would it now?'

'No.'

'No.'

She is still standing here. I turn the ignition on, putting the window up, smiling at her. It's not until I release the handbrake that she steps backwards, moving her shopping trolley out of my way.

'Bye, dear, hope he has had fun.'

'Bye.'

She waves.

I reverse off the drive, turn the corner out of our road and out of sight. I park up again. The distraction got me moving, but I haven't quite cleared up what I am going to say to Rachel yet. I knock the gear into neutral and look into the mirror. Is this the face of a man who can confront the elephant in the room? The sight of Glynis shuffling around the corner, pulling her shopping trolley behind her, forces me to adjust the rear-view mirror and move on.

We've been doing so well. We've been on a new path, a new journey. It's been working. I don't want the past to colour my future.

Is it okay to have felt happy to see her, or am I confused? Do we want her in our lives again? After what she did? After what she knows… Maybe I should just move Oli to another school.

Chapter Forty-Six

Rachel

Ed helps Oli into his school coat, juggling the books, pictures and drinks bottle that Oli hasn't managed to put into his book bag. I pick up the book he's dropped.

'There you go.'

'Thanks.' Ed takes it from me, avoiding eye contact. 'Have you had a good day, big man?'

'Yeah, look.' He thrusts his chest in Ed's face. 'Miss Fletcher gave me a sticker!' He displays it with all the pride of a gold medal Olympian.

'I couldn't not reward such excellent tidying up,' I explain.

'Wow, you can tidy up?' asks Ed, teasing Oli. 'Well done, that's brilliant,' he concedes, ruffling Oli's hair. 'Perhaps you could bring that new-found skill home.' A few more children leave, parents thanking me as they usher them out of the door. Ed straightens up, moving out of the way for a young girl and her big sister. 'Sorry,' he says to the girl.

'Dad, Dad, can I go on the slide? Jack is there, can I go too?'

Ed looks out of the door to the play area. 'Of course, mate, go on. I'll be there in a second.' He turns to me. 'How did he…?'

'Oh, fine, yeah.'

'I didn't know if he'd… you know, his mum and that.'

'No, no, he… he was fine.'

Ed nods. Something else is on the tip of his tongue, but whatever it is he can't say it.

'Have you had a good day?' I ask, then realise this is all pretence, it's all nonsense, because we don't know what else to say. 'Look, Ed. I'm sorry. If this is weird—'

'No, no! It's not… well…'

We stand awkwardly. 'How've you been?' I ask eventually.

'Oh, you know…' He shuffles Oli's bag and stuff into one hand so he can ruffle his hair. 'We're…' He watches Oli jumping on his pal's back; they collapse into giggles and a slight smile touches the corners of Ed's mouth. 'He saved me.'

His words touch me, his focus on Oli as he runs around. 'Now probably isn't—'

'No,' he interrupts, flicking his eyes briefly in my direction, before heading towards the door. 'It isn't,' he answers.

Mrs Clarke comes through the adjoining door. 'How was your first day?' she asks, bustling towards us, picking up some rubbish from the floor, her pleated skirt swinging as she does. 'You survived,' she says.

'I did,' I agree.

'Well done,' says Ed, before stepping out the door after Oli. Mrs Clarke smiles as he leaves, making it less and less possible for me to go after him. Talk to him. Apologise to him.

So instead I stand and watch him leave, wondering if he notices I'm there when he turns back to face the classroom before turning a corner out of sight.

Chapter Forty-Seven

Rachel

From the safety of my car, I dial Mo's number. It rings out for so long that I begin to think I'm going to get her voicemail, relieved when she finally picks up. 'Mo, we have a problem.'

'You think *you* have a problem? I took forever to answer because I'm stuck in the bath, only just able to get my fingertips to my phone and now wondering if I should call the fire brigade or wait until Greg gets home to rescue me.'

'What do you mean, rescue you?'

'I mean, I can't get out. I mean, I am so fat right now that my Weeble-like state is making it impossible to clamber out of this bath. All I wanted was some warm water on my aching back, but I've been in this thing for two and half hours and I cannot for the life of me escape. I'm like a stranded ladybird. Or a cow. Or any other animal that is unable to right itself in the event it finds itself on its back.' There's a slosh of water in the background. 'And now the water's cold.'

'Oh, Mo.' I giggle.

'Don't you bloody well laugh!'

'I'm sorry, I'm sorry. I didn't mean to, I just… Can't you call someone, a friend, to get you out?'

'I AM NUDE!'

'Since when have you been shy?' I guffaw.

'Since my stomach became a map of the world and my ankles morphed into those of an elephant. Now, if you need some kind of help, kindly stop laughing at my expense and tell me something that will take my mind off how cold I am and how wrinkled my fingers are. How was your first day? And how can you have a problem already?'

'Oli is in my class.'

'Oli?'

'Ed's Oli.'

'You are shitting me!'

There is a slosh of water again and I can imagine her face, open-mouthed, prune fingers in the air.

'I wish I was. But, no, Ed dropped him off this morning.'

'It's like… Oh my God, I don't even know what it is like. How did you feel? What did you say? What did he say? Oh my actual God!'

I think for a moment, trying to work out the different emotions I've gone through during the day. 'My heart stopped. I was completely thrown. I was terrified. I wanted to throw my arms around him and I wanted to run away.'

'What did he do?'

'Ed? He was pretty much poker-faced. Stunned, maybe? I don't know really. I mean, the last time I saw him he ordered me out of his house, and there I was, this morning, on one of his son's most important days, casually pulling faces at him through the window.'

'You did not.'

I go a bit cold with the memory. 'Yup. I was trying to be a cool teacher.' I bury my head in my free hand, groaning. 'So, anyway, I was thinking I'd hand my notice in tomorrow and go back to nursery nursing. Or leave the country. Or perhaps change my identity. What do you think?'

The sound of bare flesh on the bathtub suggests Mo's attempting to sit herself up in the bath. Which also suggests I'm about to be given a good talking-to, which, let's face it, is exactly the reason I called her.

'Now, look here. Firstly, don't be a dick about this. For some reason the universe has decided it's appropriate to throw you two back together again. You have to trust that it knows what it's doing.'

'The universe?'

'Yes.'

'Since when did you consider the universe in control of your destiny?'

'And secondly,' she goes on, ignoring me, 'as if you can jack your job in. You've just worked your arse off for four years to get to this point. Don't let anyone make you feel that leaving is the only option. Sure, you made a mistake. I mean, it was a big one. And quite crap.' The sick feeling that I always get when I remember what I did returns. 'But it happened. You felt bad about it. You apologised. You don't owe him any more than that, and you certainly don't owe him your first job as a qualified teacher. If he has a problem with it, he can move schools.'

'Why should he?'

'Why should you?'

I groan.

'Look, I know you'll be desperate to do the right thing here, and that is why, ultimately, you will. But don't rush into anything.' There's a muffled sound in the background. 'Oh, thank God, he's back. GREG!' she shouts. I pull the phone away from my ear. 'GREG! I'm stuck in the bath. Can you come and help me…? Thank God… Rach, give me a minute.' The phone rattles as she puts it down. I hear Greg come into the bathroom and start laughing. 'Don't you dare, Gregory Matthew Peters, you got me into this state, now you can jolly well rescue me without so much as a word.' The sound of her berating him – full Sunday name tinged with the warmth of a couple in love – makes me smile. 'Rachel is on the phone, having a crisis, and I cannot deal with it from in here. Also, make us a cuppa, I'm gasping!'

Moments later, the phone rattles as she picks it back up. 'That is *so* much better. Right, I'm wrapped in a towel, in my bed, ready to sort this out with you. So, you need to call Ed.'

'*What?*'

'You need to call him. Arrange to meet up with him. This needs nipping in the bud quick smart. Before it gets awkward.'

'Sure, because that would be awful, wouldn't it… for things to get awkward, I mean,' I say, sarcasm loaded.

'Or we can finish this call and you can work it out for yourself.'

'I can't call him, I don't have his number.'

'Do you want to come up with all the reasons why you can't do this, or pay attention and sort it out?'

'Okay, no! No. Sorry. Go on.'

'So, you call him, or speak to him at school, or whatever. You arrange to meet up. You explain. You apologise. You tell him that you are not around to make things awkward for him, and that if he'd rather have Oli moved into another class, that is fine. But that you are here to stay and while you don't expect him to forgive you, you hope you can both be adult about it.'

She was always able to make solutions seem obvious. 'I suppose…'

'The alternative – i.e. you walking out on your job – isn't really a goer, so you're going to have to do this. Dear God, my back is agony today.'

'You had any pain relief?' I ask, looking at the calendar beside my bed. She's not due for another week.

'Yes, Nurofen and a giant mug of Horlicks. Neither touched it, though the Horlicks was unexpectedly comforting. Midwife is due tomorrow, I'm sure it's all par for the course. Now, look, I need to go. Let me know when you've spoken to him. Love you.'

'Love you.'

I put my phone on the passenger seat and start the engine. Mrs Clarke bumbles across the car park, arms full of papers and folders, to a battered Renault Scenic. She waves furiously as she drives away, her face beaming, warm, friendly. A good ally for the start of my career. Mo's right. I can't leave. Moving classes for Oli might be the best plan. I guess I'll talk to Ed about it tomorrow.

Chapter Forty-Eight

Ed

'Rachel, I've thought about this all night, and, though it's an uncomfortable situation, I don't think we have any alternative but to just get on with it.' She stands beside me as I talk under my breath so as not to be overheard. 'I did wonder about moving him into Mrs Clarke's class,' I admit. 'But his friends are in this one and I'd really rather he wasn't affected by our relationship.'

Our relationship. Those are not the words I was looking for.

'So, if we can find a way to just get on with things – it's only for a year – that would be great.'

'Of course,' she says. Her face has turned pink, she bites at the corner of her mouth. 'Of course…'

'Right. Good.' I search the sea of children for Oli. I've said my piece, now I need to get out of the suffocating heat in this room. I don't know how she copes, how any of them do. 'Is it always this hot in here?' I ask.

'Erm, I don't know. Second day, I'm not really sure how…'

'No. Well.' I signal to Oli to come and give me a kiss, but he just blows one across the room then turns his back, giggling with his friends. I try to ignore the rejected child within me. It's good that he's happy. It's good that he's confident. '*I wonder how our children will grow, Ed.*

Confident? Shy? What do you think? Confidence in spades sums Oli up. Confidence in absolute spades.

'Do you think, at some point maybe, we could... well, I'd like to...' Rachel fiddles with her fingers, her back to the class as she talks to me. 'Would you consider talking to me about it all? Just so we can clear the air, put it behind us.'

I clench my jaw. 'I'm not sure there's anything to talk about, is there?'

Rachel nods as if she understands, but the look in her eye suggests otherwise.

'Look. I've been working really hard to build a life for me and Oli. It's been four years. I got your letter. I know your side of it. I think it's probably best to just move on.'

She looks hurt, which I realise makes me feel bad. I don't want to be too hard, not really; I suppose time healed the hurt. And what she did was nothing compared to how Simon handled his jail term. Or how Mum handled trying to get him to talk to me. Or how I handled the fact he flat-out rejected my requests to visit him.

And then Mum died, suddenly, and I wondered if her heart hadn't been able to cope with all that had happened, and if maybe I just needed to move on. Let things go. Not worry about if I was Oli's real father or not, because I was his father in Oli's eyes. In his needs. And as he grew older, looking more and more like his mum, he was becoming more and more my son every day. The boy I relied upon. Needed. *Need.* The idea that anything could change; that was too much. It *is* too much. I survived the worst days, weeks and years of my life because of Oli. He is my son, no matter what science might say.

Perhaps I should I tell Rachel that's why I can't talk to her about it? Because the whole thing is buried deep enough for me not to have to think about it day and night, as I did those first few months.

Except Dad said Simon will be out soon.

And then he can't avoid me any longer. And by the same token, I suppose, I can't avoid him either. Or the situation. So maybe I need to belt and brace my approach, make sure I know every last detail before I fight my case. Whatever case that may be…

The bell rings out for school to begin. Rachel signals that she needs to get on, biting the side of her mouth. 'Okay,' I say. 'Let's talk. Tonight. Where, though? I don't want to go where people know us.'

'You could come to Fulbeck, where I live. The Hare and Hounds? It's about twenty minutes away.'

'Eight o'clock? Then I can get Oli to bed first.'

She nods. I leave, not entirely sure I'm doing the right thing.

Chapter Forty-Nine

Ed

'Thanks for this, I really appreciate it.'

Glynis settles herself down in front of our telly, flicking channels and landing on some real-life crime drama. 'Oh, don't worry, dear. I'm only too happy to help. You off anywhere nice?'

'No. Not really. Just need to pop out and see someone.' She raises her eyebrows in question, but I'm not giving any more information. If I wanted everyone to know my business, we'd have met up down the village pub. 'Oli went to bed at half seven. You won't hear a peep now, he never wakes up these days and he'll be knackered after his first couple of days at school anyway, so, you know, easy.'

'Ah, he is a good boy. You've done a good job there with that one, Mr Moran—'

'Please. Call me Ed.'

'Not a chance of it, Mr Moran. I shall call you as I call you. You have done a good job with that boy and I am sure his mother would be proud.'

'Thank you, Glynis. I appreciate that.'

'She was a beautiful woman, Mr Moran.' She's staring at the photo of Ellie and Oli on our mantelpiece. 'Such a shame.'

'Yes.'

'Anyway, take your time,' she says, moving swiftly on. The volume on the television gets louder and she lounges back into the sofa, opening a bag of mint humbugs from her handbag, popping one in her mouth.

I check my hair in the mirror, pick up my coat, wallet and keys and open the door to leave as she shouts, 'Mr Moran...'

I pop my head around the door. 'Yes, Glynis?'

'You smell lovely,' she says with a wry smile on her face, her eyes not leaving the TV screen. I go to explain the aftershave: the fact I went up to shower when we got back from school and lost all sense of time, gazing out the window and wondering how a world as big as it is can actually be so small. I ran out of time and, instead of showering, splashed on some Adidas stuff that I dug out from the back of the cupboard. Of course, I don't actually have to explain to her, or to anyone. As time goes by, I begin to realise more and more I am my own man. A single man. A widower, yes, but that feels like half the story.

Driving to the pub gives me headspace. A chance to reflect on the four years since I last saw Rachel. I wasn't really living back then. Just sort of functioning, day to day. Am I living now? Sometimes, maybe. I have the job I wanted, which Ellie would have loved. I have Oli. But who am I? Does it matter that, outside of Oli and work, I don't really know?

Pulling into the car park, second thoughts swirl. What am I doing here? What does this change? What can she possibly know or do or say that could help? From the corner of my eye, I catch sight of Rachel, heading into the pub.

She's at the bar when I step through the door to the sixteenth-century pub, all exposed stone walls and aged beams. Our eyes meet in the whisky-branded mirror behind the bar and she half smiles. Some old bloke props up the bar, his dog sniffing a greeting as I pass. Rachel turns to face me. 'What you having?'

'I'll get these.' I offer a note up to the barman.

'I've already given him my card. I'm on the wine, what you having?'

'Er, a Coke then. Please.'

She repeats my order, taking a sip from the large glass of red she's just been poured. 'Over there?' She points towards two sofas that face one another by an unlit open fire.

I nod, turning back to the bar to wait for my drink. Rachel goes to sit down, perhaps not realising that I can see her in the mirror behind the bar. She hovers between the sofas, working out which one to sit in, pulling a cushion up to her when she does finally sit down. I can feel her nerves. Is that me? The situation? Is that just who she is these days?

I sit down opposite her just as her phone rings out. 'Sorry, I'll switch it off. Sorry.' She reaches into her bag, pausing then fiddling until it goes silent.

'Answer if you need to.'

'No, it's okay. It's just Mo.'

'Wow, you're still in touch with her, then?'

'Yeah, of course. She and Greg got married, they're having a baby.' She pulls her phone into view, checking the screen.

'I lost touch with Greg when I left work. I cut all ties from that time. Survival, I guess. Nice to hear they got married, though.'

'It was sort of inevitable, I think. They make a good team.' She reaches out for her glass, resting it on her knee. I notice her hand shakes. 'They're both good, anyway. They married in Vegas last December. The honeymoon baby is due any day.'

'Marriage and a honeymoon baby. Not bad for a one-night stand.' I smile, remembering the night Rachel and I left them in the club.

How much I didn't want to be there. How drunk Rachel was. 'God, that was a horrendous night. The very last place I wanted to be.' I rub my eyes. 'That's the night I walked you home, wasn't it? You dragged me to the kebab shop on the way home, do you remember?'

Her fixed smile falters. 'I do.'

It seems odd to be sat here with her now. She was overfamiliar on that night. I remember being so ill at ease with her proximity. My hand tingles with the memory of her writing her number on my hand. How did we end up, four years down the line, sitting in awkward silence, neither one sure where to take the conversation next? I wish the bar was a bit fuller, or the music was a bit louder. Maybe I wish I wasn't here. But I am. And she is. So…

'How've you been?' we both start.

'Go on, you first.' I immediately wish I hadn't said that as I don't really want to answer the question. Politeness being my Achilles heel.

'How've you been?' she ventures, tentatively, nervously, tapping a nail on her glass.

I try to decide how I've been. Because, until now, I haven't been asked this by somebody who knew me four years ago, someone who knows the detail of what went on. 'I don't know, Rachel. How can I answer that? I've been okay, sometimes. Terrible at others. I've been trying my best. I've been pushing on when it was the last thing I wanted to do. I've been lucky to have Oli, and lucky to have found somewhere new to live. Somewhere that connects me to Ellie's memory because of all the time she spent here before we met. But it's somewhere that doesn't have her breath in the walls, you know? I've been' – I shrug – 'okay,' I repeat. 'You?' She drops her eyes; her hair falls across her face as she takes a deep breath. 'How've you been since I last…' I stop myself, not wanting to revisit that time.

She laughs to herself. 'Well, I *was* shit. I got a bit better. I went to uni and sorted my life out. I…' She fixes her eyes on me. 'You know what, we can small talk this all we want, but we both know the elephant standing in that corner right there. I'm okay, but I have not, and probably never will, forgive myself for doing what I did.'

Well, I've got to give her some credit, she isn't shying away from the difficult conversation.

'Look, Ed. I don't know how you want this to go, or what you think I can tell you that will ever make what happened okay.'

'There isn't anything,' I say.

'I know. Exactly. And I don't sit here thinking there is. Or that we can be friends. Or that in time everything will be okay. I understand that moment has long passed, but…' She swallows, dropping her eyes to her knees for a second before fixing me with a look that says I have to believe her. 'I don't think anything has changed, in terms of what I think happened, since I wrote that letter. I was in a weird place. I had no idea that was the case, it's only looking back now that I can fully see it. And there's no excuse. Simple as that. I can only apologise.'

Our eyes meet.

'I am truly, totally and overwhelmingly sorry. I will always be sorry. University didn't see me invent the time-travel car in which I could go back and fix it all.' She relaxes visibly, just a little. 'Four years and all I got was a certificate and a job on your doorstep. That wasn't in the plan.'

She twists her glass on the table and I wish I'd never suggested we meet up. She looks down at her shoes and a sadness outwardly takes over; it swims around her like cartoon smoke that might magic her away any moment. It's a sadness that, as I sit here, seeps into me too. Into my heart. Because, actually, there *was* a moment, back then, when I thought maybe we might have been friends. At a time when others around me said all the wrong things, she knew the right things to say. She knew loss, she still does; perhaps that is why it hurt so much and I just hadn't realised it before.

'You let me down, Rachel,' I whisper.

Despite the late-summer evening turning to dusk, and the inside of the pub seeming hazy, I see Rachel's eyes fill. Kirsty MacColl sings out on the jukebox. I feel like shit.

'I know I did,' she answers. 'I know.'

The woman whose arms I've openly cried in is sitting before me, hands clasping her drink, refusing to give in to the emotion I can see that she feels. The woman who was there for Oli when I needed her to be. The woman I called upon to help me when I confronted Simon. And I realise that not only did she let me down by looking in Ellie's box, but she let me down by doing something that made me lose faith in her. In an outsider. The only person at the time who might have had an impartial opinion. Who wasn't coloured by family history. Someone who I hadn't realised was important on some scale or other because I was too busy grieving to notice her quietly, carefully, being there. And maybe now, with the benefit of time and distance, I can see that. Does that make me feel differently? Does that quash any anger?

'He comes out soon,' I say carefully.

'Simon?'

I nod.

She stares into her glass. 'Have you seen him?' I shake my head. 'Lisa?' I flick my eyes up to her. 'Have you seen her?'

'Not since the court hearing. Not since I saw you.' It's my turn to stare vacantly at my drink for a moment. 'I tried to see Simon, but he wouldn't have it. He rejected my visitation request, he ignored my letters, so I had to leave it.'

'Why wouldn't he see you?' she asks.

'Guilt?' I say. 'Trying to hide something?' I add. 'Shame?'

Rachel runs a finger around the base of her glass. She looks sad and tired and older. 'Do you think...' She stops herself briefly, before just coming right out with it. Again. 'Did you ever do the test?'

'No!'

She stares at me.

'Why would I? What good could it have done?' I lean back in the chair, studying her face, wondering why she asks. 'Simon had gone to prison. Even if Oli wasn't my son, he was still Ellie's.' I sigh. 'He *is* Ellie's. He *is* mine. I *feel* it.'

Our eye contact is broken by Rachel's phone ringing out again. 'Sorry, it's Mo. Again. I'll call her in a bit.' She drains her glass. 'I need another, you?' she asks. I offer up my almost full glass by way of answer.

By the time she comes back, I realise there's only one question I've ever wanted to ask her. Only one question that could ever make a difference to any of this. To us. Not that there needs to be an 'us', but if she's going to teach my son for the next year I need to be able to look at her without my thoughts flashing back to my bedroom, the DNA test in my hand, her face when she realised what she'd said. What she'd done.

'Would you have told me?'

She pauses before sitting back down. 'I think so. Eventually. Maybe.'

'Maybe?'

'It's complicated.'

'What's complicated about it?'

'Look.' She sits up in her seat. Her eyes fleetingly meet mine, then dart away again. 'I could explain, but it doesn't change things. I'd like to think I would have told you but honestly, when I think about it, I don't know. I don't know if I would have wanted to be the person to rock you that way. You know? To hurt you. Your opinion of me... it mattered.'

'My opinion!'

'Yes. Okay. It mattered. It was stupid. To be honest, I didn't even realise until Mo pointed it out.'

'Pointed what out?'

She lets out a massive sigh. 'You know what, nothing. It's not relevant. I hope I would have told you, but I can't promise that I would have. If that's what you want me to do? I can't promise it. Now, excuse me a minute, I need the ladies'.' She knocks her drink back, then disappears into the back of the pub.

Chapter Fifty

Rachel

'Fucking hell,' I say, then apologise to the girl coming out of the toilet. 'Not you – sorry.' *Oh God.*

I kick the bathroom wall, annoyed at being such an idiot. *It's fine. It's all fine.* 'It's all fine,' I tell my reflection, splashing my face with ice-cold water from the tap. 'Rachel,' I say to my reflection, reapplying some make-up, putting the mask back on. 'You have to teach the man's son. Don't play with fire. Move on or... *move on.*' I stare at myself, my chest heavy with the rise and fall of breathlessness. My eyes sting. My heart pounds. There's a fuzzy edge to my mind, the wine beginning to filter through my bloodstream. Perhaps it's time I left.

But when I get back, he's bought me another drink. 'I don't know if you wanted it, but there you go.'

I look down at the glass, full and waiting. He sits, back resting against the sofa, staring at the sofa where I'd been sat. I don't know what else he wants from me. I'm not sure what more I can say. My phone rings out again, Mo's number flashing up. 'That's the third time,' he says.

'Mo?' Heavy breath comes down the phone line. 'Mo! Are you okay?'

She breathes in and out three more times before saying, 'No. My waters have broken and Greg is currently stuck on the A1 somewhere near Edinburgh.'

'Shit!'

'Yes. And also bollocks.'

'Okay, don't panic.'

'I'm not… well, I'm trying not to. Oh fuck it, I am! I am panicking. What happens if he doesn't get here, Rach? What happens if I have to give birth alone. On the bathroom floor. With only an Egyptian cotton towel and some Dettol.' I want to laugh, but can sense she's being dramatic to hide the fear. 'How would I even cut the cord?'

'Chip away with your tweezers?'

'They're gold-plated, Rachel!'

'Okay. Come on then, you need to get to the hospital.'

'How! Have you ever had a contraction, Rachel? They may only be every seven or eight minutes, but dear God they smart.' She starts heavy-breathing again.

'Mo, that's not seven or eight minutes.'

'I know. They do keep getting a bit closer.'

'Right, you need to call an ambulance, or a taxi. Or a neighbour.' I look at my watch, then the empty glasses of wine that prevent me from getting in my car to be by her side. 'You going to Queen's?'

Ed puts his drink down, moving to the edge of the sofa. 'Everything okay?' he mouths. I shake my head.

'Yes, Queen's. Rach, I need you.'

'I know, chuck, I'm coming. Cross your legs for at least an hour, okay?' I get up, looking around. 'Can you call me a taxi?' I shout over to the bar.

Ed jumps up. 'Come on, my car's outside.'

'It's fine, really. I'll get a cab.' Mo lets out a heavy breath and a swear. 'I'm on my way, Mo. Okay?'

'That'll cost a fortune and you have to wait until it arrives. Come on, I'll take you,' Ed says.

Not really having much alternative, with Mo crying down the phone about being on her own and frightened and annoyed with Greg because she told him he shouldn't be so far away when she was so close to her due date, I relent, following Ed out to the car. I put the phone on speaker, resting it on my knee, as I buckle up. 'Right, I'm on my way, Mo. Ed's bringing me.'

'Ed?' she asks. 'Ed... Ed...?'

'Yeah.' I fumble with a twist in the strap that stops me pulling it across my body, then struggle to snap it in place.

'As in the man you have just spent the last four years trying to get over... Ed?' The seat belt snaps in and I rush to try to take her off speaker, but the belt tightening and a sudden lurch forward means I knock my phone into the footwell. 'Rach, what are you doing...' She pauses to breathe as I fumble to release the seat belt so that I can rescue my phone, which is as far away from reach in the footwell as any phone can be, especially when you don't want a conversation to be overheard. 'Rachel, teaching the child of a man you were in love with is one thing – fucking hell this hurts – but going out with him?' She stops and breathes through her pain and I wish I could do the same as I feel Ed staring at me, his elbow touching mine, so small is his car.

I finally manage to take Mo off speaker phone. 'Mo, call an ambulance,' I say flatly. 'I'll be there as soon as I can. Okay?' I hang up, turning to face him. 'I can get a taxi,' I say. But he shakes his head, and backs out of the car park in silence.

Chapter Fifty-One

Ed

A man she was in love with? Is that what Mo said? *It's one thing to teach the child of a man she was in love with…*

Is that what Rachel meant when she said it was complicated?

Is Mo right…? She's in labour; Ellie spouted all sorts of nonsense in the depths of labour and childbirth. It's probably nonsense.

Except that Rachel is staring out of the window, arms folded, silent. Distant. Wiping a tear away.

'You don't have to do this you know,' she says, pulling a tissue out of her bag. 'I can still get a cab.'

'It's fine. She obviously needs you.'

'She needs something,' Rachel answers. She flips through her phone, opening and closing apps, scrolling through Facebook, Twitter, Instagram. She switches it off, tapping it on her hand, her knee, staring out of the window as we drive the flat roads through Lincolnshire. She sighs, shifts in her seat, she groans. 'Look—' she begins.

'Don't… you don't have to—'

'I know, and… well, I just… it was a long time ago. I was a different person, I didn't even… It's not like I knew. It was Mo who pointed it out and it was too late by then and I think saying I loved you was an overstatement, anyway. I just maybe felt sorry for you, or empathised or... I don't know. Look' – she groans into her hands – 'okay, I think I probably did have feelings, but not any more, okay? So don't panic.'

I pin my eyes on the road ahead.

'And I don't for a second expect you to feel positive about any of this so I'll move schools. Leave Oli where he is. I'll go. This is all too close for comfort and though it didn't mean anything – *doesn't* mean anything – let's face it, it's just a bit awkward, so it's fine. Just drop me in Nottingham. Thanks for the lift, I appreciate it – Mo will appreciate it – but leave me there. I'll sort everything else out. You don't have to see me again.'

She pulls her bag into her stomach, staring out of the side window again.

'Rachel—'

'Don't.' She holds her hand up. 'Please. This is awful enough as it is.' She rests her elbow on the side of the door, wiping her eyes in such a way that I think she thinks I don't notice. She chews on her cheek, her finger, her top lip. She leans her head back into the chair, hugging her handbag like her life, this journey, depends on it. I feel bad for her.

We travel for an hour in silence, neither knowing what to say. Maybe neither wanting to say anything. But her demeanour changes as we take the ring road down to the hospital. Pulling into the car park, she turns to face me, not quite looking, but not avoiding eye contact either.

'You know,' she begins, quietly, uncertainly, 'I don't know what it's like when you lose a partner, I can't imagine it.'

I wish that I couldn't.

'But, I've realised... maybe in the last few years, I don't know, maybe in the last few minutes... I've realised that losing a parent skews your view of love. Of life, maybe. You probably can't ever imagine loving again... a partner, I mean. The idea must be too painful. I don't know.'

A barrier up ahead bounces in its holder each time it drops closed after a car passes through.

'I think. It skews your view of love. Of life, maybe. Love becomes everything we need. It's as though we seek it out, that depth of feeling, that need. That emotional black spot needs filling. When Mum died, it was Mo. She got me through that time. I loved Mo so much, I still do... despite this, now... I mean, right now I could throttle her and her unborn child. But then... it was like her friendship was the only thing to keep me breathing. And maybe it's the same with work, with the kids at nursery and now at school... you want to be needed, to be loved almost. You need to fill your heart with things that mean something... a love, of sorts. I don't know. I'm rambling. I guess... I just think... maybe I *thought* I had feelings because we shared loss. Maybe I did have feelings, *because* we shared loss. Whatever it was, it was no excuse for my behaviour and I don't expect you to forgive me. I'd hoped we might be able to find a way to work things out, but perhaps that was naive, or maybe now it's untenable. But don't worry, I don't expect anything from you. Just know that I am sorry. For everything. Truly.' Her eyes fill up again, but she blinks the tears away. 'Thanks for the lift, I appreciate it. I'll talk to the school, I'll make it right.'

And as she walks away, I realise that she already has.

She didn't need time travel after all.

Chapter Fifty-Two

Rachel

I've just spent the last ten minutes breathless sobbing in the bathroom. The kind of crying I haven't done in years. The kind of crying that makes one of the cleaners push their trolley up to the door, tap gently and ask if you are okay. The kind of crying that makes you hiccup a 'yes' like you really think you can pass it off as the truth. And now I'm making my way to the delivery suite, desperately trying to put my emotions in a box so that I can adopt the role of birth partner... should Greg not make it back in time.

'This way,' summons a nurse, when I explain who I am. 'She's getting pretty close. In here.'

I follow the nurse into a room empty of other people except for Mo, who crumbles into a snotty mess at the sight of me. 'Oh my God,' she wheezes. 'You're here, you're here!' She's leant over the bed, waving her arse from side to side. She grabs hold of my hand, growling into it, and I resist the urge to ask her to go steady as her nails dig into the fleshy part of my thumb. 'Greg's going to miss this,' she says. 'The fucking idiot.' Not so close to delivery that she's lost her ability to be cross, then. 'I told him, I told him not to go today. I just knew.'

'But you've still got a week left,' I say, rubbing her back. 'Don't they say first babies are always late?'

'Of course they do, but since when have you known me to do things the way everyone else does? And please stop rubbing my back,' she growls. A nurse crouches beneath her, her arm lost up the blue of the hospital gown that barely covers Mo's modesty. If there's any left.

'Wow, childbirth is dignified,' I say, averting my eyes.

'Funny, when your contractions hammer through your womb every ninety seconds, dignity is the last thing on your…' But she can't finish her sentence; another wave of pain consumes her, taking her inside of herself and, without warning, her growl turns into some kind of grunt.

'That's it, love. That's it,' says the nurse, now positioned on the floor beneath Mo. 'Baby's on its way,' she says to me, briefly lifting her head from beneath the gown before going back to focus on the task in hand. Mo crouches and grunts and pushes, pulling on the bed, squeezing my hand. I'm so wrapped up in the moment, the ferocity of it, the grit, that I lose all sense of self-control, my head next to hers. I tell her that she's amazing, that I love her, that I can't believe she is doing this and how proud I am of her until, finally, with one final grunt, bend and downward push, the nurse declares, 'That's the head!'

And I think, *The head! Is that all we've got after all of that?*

After a moment to breathe, a moment in which I can't bring myself to look anywhere other than at Mo's face, eyes closed, cheeks pink with effort, the nurse says, 'Okay, one more push.' And Mo pushes, she pushes and breathes, she judders and, in a final flinch, my best friend in the whole wide world becomes a mother as a tiny, purple, bloody, creamy baby is placed into her arms and she collapses, exhausted, onto the side of the bed. 'Welcome to the world, little girl,' says the nurse, rubbing at her chest and face to clear it of childbirth goo.

Mo looks down at this tiny person wriggling on her bare chest, then up to me. 'I fucking did it!' she says, through tears and exhaustion, her baby letting out a cry. 'Look! Look, Rach! I fucking did it!' she says again, gazing down, completely and totally in love. The nurse guides her onto the bed, but Mo doesn't take her eyes off the baby for a single second. And I don't take mine off Mo, aware that I'll never again witness anything so beautiful, significant and so terrifying in equal measure.

'You bloody well did,' I sob. Moving to her side, taking the baby's tiny, curled up fingers into mine. 'And look Mo, she's so beautiful. She is so….' But I can't finish what I was going to say, because I realise that I am looking at the face of the most incredible, precious gift anyone can have, and I love her. With all of my broken, stupid heart, I love her.

'Say hi to your godmother, baby Elizabeth.'

And that's when I lose it all together, looking up at Mo, whose eyes are also brimming. 'Mum's name,' I just about utter, and Mo nods. 'It's perfect,' I say. 'She's perfect.'

The nurse dials Greg's number for Mo to tell him the news. I'm invited to make her some tea and toast while they tend to Mo's nethers… something, no matter how close we may be, I really don't need to witness. It's several hours until Greg finally arrives. Mo has drifted off to sleep, Elizabeth too, so I leave him to get acquainted with his new family.

Heading out into the dawn, an early-morning, heatless sun makes Nottingham glisten around me. I walk up to the top road, birds beginning to wake, looking for a bus or tram to get me over to Dad's. I call work, leaving a message to tell them I'm sick for now. Then I text Dad so he gets it as soon as he wakes. I'll crash at his place. Some Dad chat will help. Decisions about my future need not to be made after a night of acute embarrassment and childbirth. I need time.

Chapter Fifty-Three

Ed

Seeking her out through a crowd of parents is tricky when children queue up at the door, completely obscuring my view. Did she make it home last night? Is Mo okay? Is Rachel okay? How does she feel about everything she said?

When the bell goes, a teacher I don't recognise welcomes the children in. I strain to see past her. If I could just check Rachel's face, I'd know either way. It's weird; on the drive home I thought about what she said, what Mo said. I tried to imagine how I'd feel if that happened to me; embarrassed, tormented even. But I also tried to imagine what I'd do if I had feelings for someone and thought that one action might help. Would *I* do it? And, though I couldn't say that I would, if I was being honest with myself, perhaps, I couldn't say that I wouldn't.

Which makes me realise that it's easy for me to be angry when, in fact, the whole situation is more complex than that. *We* are all more complex than that. Whichever way I look at it, maybe Rachel was doing the best she could at that time. What is it people say? You never know what inner battles people fight. She knew she'd made a mistake, she knows it now. She didn't shy away from it; that's something, isn't it?

'Good morning, in you come.' The teacher stands by the door, a wide, welcoming smile for all the children. 'There's no Miss Fletcher this morning, I'm afraid, but I'm very excited to be having the day with you. I've heard all about what you've been learning and… Yes…? Just over there,' she instructs a child who is full of questions.

'Is… er… is Miss Fletcher okay?' I ask when Oli and I make it to the front.

'I don't know. She called in sick today. I'm sure it's nothing to worry about, though.' She smiles. 'In you come, children, on the carpet, please… Lovely.'

Oli stands by my feet, waiting for a kiss goodbye. 'Did she say what was wrong? Or when she'd be back?'

The teacher looks at me as if there's a line and I'm midway through crossing it.

Oli tugs at my coat. 'Sorry, ignore me. Hope she's okay. Right. Sorry, Oli. Bye, have a good day, love you.' He waves as I leave.

I jog when I'm out of sight, mixed emotions surprising me. Is that what Rachel meant when she said she'd sort it? That she was going to leave? If she does, maybe that is better for us all. Maybe it would just be too awkward for her to carry on. But it seems unfair. On Rachel, on Oli. On me? I don't know. How easy is it for a newly qualified teacher to get a new job? I don't want to be responsible for her being out of work. It doesn't have to come to this.

And why does her potentially leaving matter anyway?

I climb into my car, pulling out my phone. Maybe I should message Greg. It's been a while, but he wouldn't mind passing a message on, would he? Or maybe Rachel and I should talk some more… What is there to be said, though? She seemed pretty done to me.

Greg's profile comes up first when I open Facebook: a photo of Mo and the new arrival. Baby Elizabeth with my amazing wife. I hope she forgives me, one day.

What time did he make it, I wonder? Either way, the look on Mo's face suggests she has forgiven him, or that him being late, or perhaps not even there, for the arrival of their baby is small fry now that she's arrived.

Staring at the photo attracts a cloud, a sadness. Those feelings of being a new parent, the love you feel for the woman who made you a father; for all she achieved, all she went through. How incredible and strong and beautiful a woman is when she becomes a mother: how fierce and fearless. At least, that was Ellie. I could barely hold myself together when she had Oli. I was a mess, crumbling to see her in pain, fainting at the sights, then in absolute bits when he arrived, squawking, onto her chest. This fidgety, scrawny, bird-like baby who, in that very second, I would have moved mountains for. Who I'd still move mountains for. Who teaches me about love and patience and forgiveness every day.

Love. Patience. Forgiveness.

I tap out a message to Greg:

Just seen the news, congratulations, mate. I'm thrilled for you both. Take care of yourselves and each other. I know you'll be busy, but if you could, can you pass on my number to Rachel? I could do with talking to her. Thanks. Let's catch up soon, wet that baby's head.

I throw my phone onto the passenger seat, a sense of worry, or disappointment maybe, weighing down on the gloom, the black that threatens to consume me. A message comes back pretty quickly:

Thanks, mate. Fuck, this is mental. I can't believe how I feel about them both. They're resting before I take them home after the doctor's been round. Can't believe I'm a dad! Will pass on the message to Rachel now. She was bloody amazing, stayed with Mo the whole way through. I can't believe I wasn't here… What a crap start to fatherhood. Guess I'll be making up for it for a while! See you soon, be good to catch up.

How did Rachel feel, watching her best friend give birth? Does she think about having children? How was she in a crisis? I'd imagine cool, calm. Focused. I pull away, turning the volume up on the radio, then down slightly, in case Rachel calls. I just want her to know she doesn't have to leave. It feels important.

When I get home, an unfamiliar car is on the drive. My first thought is it's hers, but it's obvious pretty quickly that it isn't. Turning around and pretending I haven't seen him is an appealing option, but as he climbs out of the car I find myself emotionally armouring up, climbing slowly out of mine, coming face to face with my brother.

'Ed.' A cleaner, healthier-looking version of the man I last saw comatose in his bedroom stands before me. 'I…' His voice falters, he coughs, clears his throat and tries again. 'I called, last night, there was no answer.'

'I was out.'

'Well, I wanted to let you know I'd be here today.'

'Let me know?' I say. 'Not ask?'

'No,' he answers. 'This is important.'

We're face to face. There's no trace of alcohol on his breath. No vacant glassiness in his eyes. He's nervous, I can feel that. I could always tell his mood, from us being kids. But unlike times gone by, he doesn't fidget or move to get away.

I glare at him a second before leaving the front door open for him to follow me into the house. In the kitchen, I flip the kettle on, sort out paperwork from the side, clear breakfast pots away. I'm waiting for him to take control of the situation he wanted to have. Eventually, I turn to face him, arms folded, teeth clenched. 'Well?'

'I want to talk to you. I want to explain.' *Two people in two days. Lucky me.* 'There's no easy way to talk about this.'

A photo of Ellie hangs on the wall behind him and feelings long buried come flooding back without warning, punching me in my chest. The questions, the uncertainty, the fear. Stuff I've hidden for the last four years because that was the only way to survive. The reason I stopped looking at the photos, now hung for Oli more than me. 'You're ready now, then, are you?' I can't hide the contempt I feel. The anger that now he wants to, he thinks he can just walk in and have his say. What happened when I needed to talk to him? Why should I bend over and take it on his terms?

'What if I'm not? What if I don't want to hear it? What if I never want to hear it?' I hiss.

'I wouldn't blame you. I couldn't. But I think we both deserve closure.'

'You don't deserve anything!' I step towards him, taking some satisfaction in the fact he tries, yet fails, to hide an urge to move back this time. 'You had my newborn son in your car; you had my wife. And yet, whatever was going on in your own life, with your own wife, was more important than their safety. You drove like an idiot, and now Ellie's dead. Because of you.' Anger spits in my belly, everything forcing its way to now. 'And I wanted answers, Simon. Okay, so not straight away. I couldn't talk to you at first, I was too angry, I was grieving, and I don't blame myself for keeping my distance to begin with. Yet you had no respect for that. You couldn't wait until I was ready, so instead you just sent a text message. A text message, Simon! To say sorry. Like you'd accidentally broken something, or lost something. "Sorry I killed your wife. Oopsie! LOL." I stare at him, my breath heavy. 'And that was enough to make me want to talk to you. To try to understand what the hell was going on in your mind. To get to the bottom of why you thought the message was okay. To get to the bottom of the stories Lisa was giving me about why Ellie was in your car in the first place. I needed to talk to you and you were nowhere to be found.' I take another step towards him but he still doesn't move. 'You know something? When I read the report, when I heard what the investigation said, I wanted to hurt you. I wanted to make you feel just one tenth of the pain I was feeling. I wanted to pull it off me, de-cloak, and lie it firmly on you. Smother you in it, offload, share, suffocate you; anything to get rid of it.'

'I don't blame you.'

'You don't!' I laugh angrily. 'That's big of you. Congratu-fucking-lations, forgiveness must be a beautiful thing.' I twist away, my hands clasped behind my head in a desperate attempt to keep hold of myself. The words 'love, patience and forgiveness' return, but they're less palatable in this instance, further from grasp.

Resting against the worktop, I hold myself in. 'So, why now? Why do you want to talk about it all now? How is it that I'm doing this on your terms, again?'

'I've served my time, Ed. I've had the space to reflect. Time to get help. I was drinking, I was hurting. I couldn't think straight. It's not an excuse, Ed, but it is a reason. And why now? Because you have a right to know. Because I owe you. Because I want the opportunity to stand in front of you and tell you how sorry I am. How totally, truly, sorry I am. How I have had to learn a way to forgive myself for what I did, but I don't expect you to.'

'You know, I didn't believe it to begin with. I refused. I didn't feel that she would have ever done anything to hurt me. To hurt Oli. But Lisa planted these seeds, you know. Seeds of doubt that grew; they wove their way around my heart until doubt constricted me. I'd find myself staring at the sky, desperately asking for a sign, anything! Anything to let me know that I could still trust Ellie, that our love was real, that our marriage was built on the foundations I believed in.' My voice rises, volume an alternative to physical violence. 'Do you know how hard that is? Hmm? Do you? To be grieving, to find it impossible to function some days? Only getting out of bed because I had to? Because of Oli? And then' – Simon goes to speak, but I hold my hand up – 'I'm not done… And then, to have your own son dragged into it. To question who he is, to not know if he even is your son… *my* son.'

'I don—'

'I almost don't want to know now. I almost don't want to hear what you've got to say, because I've found a way to live and surely that's all that matters now? Because the day I came home to pack up our house, finding more evidence that he might not be mine, was the day I realised I couldn't think about any of it any more. You were out of the picture, Oli needed a father. What choice did I have?'

'Ed—'

'And then, when I tried to visit you, when I tried one last time to get the truth, something I had every right to hear, you rejected my request for a visit. It could only be the last act of a guilty man, couldn't it?'

'I was ashamed,' he answers quietly.

'Yeah?' I step forward, my knuckles twitching and itching. My hands are aching from holding them tight shut. I reach on top of the fridge; a wicker basket contains Ellie's memory box. I blow the dust off, lifting the lid to reveal the DNA test on top of all the papers. I throw it across the room at him; it hits him in the chest, then tumbles to the ground. 'Ashamed, were you? Well, you fucking want to be, because if you did this, if the thing you had to tell us was this—'

'What do you mean?'

'Ellie's voicemail. On your phone. I heard it the night I came to see you.' I step closer to him again. 'She said you had to tell us. That it was going to be hard, but it was necessary.' We stand, nose to nose. 'If you and my wife were having an affair, I'll fucking kill you.'

'Of course we weren't!' Simon's heavy breath is hot on my face. 'Ed! Of course we weren't.' I stumble back into a chair. 'I can't believe you'd think that. Is that what you've thought all this time?' I stare at him. 'And you thought Oli…'

My strength is evaporating. 'Ellie had a test, I found it. A DNA test.'

'I know, she told me.' I narrow my eyes, waiting for the explanation. 'Lisa sent it. Ellie was opening it one day when you came in. She said she hadn't known what to say that wouldn't make you start asking questions. I think she shoved it in her wardrobe out of sight so that she could dispose of it somewhere you wouldn't find it.'

'Why would Lisa send it?'

Simon pulls up a chair in front of me. 'I saw quite a lot of Ellie in those last few months of her pregnancy.' I shift, uncomfortable, not sure if I can listen to him. Not sure if I trust him. He takes a moment; the room falls silent except for the quiet tick of the kitchen clock. '*I hate that clock*,' I hear Ellie say, and realise it's the first time in a long time that I've heard her.

Eventually, Simon starts again. More controlled this time, as though he's detached himself from the words. 'I don't know if you remember the baby shower Ellie's friends threw for her?'

'They went for a meal at Hart's.'

'Yes. Well… Ellie saw me there with a colleague.' I narrow my eyes, trying to see where this is going before he gets there. Searching for the sense that this is true. 'I met someone at work… we weren't having an affair,' he says quickly. 'We'd just spent time together, on a course, realised we had things in common. I liked talking to her – Sally – she was kind. She made me laugh. She didn't make me feel like I was a piece of shit. She didn't belittle me, she didn't chide and rile me. She didn't try to get a rise out of me every time she opened her mouth.'

'As opposed to Lisa?' I say, not really in need of clarification. If I look back, I can probably see the slow dismantling of his confidence.

'Exactly. And the more we talked, the more I wanted to find a way to be with her, but I didn't have the strength or the confidence, maybe. I didn't even know if Sally liked me that way, but when Ellie saw us she joined up the dots.'

'She was smart.'

'She was trying to get me to leave Lisa, not necessarily to get together with Sally, just to leave an unhappy marriage. She told me that she wouldn't tell you, or Lisa, about what she'd seen, because she knew that Lisa would use it against me, but that she didn't like to lie. She told me that she needed me to find the strength to be happy. To end things with Lisa. But it started getting complicated. I tried to leave and Lisa kicked off. She started making accusations about me. She saw messages from Ellie on my phone and put two and two together and came up with three. She used it against me. I don't know if she ever really believed it or just found it a useful tool to hurt me even more.'

'I still don't understand why Ellie was with you that day.'

'She told me she was going to talk to you. That she couldn't deal with the pressure any more. The stress of it – Lisa was being vile to both of us. Ellie had just had Oli; she was exhausted and didn't want the distraction. I panicked, I didn't want her to tell you because I knew you'd kick off about Ellie being caught up in it all, especially given Oli. And I just… I needed more time, I was upset. I'd told Sally that I was definitely going to leave Lisa and asked her if she thought we had a future together. But she told me she wasn't sure. That she didn't want me to leave Lisa for her.'

'Rather do it for yourself?'

'I guess so, but I didn't understand that at the time. I felt stuck, I felt weak, I felt totally lost and useless. I didn't… Ed… I didn't…' But he can't finish the sentence because my little brother, the one I should be there for, the one I should protect, the one I see now that I should never have judged this way, has just lost it right in front of me. And the pain I can hear, coming from his boots, it's too much. It's too much. I lean over to him, resting my arms across his back, holding him until he has enough strength to catch his breath. Because it's clear to me now that this was the most awful, accidental, terrible thing to have happened and despite all that I've believed for the last four years, my brother wasn't to blame.

It's also clear, in the most painful way possible, that I have spent the last four years questioning the one person who, deep down, I knew wouldn't do that to me and yet I was dogged by doubt. I was wrapped up in the possibility of something I couldn't prove or disprove and I let that take over my life. I let it twist my memories. I lost faith in the one person who would never have lost faith in me. *I'm so sorry, Ellie. I'm so sorry…*

Chapter Fifty-Four

Rachel

Greg messaged me hours ago. I keep pulling my phone out and checking what it says, seeing if there are lines for me to read between. I've dialled Ed's number several times but never got as far as pressing 'call'. I've tapped out messages, imagined conversations. And now, at teatime, I'm still no clearer on what to do.

I told Dad about it all. Reminded him what I did. He pulled me in for a hug and said that everything happens for a reason. That maybe our story wasn't over. I wasn't aware Ed and I had a story, and if we do, I don't know if I want to read until the end.

Mo's messaged me. A photo of Elizabeth and a love heart. I'm so happy for her, I really am. Which makes it harder to understand why my heart hurts whenever I think about the fact my best friend is now a mother. I've had time to prepare, I knew this was coming. But perhaps now, having seen the beauty of it for myself, I'd be kidding myself to think I don't want that too. Thirty-one, the age Mum was when she died. I'm at the start of a new career and contemplating the need for a child of my own. Is it an age thing? Or a love thing... a mum thing, even? Or just a last-twenty-four-hours thing?

Dad said I shouldn't leave the school. And I don't really want to. I just want to do the right thing, by me, by Ed. If only I knew what the right thing was.

My phone lights up with a news alert; it draws my attention to it. Doing the right thing is harder when you're assuming you know what that is. But doing the right thing is important when you've made so many bad decisions. And he did ask me to call. I dial Ed's number.

'Hello?' His voice is weary.

'It's Rachel.'

'Rachel, hi.' He sighs down the phone.

'You asked me to call you, are you okay?'

'Honestly? I don't know. I've got no idea what I am at the moment, but, yes, I did ask you to call. I just…' He breaks off. 'Yes, Oli?' Oli's voice is muffled in the background, making it hard to work out what he's saying, not that I need to. 'Sorry, Rachel, I'm back. Look, I just wanted to say to you that I don't think you should resign. If that's what you were thinking. Anyway, you just said something about sorting it… And then you weren't there this morning, and it made me see that I don't want that. I don't want you to leave because of me, out of some sense of duty, or guilt or whatever.'

'Thanks,' I say, wishing he sounded more like he actually means what he says.

'That was it, really. I just… I had to say something. We can be grown-ups about it, I'm sure.'

'I appreciate that. Truly.'

'The truth is, none of it matters anyway. It changes nothing. We're all human. If there's anything I've learnt in recent years it's…' He trails off again.

'Ed, you don't sound okay.'

He groans. 'I'm not. Not really… Simon's out.'

'Oh.'

'He came round today; he told me everything.' I close my eyes, a picture of his face in my mind. 'It just hurts again, you know?'

'Can I do anything?'

'No… it's fine. I need to cuddle up on the sofa with my boy. I need to think about a way I can put things right with Ellie's memory. I need to…' I wish I could take his hand. 'I need time.'

'Of course.'

'Rachel?'

I hold my breath.

'Promise me you'll be at school tomorrow.'

Against every bone in my body, I make him the promise. I suppose I owe him that much.

Chapter Fifty-Five

Rachel

Mrs Clarke follows me through her classroom to mine. 'Good morning, are you feeling better?'

'Better than I was, yeah. Thanks.' I busy about with key words, the register, stuff to distract my brain from the sensation of butterflies in my stomach.

'Good. Here's your sheet for parent teacher meetings.' She hands over a piece of paper, with dates and times in boxes across it. 'The sooner you get them booked in the better. They can drag on otherwise. Some people just don't want to see us.'

'Already? They've only just started.'

'It just helps us get to know the parents a bit better, understand their view of the kids. Lets them know that we understand their children. It doesn't take long. Five minutes or so per parent, but I find the sessions work quite well.'

She smiles, then heads back to her own classroom, leaving me to stare at the paper before attaching it to the top window in the double door, along with a pen. My first ever parent teacher sessions. What am I supposed to say about them all? We barely know each other yet. And oh God, that means I will have to meet with Ed too. My stomach drops to my shoes, then through the floor when the bell goes and I notice Oli is now pressing his face up against the bottom window again. I resist mirroring him this time, opting to wave instead. He beams back at me.

'Come on then, everyone, in you come. Coats off. Whiteboards out, please.' The kids, for the most part now confident to come in on their own, kiss parents or carers, grandparents or family friends, before skipping through the wide-open door.

Ed watches Oli through the window, then moves to the door as everyone else begins to leave. 'Good to see you,' he says quietly.

'Thanks.' I half smile. 'You okay?'

He gives a shallow nod. 'I will be.' He smiles, his eyes meeting mine. 'I will be.'

'There's a form on the window, parent teacher meeting in a few weeks. It'd be good if you could put your name by a time,' I say, quickly back to business.

'You got a pen?' I nod over to the one that hangs from the form. 'Cool. I'll put my name down then.' He pauses, looking at the dates, looking down at his shoes, before scribbling his name on the last session on the last day. Great, so I have to build myself up to sitting in front of him in a one-to-one situation. That's just what I needed.

The kids wait for me on the carpet, each practising writing this week's words from the board. I weave through them to take up my position at the front of the class, by which time Ed has gone. Six hours before I have to see him again. Six hours to concentrate on the kids, on teaching. God, I hope this gets easier with time. I'm not sure if I can do this if it doesn't.

Chapter Fifty-Six

Ed

It's been three weeks since Simon came round. He's gone underground again. Out of sight. I think I'm happier that way. It's too painful to see him at the moment. I forgive him, I do, but, it's still too hard. Apparently Lisa's been sniffing around again. I just hope he can find it in himself to tell her where to go for good. Maybe I should reach out to him, let him know I am here if he needs me, despite it being the last thing I want to do.

I check my watch. I need to go for my parent teacher meeting with Rachel. Paper and scribbles are strewn about my desk. Doodles I've done under the guise of work. Deadlines loom yet the muse has gone. Creativity eludes me. It has for weeks now and it feels like there's unfinished business, but I don't know what it is. Or how to fix it. I suppose I could start with Simon; maybe that's part of it. I pull out my phone.

Hi, how are things? Hope you're managing okay. Call if you need anything. Stay strong.

Is that the wrong thing to say? 'Stay strong.' Does it imply I think he might not, and what even is strong? Perhaps I should just have said 'stay clear of Lisa'.

I sling a jacket on, briefly checking my hair on the way out of the door. Glynis is out in her garden, clipping at roses. She throws me a wave as she hurries across the road. 'Mr Moran, how are you? It's good to see you. Did you remember it's the village Autumn Fete this weekend? It would be lovely to see you and Oli.'

'Oh, thanks. Yeah, we might come.' She stares at me, two blousy late-summer roses in suede-gloved hands. Ellie's voice comes to mind. *'Eurgh, roses. They look beautiful, but they're thorny as hell. Not unlike some people, Ed.'*

'My granddaughter will be there, Olivia. She's probably going to be on her own so you'll have young company if you need it. She's a lovely girl, smart, funny. A little on the plump side, but still, she's a very pretty face.' I stare at Glynis, gobsmacked at the description and suspicious of what she's suggesting. 'She'll be staying for a few weeks, I think. She's got some work on in Sleaford. I don't really understand it, but I just thought... what with you being single—'

'Erm, right, yes. I've got to—'

'I'll tell her to pop over,' Glynis says, hobbling back over the road, waving the roses above her head.

'Well, I'm quite busy at the moment,' I shout after her. It's not clear if she doesn't hear me, or chooses to ignore me.

On the journey to school, I think up all the various excuses as to why we can't go to the fete. Maybe we could go away this weekend. By the time I get to class, the bell has gone and on seeing me, Oli comes running out. 'Are you seeing Miss Fletcher today?'

'In half an hour, yeah. Let's wander over to the shop. Get you a drink and a snack while we wait.' Oli gives me a squeeze then skips off ahead of me, occasionally looking back to make sure I'm still there. When we get to the shop, after he's taken ten minutes to choose between snacks, we wait in the queue to pay.

'What's that, Daddy?' he asks, pointing to a poster by the till.

'Oh, erm. It's…' I search for inspiration on what it might be, aware that the second he hears about a fete he's going to want to go, but we're at the back of a queue of locals and I can't really lie. 'It's the village fete.'

'Like the one we went to last year with the donkey rides and that little fairground. Can we go? Can we, can we, can we?' He jumps up and down in front of me, his hair bouncing across his eyes. Eyes just like his mother's.

'Maybe,' I say, not wishing to promise in case I can come up with a reason why not to go. I don't suppose telling him our neighbour appears to have a touch of the matchmaker about her would help.

Walking back to school, Oli relives every second of last year's fete visit, including the tombola in which we won a bottle of bubble bath that still sits on the side of our bath-free shower room.

'Goodness, you're excited,' says Rachel as Oli bounds back into class.

'We're going to a fete on Saturday, Daddy said.'

'Well, I said it was on…'

'You said we could go. I'm going to go on a donkey and eat candyfloss and there might be a bouncy castle.'

'Oh, yeah, apparently they're raising some funds for the school there too.'

'Come!' he says, and I wonder who is more inappropriate, Oli or Glynis.

'Oh, I… er, we'll see. I mean, I do love a bouncy castle but…' she says, colouring. 'Now, go on, little man, go over to the book corner and practise with your white board while I have a chat with your dad.' Oli hops on one leg to the corner of the classroom, sinking down behind a bookshelf. 'He's a joy!' she says, smiling sadly.

'He is.'

Rachel looks at the file on her knee, tapping her pen on it before she looks up at me, clearing her throat, tears in her eyes. 'He is doing great, really well. I'm really pleased with his progress and you've nothing to worry about,' she says.

'What's the matter?'

She lowers her voice so Oli won't hear. 'Ed, I wasn't going to do this now. It's all kinds of inappropriate, but I seem incapable of keeping myself in check. I keep trying to make this work, I do. But, it's no good. I can't do this. It's too hard.' She holds her hands tight, clasped, resting on the folder. She bites at the corner of her mouth, sitting upright. 'I thought it would get easier, after we talked. I thought it would be okay. But it seems it's not. I am angry with myself, I am confused. I spend each day counting the minutes until the day is over and I can go home and hide. I'm going to have to leave.'

'Hide from what?' I ask, pulling my chair in closer to her. She leans back, reinstating the distance we had until I moved. 'Rachel?'

'Look, this isn't a discussion for here. It's not really a discussion to be had at all. I just wanted you to know from me that I'll be handing my notice in at half term. I'll be leaving at Christmas. I'll find something else, and we can both put this all behind us.'

'Don't rush into anything, Rachel. Please. What if you regret—'

'What does regret mean?' asks Oli, who has tiptoed back, book in hand. 'Daddy, what does regret mean?' he asks.

'It means you feel sad, or unhappy about something.' Rachel gets up from her chair. 'About something you said, or did, or maybe didn't do and you wish you could change.'

'Oh, like that time I drew on one of your pictures and you told me off and I was really sorry.'

'Yeah, I suppose.' With her back to us both, Rachel wipes her eyes, before turning round to us.

'Some people don't think you should have regrets,' I say, fixing Rachel with a look so she knows this is one hundred per cent directed at her. 'They think you learn from the things you do, or wish you hadn't. That we are all made up of the choices we made in our lives; we're richer for them. We know more.'

'I don't really know what that means,' Oli says.

Rachel blinks. 'See you tomorrow, Oli,' she says, then picks up some files, slinging them into a bag as she quietly waits for us to leave.

Chapter Fifty-Seven

Ed

Oli and I traipse across the village green, his eyes fixed on the prize of freshly cooked doughnuts. The sweet smell reminds me of Skegness. '*Oooh, I love a doughnut.*'

'Cooee, Mr Moran,' sings a voice behind us and I wonder if it'd be rude to run. Glynis catches up with me, heavy breathing as she grabs my arm. 'Didn't you hear me calling you, goodness…' She takes a moment, rooting around in her handbag for a humbug, popping it in her mouth like it will replenish her lungs with all the air she's ever needed. 'There, that's better. Did you remember my Olivia was coming to stay? I just wanted to introduce you to her. Edward, Olivia. Olivia, Edward.'

A woman in her mid-twenties stands beside Glynis. She extends her hand with a look of deep-seated embarrassment. 'I tried to tell her you'd probably be busy with your boy.'

'Nonsense, Olivia, Ed's got time for everyone, haven't you, love?'

'Erm, sure. Of course.' The three of us stand awkwardly in a triangle. 'Doughnut?' I point to the van.

'Oh, look, there's Mr Sharpe from the butchers. You'll have to excuse me, I want to have words with him about his turkey crown.'

Glynis walks in Mr Sharpe's direction, swinging a handkerchief in the air to catch his eye.

'Oh my God, I am so sorry,' says Olivia, turning her back on her grandmother. 'I did tell her not to do this. She is obsessed with trying to matchmake whenever I come to see her.'

'Daddy, have you got that money. The doughnuts are ready.' Oli tugs on my jacket.

'Course, here you go.' I give him a pound coin and he skips off to join the queue. My heart fills with pride at his confidence.

When I turn back to Olivia, she's smiling in his direction too. 'Cute kid.'

'Thanks.'

'Never fancied them myself,' she says.

'No?'

'No. It's why me and my girlfriend split up. She was ready to settle down and have kids and I just don't see it in my future.'

'Your girlfriend?'

'Yup. I have told Gran. She even met Becks. I think she thinks if I got a boyfriend I'd realise I did want children after all. Doesn't want me to follow in her footsteps.' I look at her, confused. 'She's my step-gran. Married my mum's dad when I was a baby. Only ever had Michael, with her first husband who passed when she was young. Wanted more kids, a football team I shouldn't wonder, but remarried too late in the end.'

'Ahhh,' I say.

'So, you'll have to forgive me, I'm sure you'll be disappointed, but you're just not my type.' She winks.

Oli comes back, his face, fingers and mouth full of sugar and doughnuts, grinning. 'They gave me extra,' he declares. 'Donkeys?'

'Sure.' I laugh. 'You wanna?' I motion for Olivia to join us. She nods and follows on.

'So, how come you're single then?' She gets out a pack of tobacco, making herself a roll- up. 'Where's his mum?'

It's been a while since anyone asked me that outright. The reaction always makes me feel awkward. For the person asking the question, mainly, as you can see the desire for the world to swallow them whole flash across their face. 'She died. Almost five years ago now.'

'Shit, sorry! Fuck, that's… wow… Gran might've mentioned that one.'

'It's okay, don't worry. The mere mention of it no longer sends me into a fit of despair.' Lightening the mood never really seems to work. 'Yes, it's shit. But, we have to live on. She'd be furious if we didn't.'

'You've been on your own ever since then? With Oli.'

'Yeah, that's how we like it.'

'You must get lonely, though?'

'Of course. And I guess I do sometimes wonder what it might be like, to meet someone new.'

'Granddad always said losing his first wife was the hardest thing in the world, but meeting my gran was the easiest.' I look at her, not understanding. 'They'd been neighbours, friends, while it all happened. Gran knew what he'd been through. She understood. She never let him feel he couldn't still be in love with Mum's mum, despite them two getting together.'

'Right.'

'You watch, bets on you already know her.'

'Who?'

'Your second wife.'

I shake my head. 'Thinking about being alone is not the same as thinking about remarrying.'

'Sure, but how old are you? Early forties? Marriage or not, there's more happiness in your future. When you're ready to let it in.' She takes a drag on her newly lit cigarette, catching sight of something of interest across the field. 'Look, I've gotta go. I think I see happiness in my future too,' she says, sauntering in the direction of a bar, a pretty blonde, and an embrace that suggests the two of them know each other already.

'I'd like a new mummy one day,' says Oli, simply.

'Pardon?'

'What you two were just talking about. I'd like a mummy. And maybe a brother or a sister. Well, a brother. A sister could be boring. Though a brother might steal my toys. Which would be better, do you think?'

I stare at Oli, open-mouthed.

'Oh, look, Daddy! It's Miss Fletcher!' My heart lurches as he pushes past me, running over to Rachel, who's walking across the green, her cardigan pulled tightly around her waist. Her face briefly lights up when she sees him, then drops as she looks around to find me. He pulls upright in front of her, chattering, waving his arms around wildly.

When Rachel spots me, something in my belly flips. And something in Olivia's words seeps through. And I remember what Ellie said, that night we celebrated with friends. The house-warming in a house that seems like a lifetime ago. *'You'd be terrible without me, Ed.'* I'd tried to deny it, told her I would cope. When we cuddled in bed, alone, later that night, she lay her head on my bare chest. *'You don't have to cope, Ed. None of us do.'* She lifted her head, resting her chin on her hand, hand on my chest. She drew a heart on my heart then said, *'If anything ever happens to me, promise me you'll find someone to love.'* Rachel waves, shyly, and I wonder if I ever could. And if I did, is Olivia right? Do I already know her?

Chapter Fifty-Eight

Rachel

I'm not sure what changed in the last few months: it started out with friendship. The late September weekend when I collected a cheque at the fete, the donation for our school, was the start of things. Ed came over and told me he wanted us to be friends, that he didn't want me to leave, that I was important to him. I didn't know what I felt at the time, or how it would turn out. I had my letter of resignation penned out. I was planning to give it in two weeks later, when we broke up for half term. But I didn't, and then the weeks passed. And things got easier, almost comfortable; brief chats in the playground; we'd share a joke. It's been gentle, steady, but sort of definite. Certain. Certain of what, I haven't been sure, but certain of something.

'Oli is devastated, Floyd was his mum's cat. It really would mean a lot to him if you could be here,' he had said.

'Of course, of course I will.' I didn't hesitate.

'There's just one thing,' he'd added. 'I know this might seem a bit… odd, but…. it's fancy dress.'

'Pardon?'

'Fancy dress. Glitter-red shoes and sky-blue gingham.'

'Okay…' I answer slowly.

'I can't explain. It's a *Wizard of Oz* thing. Just… just go for it, okay?' he said, and something in his voice made me certain this wasn't a joke, which is why I'm standing here in my living room, at the beginning of December, dressed head to toe as Dorothy.

'You look amazing,' says Mo, who insisted I FaceTime her to show off my costume. She dangles plastic keys above Elizabeth, who follows them, gurgling and cooing at the toy.

'Oh, she is so adorable!' I say, watching as she fiddles with her hands before attempting to stuff an entire fist in her mouth. 'Wow, I see her mouth's as big as her mother's!'

'Funnily enough, that's what Greg said when it was his turn to get up in the night and didn't do it quickly enough!' Mo pulls faces at Elizabeth, who giggles at her happily. 'Ed's going to love that outfit, isn't he, baby,' she coos. 'Just think, Baby Bette, your aunty Rachel might be about to get a boyfriend.'

'Mo! That is not what is happening here,' I say, looking in the mirror, feeling faintly ridiculous. 'Oh God, what am I doing? I look stupid,' I say, picking at the pigtail wig that is itching my scalp.

'How have I never seen it before? You are a total ringer for Judy Garland! Isn't she, Greg?'

I hear him in the background. 'Rach? Judy Garland? The spit!' he agrees.

'A million per cent.' Mo nods furiously, disappearing briefly with Elizabeth, then picking the phone up.

'A million per cent is not a thing,' I correct her.

'Don't you get all teacher on me,' she says, wagging a finger at me. Greg takes Elizabeth from Mo's lap, moving her into a fat pink seat-type thing in the background.

'What the heck is that?' I ask, peering at the phone for a closer look.

'A game changer,' says Mo. 'If you ever decide to have a baby, make sure you buy a Bumbo. They love it, and your hands are free to pick up that cup of tea that would otherwise, undoubtedly, be stone cold.'

'Okay, then. Fair enough. Well, look, I'd better go. I don't want to be late.'

'Call me later, or tomorrow. Just call me, okay? I want to know every single thing.'

'Yup, okay. Love you.'

'There's no place like home!' she shouts as I hang up.

I take one last look in the mirror, scratch beneath my wig, pull down the gingham dress and wiggle my toes in too-tight ruby-red slippers. I've never been to a cat funeral before…

Chapter Fifty-Nine

Ed

Smoke from the garden incinerator weaves across the garden; I toss the letter I wrote to Ellie into the flames. A gentle breeze picks up the grey and wafts it straight into next door's washing. I should have mentioned something to them, but it's December; I didn't realise people still pegged stuff out at this time of year.

I set out the hot dogs and buns, get the ketchup out of the fridge and search for a rack to place over the flames to cook our food.

'Dad, look!' says Oli, who skids in dressed in green shorts, striped socks and a matching checked shirt. 'Have we got any face paint? Weren't their faces orange?' He digs around in his art box for something suitable. I admire his commitment to the cause, though relieve him of the orange felt-tip pen.

'You're thinking of Oompa Loompas. No orange face required. Careful now,' I say, as he climbs up on a bar stool. 'Don't fall.' I shift him to the back. His face drops. 'Hey, buddy. You okay?'

'I miss Floyd,' he says.

I take a deep breath. 'Me too, fella, me too. But, you know what? Maybe he's with Mummy now.' I pull him in for a cuddle and he nods into my chest. The photo I always kept in my pocket is Blutacked to the kitchen cupboard behind him. I look at her face; how alike they are. How proud she would have been of him. How proud would she have been of me? A shard of guilt splinters: *I'm not leaving you behind, just doing as you asked.*

But before I can let the moment take over, the doorbell goes and my stomach drops to my knees. I haven't really got a handle on my nerves yet today. It's been building since I asked her to come over. When I woke this morning, I wasn't sure if I was actually coming down with something. I'd held my phone in my hand, all ready to cancel, until Oli jumped on the bed asking if it was time for him to get ready yet.

He leaps off the side of the counter, his sadness evaporating. 'She's here, Dad, quick, put the music on! Where's Floyd?'

'In that box,' I say, nodding in the direction of the candy-striped memory box, just like all the ones that store Ellie's precious things.

I steady myself against the kitchen table, glimpsing a glisten of my costume in the microwave. It's probably too late to hide. Or change. This costume is ridiculous and, I now realise, very difficult to move about in. I hobble over to the iPod and press 'play' on the soundtrack: 'Ding-Dong! The Witch is Dead!' sings out into the garden from speakers stacked by the kitchen door. Rachel's voice filters through the lounge and finds its way to my bowels. Nerves kicking me in the gut. I busy myself around the kitchen to put off the inevitable moment of standing face to face for the first time since I decided how I felt, not really knowing if I'd left it too late.

'Wow!' she says from behind me. 'You look amazing!'

Dressed head to toe in gingham and glittery shoes, self-consciously pulling her skirt down, Rachel stands before me. In my kitchen. Here. And suddenly I'm grateful for the silver face paint. Not only does it make me look like the Tin Man, but it might also be hiding this shade of crimson I can feel myself turning at the sight of her.

She clumsily edges towards me, handing out a bottle of wine. 'Sorry,' she says. 'About Floyd. I know he was... special.' She blows away a bit of wig hair that has crept into the corner of her mouth. 'Not the best wig, I'm afraid,' she mumbles, scratching the back of her head, causing the wig to move about, lopsided. 'I couldn't plait my own. It kept dropping out...' She fixes it straight in her reflection in the glass. 'My plaits kept dropping out, that is, my hair didn't. Although it can do sometimes, especially after I've washed it and brush it wet, then it—'

'You look great!' interrupts Oli, saving me from having to give her an answer.

'Do you like hot dogs?' I ask. 'Because we have a lot. Also burgers. And there's turkey and cranberry over there, beside the salad. Something a bit festive, you know? Drink?' I ask, offering her a can of Coke as Oli drags her down the yellow brick road he coloured in yesterday, and onto the patio. 'I'm afraid that's less Yellow Brick Road and more Yellow Brick Welcome Mat, as Oli got bored and gave up before he'd coloured it all in. We cut off the part he hadn't got to.'

Rachel smiles knowingly, presumably having come across his penchant for cutting corners while at school. Oli rolls his eyes at my dropping him in it, and runs off down the garden. Rachel and I stand watching as a Munchkin scales the side of the slide I built two years ago, which is now too small, too short. The sight of him plumping on the ground makes us both giggle, his costume caked in mud as he runs back around for another go.

We watch him for a few moments before she breaks the silence. 'Ed,' she begins. 'I just want to say thank you...' I look across to her. 'For asking me to stay.' She looks to her feet. 'I'm glad I did.'

'Me too.'

* * *

I get the box containing Floyd, aware Rachel is watching my every move. Oli sees what I'm about to do and moves over to stand beside her, his head low. 'You ready, fella?' I ask him, and he nods, shifting his weight to lean against Rachel. She puts her arm around him and gives him a squeeze. 'Okay.' I kneel, laying the box in the ground. The smell of damp soil brings unwelcome memories of that day, almost five years before. If I close my eyes I can see the open ground. I can hear the cries behind me as I dropped flowers on her coffin. I can feel the disbelief I felt at the time, the pain in my chest and the exhaustion from lack of sleep.

'Ding-Dong! The Witch is Dead' comes to an end and Oli's choice of 'Follow the Yellow Brick Road/You're Off to See the Wizard' kicks in, bringing some much-needed light to a moment I don't want to relive. Not because I don't want to think of Ellie any more, I just want it to be the happy times. The good stuff. The memories of us building a life together, a life that, despite being cut short, brought us my wingman. My right-hand man. My perfect companion in life. The one who has stepped forward to drop a catnip mouse on top of the candy-striped box.

'Bye, Floyd,' he says, as I drop earth back into the hole, burying Ellie's beloved pet. I kneel beside the mound, giving Oli a hug. 'Don't be too sad, Daddy,' he says, giving me a squeeze, and I throw my arms around him, lifting him up into a hug.

Over his shoulder, Rachel stands, patiently watching, and I wonder where we go from here. Smoke twists into the sky, taking the letter I wrote up into the heavens. A letter apologising for everything I let myself believe. A letter telling her I loved her then and always will. A letter that included a sketch of her funeral, a congregation wearing glittery red shoes with her observation: '*They might just have lifted the mood.*' And I know that if she was ever able to look down, after she'd finished laughing at me dressed up like an idiot, she'd be nudging me towards happiness.

Oli gives me a kiss, tells me he loves me, then jumps down. Rachel moves beside me and I let smoke sting my eyes to disguise my tears. 'Is he okay?' she asks, and I nod. 'Are you?' she says, and I look at her, here in my garden, dressed as Dorothy.

'I think so,' I say, giving her the best shoulder nudge my Tin Man costume will allow.

Then I quickly move away, because being so close to her suddenly gives me butterflies.

Author Letter

Dear Reader (and perhaps specifically, dear aspiring author),

I don't know if you know, but this is my second published novel. And in an odd twist of fate, it's also the second novel I ever wrote, back in 2012–13. Coming back to it after some four or more years away was a fascinating insight into the writer I was when I started out. Editing it was a task, I'll be honest, because when I set out to write *The Lost Wife* that very first time, on a Tuesday morning in September, the kids safely deposited at school and my bum placed firmly in the chair, I hadn't fully identified my voice. I didn't know the style of writing I wanted to achieve, the kinds of stories I wanted to tell; I didn't really know what I was doing! Going back to it in 2017 was like the return to the old box room I slept in as a child. It was comforting, it was secure… it was a little bit small and the Bros posters were devastatingly cringe, but there were a number of times when I sat and stared at my laptop, wondering how to edit the words that stared back at me into something that people would want to read. Until I remembered I had a delete button, and that – just as I had ripped down my posters of Matt, Luke and Craig (sorry, boys) – I could take the words away and rewrite them in my new style. With my new approach. With a more assured voice.

Do I know what I'm doing now? Who knows, but I know that the completed novel is something of which I'm very proud. I love this book for lots of reasons, but mostly because it taught me a lot, and also gave me a lot. It gave me things I needed at the time I needed them most. Like award nominations and competition shortlistings. It gave me bursaries for editing, when I needed someone else to read my words and give me an opinion that was slightly more constructive than the words of friends who told me they loved the novel. Which, to be fair, also gave me great encouragement, hence it being dedicated to Mel. Because her total love for it gave me a real boost when I needed it. I hope she still likes it; it's changed quite a lot! This book also gave me interest from agents that, while never resulting in a dotted line on which to sign, gave me the feedback and confidence to keep on keeping on. It gave me more beta readers who laughed and cried and it gave me a sense that maybe, just maybe, I could do this… if I didn't give up.

So, I didn't. And now I'm doing it. How blooming lucky am I!?!

The moral of this story, in case you're interested, is that I *didn't* give up. And if you're reading this because you write too, but you haven't yet achieved your dream… in whatever shape that may be… don't give up. Don't give up. Don't give up!

I hope you have enjoyed *The Lost wife*. If you get chance to leave me a review, it really does help. You can also sign up to my mailing list here: www.bookouture.com/anna-mansell. And, finally, I love to hear from readers via my social media platforms: @annamansell or Facebook.com/AnnaMansellAuthor. If you've anything you'd like to tell me, please do get in touch! Letters and messages from readers really are the best.

Thank you for reading this letter and my book. Truly! I do appreciate it!

Love,

Anna x

Acknowledgements

Goodness, a chance to say thank you again! Where do I begin? Firstly, I should say thank you to every one of you who has read this book. Thank you so much for taking the time to, I really hope you've enjoyed it. And if you read my first novel, and have come back for more, thank you thank you thank you! That really makes my day.

To the book bloggers in this fine land, wow, they are amazing. Their support and encouragement and reviews and retweets and shares and… Honestly, they are amazing. I genuinely don't know how they get through all those books, or find time to write the questions, to update their websites and support our cause. Thank you from the bottom of my heart. With my first novel, I learnt a lot from what people said. I was encouraged, I was made to think and question, I was nurtured and I was inspired. I await your thoughts on book two with bated breath and butterflies in my stomach. If I could high five you all, I blinking well would!

The Bookouture team are incredible, every single one of them. Thank you Abi for your patience when I send email after email. Celine, once again, you saw what I was trying to achieve and pointed me in the right direction. I wonder if I could have you live in my pocket? To all the other authors in 'the lounge', gosh, you're a tonic. I feel so lucky to have you all in my laptop. You really do make a difference.

And speaking of making a difference, Kim... how many dedications, acknowledgements and thanks can one woman have? I'm adding you to the list because you deserve them all. Thank you, what a wonder you really are!

To the beta readers, who read early versions of this novel. Mel, I've dedicated it to you because your love and total understanding of what I had written made a difference. You forgave the flaws in the story, in fact, I seem to remember you saying you didn't see any... there were plenty, hopefully I've ironed them all out and you will still love it. To Jo, you said you could see it as a film, which is funny 'cause I saw that opening chapter in the exact same way. To Li, I promise I'll ensure they play 'Ding-Dong! The Witch is Dead' at your funeral. I'll be the one in the open-toed slingbacks with talc in my hair.

I should also take this opportunity to say thank you to the staff at Basingstoke and North Hampshire Hospital. I had cause to accompany my mum there for a few weeks as she received treatment from their incredible, superhero team. In fact, I type this sat by her bed, surrounded by monitors and wires and drips and dedication. The doctors, nurses, consultants, specialists, cleaners, tea makers, food suppliers... other patients and their families, thank you for letting me plug myself in and work by her bedside. Thank you for making her better. Thank you for the laughs and the chats and the support at a really tricksy time. The NHS is a remarkable, vital and incredible thing full of people of all makes and models who are committed to the very best care. I doff my cap in their direction, which is nothing like what they really deserve.

And finally, thank you to my beautiful family. My him indoors who continues to support, congratulate, commiserate and celebrate my achievements. I am indebted to him for giving me the space to write and the forgiveness when I'm throwing some kind of writerly tantrum. He is the best. My kids, who are the most brilliant, funny, kind, silly and special people in my life. I am nothing without them. And our Olive Dog, my companion and confidant. She interrupts me when I need it least, she accompanies me to the toilet, and she has a total disregard for my 'dance space'... and there is nothing about her that I'd change.

And if you're reading this, hopeful of a mention, and are disappointed – know that it's because I am rubbish, and not because you have not made a difference in my life or my writing. I am very lucky to be surrounded by brilliant people; know that, name-checked or not, you are never taken for granted.

68357061R00175

Made in the USA
Middletown, DE
15 September 2019